All I Want From Santa

Books by Lisa Jackson

Stand-Alones
SEE HOW SHE DIES
FINAL SCREAM
RUNNING SCARED
WHISPERS
TWICE KISSED
UNSPOKEN
DEEP FREEZE
FATAL BURN
MOST LIKELY TO DIE
WICKED GAME
WICKED LIES
SOMETHING WICKED
WICKED WAYS
SINISTER
WITHOUT MERCY
YOU DON'T WANT TO
KNOW
CLOSE TO HOME
AFTER SHE'S GONE
REVENGE
YOU WILL PAY
OMINOUS
BACKLASH
RUTHLESS
ONE LAST BREATH
LIAR, LIAR
PARANOID
ENVIOUS
LAST GIRL STANDING
DISTRUST
ALL I WANT FROM
SANTA

Cahill Family Novels
IF SHE ONLY KNEW
ALMOST DEAD
YOU BETRAYED ME

**Rick Bentz/Reuben
Montoya Novels**
HOT BLOODED
COLD BLOODED
SHIVER
ABSOLUTE FEAR
LOST SOULS
MALICE
DEVIOUS
NEVER DIE ALONE

**Pierce Reed/Nikki Gillette
Novels**
THE NIGHT BEFORE
THE MORNING AFTER
TELL ME
THE THIRD GRAVE

**Selena Alvarez/Regan
Pescoli Novels**
LEFT TO DIE
CHOSEN TO DIE
BORN TO DIE
AFRAID TO DIE
READY TO DIE
DESERVES TO DIE
EXPECTING TO DIE
WILLING TO DIE

Published by Kensington Publishing Corp.

All I Want From Santa

LISA JACKSON

KENSINGTON
PUBLISHING CORP.
www.kensingtonbooks.com

KENSINGTON BOOKS are published by
Kensington Publishing Corp.
119 West 40th Street
New York, NY 10018

Printed in the United States of America

ISBN 978-1-63910-050-7

CHAPTER 1

"I GOT A letter for Santa Claus!" Amy sang out as she burst through the door. A four-year-old dynamo with black curls that had fallen from her ponytail and were now dusted with snowflakes, she torpedoed into the cabin as she peeled off her jacket and backpack.

Through the open door, Veronica spied her sister Shelly's huge Chevy wagon idling near the garage that they'd converted into a warehouse. In the paddock nearby her horses sniffed at the snow-covered ground searching for a few blades of grass.

"Gotta run, Ronni, the twins are starving," Shelly yelled, waving through the open window of her car. Her boys, Kent and Kurt, were arguing loudly enough to wake the dead.

"My turn tomorrow," Veronica called and in a plume of blue exhaust the old station wagon lumbered out of sight. Closing the door behind her, she saw her daughter delving into the front pocket of her backpack. "What's this about a letter?"

"For Santa," Amy repeated, retrieving a single sheet of paper with a Santa sticker in one corner and a four-year-old's uneven scrawl across the page. "Come on, Mommy, we gots to put a stamp on it and mail it."

"First take off your boots and tell me about preschool today, then we'll mail the letter in the morning." Veronica poured a cup of coffee and settled into a corner of the couch, where she patted a worn cushion to indicate a spot for her daughter.

She was glad to have Amy home. It was early December and all afternoon she'd felt ill at ease on the mountain where she worked as part of the ski patrol. There had been record-breaking snowstorms in the Cascades this year and more skiers than ever were gliding down the slopes, challenging the mountain. Thankfully, despite her premonition, there hadn't been a serious accident on the mountain today. Still, she was cold deep in her bones, though she'd left Mount Echo nearly an hour before.

Amy's eyes, so like her father's, sparkled. "Promise you'll mail it?"

"Cross my heart," Veronica replied with a laugh as she dragged a finger over her chest in an exaggerated motion. No matter how melancholy Ronni felt, Amy had a way of making the gloom disappear.

"Okay!" The little girl dashed across the room, her stockinged feet sliding on the hardwood until she reached the braided rug. The cabin they lived in had no formal rooms, just living areas separated by sparse furniture groupings. Everything on and around the blue-and-white rug was considered the living room, the rest of the downstairs was the dining room and kitchen. A small half bath was located on the far wall and the loft above supported a bedroom, full bath and open den area where Veronica slept. The mountain home was small, but cozy, and big enough for the two of them. "Miss Jennie helped me with it."

Miss Jennie was Amy's preschool teacher. A patient woman of about twenty-five, Jennie Anderson was a godsend on the days that Veronica worked in her small mail-order shop in her garage-warehouse, shipping a variety of Northwest items to eager customers.

"So, I suppose you told Santa what you want this year," Veronica prodded, her gaze straying to the boxes of ornaments and lights that she'd hauled out of the attic and stacked near the bookcase. Christmas. It used to be her favorite holiday, but ever since Hank's death . . . She closed her eyes for a second, refusing to dwell on the past.

"I want a puppy," Amy said, climbing into her mother's lap while the fire crackled and hissed behind an ancient screen.

"Oh, now there's a surprise!" Veronica teased as she kissed the curly hair of Amy's crown. "You're like a broken record when it comes to a dog. We've already got the horses."

"But I want a puppy!"

"I know, I know." Ronni tried a different tack. "Anything else on your list?"

"A daddy."

"A what?" Veronica silently prayed she'd heard incorrectly.

"A daddy, like all my friends have." Amy said the request matter-of-factly, as if her mother should be able to see the perfect logic of it all. "Then you wouldn't have to be alone."

"I'm not alone," Veronica protested. "I've got you." She squeezed her daughter and Amy giggled, then squirmed off her lap to run to the bathroom.

Veronica was left with a cooling cup of coffee and a Christmas wish list she couldn't hope to fill. She stared at the crayon-written letters and sighed. Sooner or later this was bound to happen, but she'd been counting on later. Much later. She'd been married to Hank, her high school sweetheart, three years when she'd learned she was pregnant. Their happiness had been complete. Tears shimmered in her eyes when she remembered Hank's reaction to the news that they were going to have a baby, how his handsome mouth had stretched into a smile and the sound of sheer joy when he'd laughed out loud, grabbed her and twirled her off her feet. She'd counted herself as one of the truly blessed people in the world. Amy's birth had been incredible. Hank had been with her in the delivery room and when he'd first held his little daughter, he'd cried silent tears of joy.

Then, within a year, he was dead, her life shattered with no way to put the jagged and crumbling pieces together again.

Veronica closed her eyes. Maybe no one was supposed to be as happy as they'd been. Maybe everyone was supposed to suffer, but it wasn't fair. It just wasn't fair. Big, blond, strapping Hank should have lived until he was in his nineties. Instead, he'd been cut down at twenty-six. Almost four years ago. Four long, lonely years.

He was simply irreplaceable.

She blinked rapidly and told herself that it didn't matter. Even if Amy wanted a daddy, they could do very well without one. Veronica had long ago determined that she could be both mother and father to her little girl. She held her cup to her lips and grimaced when she noticed she was shaking.

Amy was back quickly and scrambling onto the couch.

"Did you wash your hands?" Veronica said automatically.

Amy nodded and Veronica saw that her daughter's fingers were still wet. One thing at a time. They'd tackle drying those little fists another day.

"Hey, lookie!" Amy was standing on tiptoe on the cushions of the couch, leaning against the back pillows, her nose pressed against the glass as she stared outside. Veronica twisted to squint through the frosted panes. Icicles glistened on the eaves of the porch and snow touched by silvery moon glow blanketed the ground. "Lights," Amy said. "New lights."

She looked through the branches of the trees and noticed the warm glow of lamps shining from the house across the lake. "Well, what d'ya know? Someone must be staying at the old Johnson place." That thought bothered her more than it should have, she supposed, but she couldn't help her dream of someday owning the old lodge by the lake and converting it into a bed-and-breakfast inn. The lodge had special memories for her, memories she knew she would cherish to her dying day. Her father had been caretaker of the grounds and she'd grown up swimming in the smooth water of the lake and chasing her sister through the long grass of the shoreline. In winter, her father would let them build camp fires on the beach and cross-country ski along the old logging roads.

"It's creepy there!" Amy shuddered theatrically at the mention of Johnson's property.

Ronni laughed. "No," she said, squeezing her daughter, her melancholy chased away by Amy's analysis of a place she found absolutely charming. "It's just that the house is big and rambling and has been vacant for a long time. Believe me, with a lot of money and a little bit of elbow grease, it would be the nicest place around for miles."

Amy wrinkled her nose. "Elbow grease?"

"It means hard work. The old lodge needs TLC—that means tender loving care."

"I *know* that. But it has cobwebs and broken windows and probably snakes and bats and ghosts!" Amy said, obviously remembering the walk they'd taken down the winding lane that ran past their property and ended up at the Cyrus Johnson estate.

Veronica had ignored the No Trespassing signs and helped Amy over the gate so the little girl could observe ducks and geese gather on the private lake. It had been early morning, they'd watched in awe as the sun rose over the mountains, chasing away the shadows of the land as a doe with her speckle-backed fawns drank from the water. An eagle had soared high overhead and on the ground chipmunks had scurried for cover.

But Amy remembered the spiders and imagined the ghosts of the rambling old lodge. She'd never wanted to go back to the lake again, and Veronica, hoping her daughter would outgrow her fears, never mentioned that it was her secret dream to buy the place someday—to create the same haven for Amy that had sheltered her. Even the old caretaker's house could be rented out—maybe to Shelly.

The Johnson property had been on the market for nearly a year and no one had shown any interest. A real estate agent and friend of Veronica's, Taffy LeMar, had promised to call if she heard any gossip about a serious buyer.

Not that Veronica had any real hope of owning the hundred-plus acres. As rundown as it was, the lodge and property were worth over half a million dollars. Financially she was doing all right but she couldn't hope to secure such a large mortgage.

"I wonder who's inside?" Veronica thought aloud. Apparently not anyone who was taking up permanent residence, or Taffy would have called her. But Veronica was left with an uneasy feeling—that same inexplicable sense of dread that had clung to her all day.

"Ghosts and witches," Amy insisted. "That's who lives there!"

"I don't think so." Rubbing her chin, Veronica tried to imagine who would move into a drafty old lodge in the middle of winter. They were probably just renting it for a week or two—an eccentric couple looking for a rustic retreat for the holidays. Or they could be trespassing. The electricity wouldn't be turned on but they could use kerosene lanterns for light, a camp stove to cook on and camp fires for warmth. Water would be the only problem as the pump was probably fueled by electricity, but they could always carry buckets from the lake. She gave herself a swift mental kick for letting her imagination run away with her—she was as bad as Amy.

"Creepy," Amy said again before being distracted by the sparkling ornaments. She dashed across the room and searched through two boxes of Christmas decorations before dragging out a piece of red tinsel and draping it around her neck like a glittery feather boa. "Look at me, I'm a Christmas tree."

Veronica grinned widely. "No way. You're an angel."

"Not an angel." A look of sheer vexation crossed Amy's small features. "A tree."

"You need a star on top, don't you?"

Amy's eyes rounded. "Do we have one?"

Shaking her head, Veronica said, "I can't remember. Seems to me it broke last year when I was putting it away. We might have to buy a new one." That thought brought her no joy. All the Christmas ornaments she had she'd bought with Hank. Their first tree had been a little tabletop pine with one strand of lights and a few red balls that reminded them both of the animated tree from *A Charlie Brown Christmas*, and each year they'd purchased a larger tree and picked out new decorations. Each Christmas Eve, they had opened a small gift in their stockings, which traditionally had been a special ornament with the date inscribed across it. Once the stockings were empty, they hung their new little decorations on the tree, sipped mulled wine and made love beneath the branches. With only the light of a few candles on the mantel and an old afghan and each other for warmth, they had stayed awake until midnight when it was officially Christmas Day.

A deep, grieving sadness stole through her heart as it always did this time of year. If it weren't for Amy, she'd chuck all her Christmas traditions. Oh, Shelly would probably demand their little, fragmented family still get together. But Veronica was certain that were it not for her daughter, she would probably just give Shelly, her sister's husband and the boys each a gift certificate to their favorite store and forget the cards, decorations, stockings and tree. She would fly away for the holidays and spend the last two weeks of the year soaking up the sun somewhere, lounging around a tropical pool, sipping iced tea and pretending that the Christmas season had never existed.

"Can I buy the new star?" Amy asked, dragging her back to the here and now.

"Sure you can. Whatever star you want," Veronica replied, forcing a note of gaiety into her voice. "I bet we'll be able to find one at the church bazaar. Now, come on, you can help me make dinner."

Amy followed her into the kitchen area, tinsel dragging on the floor after her like the train of a bridal gown.

"Can we have macaroni and cheese tonight?" Amy had asked the same question every night for the past five.

"I was thinking about turkey soup and hot bread. See, I was cutting up carrots when you came home."

Amy wrinkled her nose. "Don't like—"

"We'll even add this pasta I bought," Veronica added quickly, forestalling her daughter's protests. "Here, take a look." Reaching into her cupboard, Veronica pulled out a wrapped package of red, green and yellow pasta shaped like miniature Christmas trees.

Amy's mouth rounded into a gasp of pleasure. "Can I do it?"

"You bet. When the broth's boiling and if you're very careful so you don't get burned, you can help me by tossing in a handful or two."

"I can do it," Amy vowed. She threw another loop of tinsel around her neck and pushed a chair near the counter all the while singing the first few words of "Oh, Christmas Tree" over and over again.

"I can't believe there's no cable," Bryan grumbled for the dozenth time. At fourteen, he seemed to think it was his God-given right to watch MTV around the clock. He adjusted his Seattle Mariners cap, twisting it so that it was on backward, the bill pointing down his back, his brown hair poking out around the edges.

"No TV, period," his father reminded him as he lugged a basket of kindling and set it near the riverrock fireplace which rose two full stories to the ceiling. The place was dusty, drafty and needed so much work that Travis second-guessed himself for the first time since moving from Seattle. The rooms were barren and the moving van wasn't scheduled to show up for a couple of days so he and Bryan planned to work together—kind of a father-and-son project—to put the old house in order before their things arrived. So far, the son part of the team couldn't have been less interested.

Travis had decided they'd shore up the sagging porch, clean the floors and windows, determine how much rewiring and new plumbing was needed and just spend some time getting to know each other again—to make up for lost time.

Bryan dropped his basket onto the hearth and glanced up at the chandelier, which was constructed of deer antlers that supported tiny lights, most of which had probably burned out years ago. "This place stinks. It looks like something out of *The Addams Family*!"

"You don't like the haunted-house ambience?" Travis asked, smiling and dusting his hands. The kid needed to be jollied out of the bad mood that he'd hauled around with him for the past week.

"I hate it, okay?"

Boy, Bryan was pushing. Travis told himself not to explode and tell his son to find a new attitude. "It'll be great if you give it a chance."

"Are you crazy? It's a pit! Beyond a pit! Should have been condemned fifty years ago. Probably was." Bryan flopped down on one of the two mattresses they'd brought. He propped his head on his rolled sleeping bag and scowled at his new surroundings as if he'd just been locked into a six-by-twelve prison cell.

"Give it a rest, Bryan," Travis warned, even though he, too, saw the problems with the old lodge, maybe clearer than his son.

Cobwebs trailed from the ceiling and the leftover meals of spiders—dead, drained insect carcasses—vied with mouse pellets for space in dark corners. The pipes creaked, the lights were undependable and all the old linoleum would have to be replaced. Toilets and sinks were stained and the grout between what had once been beautiful imported tile had disintegrated. Fixing the place up would probably cost him as much as his original investment, but it would be worth it, he silently told himself, stacking kindling on ancient andirons. Any amount of money spent would be cheap if it meant saving his boy.

He glanced over his shoulder at Bryan and saw the sullen expression in his son's eyes, the curled lower lip, the ever-present baseball cap on backward and tattered, black clothes that were three sizes too big for him. His fashion statement wasn't really the problem, nor did Travis object to Bryan's earring or the streak of bleached-blond hair that contrasted with his natural deep brown. But Bryan's general attitude needed an overhaul, and fast.

"You're gonna love it here," Travis said, striking a wooden match on the hearth. Sizzling, the match flared and Travis touched the flame to bits of old newspaper wadded beneath the firewood.

"In your dreams."

"Give it a chance, Bryan. I've heard that you can see eagles and deer, maybe even elk and rabbits."

"Big deal."

The fire began to crackle. "We both agreed that we needed to change—"

"No, Travis," he said, rarely calling his father anything but his given name ever since the divorce. Jabbing a thumb at his chest, he added, "*I* didn't agree to anything. This was your deal. Not mine. I would have stayed in Seattle, with my friends."

Travis bit down hard on his molars so that he wouldn't make some snide comment about the friends Bryan chose, not necessarily bad kids, but the kind that seemed to scare up trouble wherever it was hiding. Bryan's choice of friends had been one of the reasons that had prompted this move to Oregon. One kid had been caught smoking marijuana several times; another had convinced a few pals to skip school, which ended in a joyride cut short when he wrapped the car around a telephone pole, sending several boys to the hospital; and a third had attempted suicide. Not a healthy environment. "Staying in Seattle wasn't an option."

"Yeah, because I don't have any say in anything that happens to me."

"Not true, Bryan."

His son's lips folded over his teeth in annoyance and he popped his knuckles. "Did anyone ask me what I wanted when you and Sylvia got divorced?"

"Your mother and I—"

"Got married 'cause she was pregnant with me and then you found out that you didn't love each other. The only reason you stayed together so long was because of me." He made a sound of disgust in his throat and glared at the ceiling. "I don't know why you bothered."

This was getting complicated. Travis walked to the vacant mattress, which lay only a few feet from Bryan's.

He sat on his rolled sleeping bag and clasping his hands together, hung them between his legs as he looked his boy straight in the eye. "Your mother and I weren't the greatest match, it's true, and yes, she was carrying you, so that pushed up our wedding plans, but we'd already committed to each other. We were going to get married and have kids, one way or the other. It just didn't work out."

Bryan's lips tightened.

"We tried."

"Who cares?"

"You do, I think, and I feel badly that you got hurt."

"I'm *not* hurt, okay?"

Travis felt like giving up, but he gritted his teeth.

"I just want to move back home," Bryan said.

"This is home now."

"Never," Bryan muttered.

"Look, Bry, it's complicated and hard, I know, but you have to realize that Sylvia and I each love you very much."

Levering himself up on an elbow, Bryan stared straight at his father, his gaze, so like Travis's, boring into him. "So that's why she took off for France."

"She needed time and space."

"It's been three years!"

"She likes it over there."

"So she can be away from me. Doesn't have any responsibility then, does she? She can hang out with that gigolo—you know, Jean Pierre or whatever his name is."

Damn! Travis had to bite his tongue. His ex-wife wasn't a bad person, just incredibly self-centered. Half of what Bryan was saying about her was true. Sometimes it was impossible to explain that whimsical woman who thought more of herself, her "freedom," than she did of her family. But then she alone wasn't to blame for the divorce. Travis, in his own way, had neglected her and their son. "Your mother's just unconventional. Always has been."

"Does that translate to basket case?"

"No."

"Then it must be a fancy way of saying she doesn't give a damn about me!"

"Bryan, listen—"

"Oh, just forget it." He flopped back on the sleeping bag and stared at the ceiling again. Making an angry motion with one hand, he said, "I don't want to think about her, anyway. I don't want to think about anything."

"Things have a way of working out," Travis said, cringing inside at the patronizing ring to his words. "You'll get used to living here, maybe even like it."

"Why? Why would I want to live in some little Podunk town?"

"You needed a change."

"You mean you did." Bryan eyed his father disdainfully and Travis was suddenly painfully aware of his jeans and flannel shirt as opposed to the suits that Bryan had seen him wearing since the day the kid was born.

He couldn't deny the fact that he'd been little more than a part-time father at best, spending more hours with his fledgling businesses than with his son in the first few, formative years of the boy's life. He'd kicked himself to hell and back for his mistakes, but it didn't make any difference. The past was the past. Now it was time for a new start.

"Look," Travis said, climbing to his feet. "We worked hard today. Let's spoil ourselves and go skiing tomorrow afternoon."

"What? No more chopping wood? Splitting kindling? Mopping floors?" Bryan sneered.

"Careful, or you'll find yourself doing just those things," Travis warned, though he smiled. "We'll check out Mount Echo. May as well since it's practically in our backyard. What do you say?"

"*Anything's* better than hanging around this place," Bryan growled, but Travis had noticed a spark of interest—the first since they'd moved here—in his son's sullen eyes.

The next day Travis and Bryan headed to Mount Echo. After skiing together for a while, they split up and agreed to meet at two o'clock. Now, Bryan was looking down a very steep run. He had heard about Devil's Spine from Marty Sinclair, a friend of his in Seattle who had bragged about "getting twenty feet of air," by jumping off the spine. Marty had bragged and laughed as he'd rolled a joint and offered it to Bryan, who had declined and been rewarded with a cloud of smoke exhaled in his face. Bryan had determined for himself that if Marty could make the jump, so could he. Never mind that he was already late meeting his dad at the lodge, never mind that the run was obviously closed and he'd had to cross-country it over to the ridge, never mind that he was cold and tired and was, deep inside, a little bit chicken about doing this. He had a point to prove. To Marty. To his dad. And especially to himself.

He'd eyed the jump and it was nowhere near twenty feet. Maybe six or eight, but twenty? No way. Poised at the top of the narrow canyon that wound steeply between trees and cliffs on either side, he screwed up his courage, planted his poles and took off. Tucked low, faster and faster he sped, his skis skimming over the trail. The snow was glazed with ice, bumps carved into the pack so hard they sent shock waves through his legs as he raced through the narrow channel. But there was no turning back. Fir branches slapped at his face, but he didn't care. He took the final turn and the world seemed to open up as the trees gave way and there was nothing in front of him but cloudy sky. With a final push, he was airborne, soaring through the frigid air, wind rushing at his face, his entire body free and sailing through the sky.

Adrenaline charged through his bloodstream as he looked over the tops of trees. His heart nearly stopped when he finally glanced down, preparing for his landing. He braced himself, keeping his knees loose. *It'll be okay. If Marty can do it, so can I!* But his heart was pounding in fear. His mouth was dry. What if he didn't land right? What if he turned an ankle. What if—

Bam!

His skis slammed into the ground. His body jarred. He was speeding downhill. He'd done it! Exhilaration swept through him just as his right ski caught an edge. He tried to right himself and overcompensated. Before he knew what was happening, he was falling, head over heels. One binding released. His ski flew off and he was tumbling ever faster toward a small fir tree. The second biding broke free. He tried to break his fall, but couldn't dig in. The sky and ground blurred. "Oh, God," he yelled, snow filling his mouth.

He careered into a tree, his body jerked by the force. With a yowl, he felt pain—intense, blinding and hot— scream up his leg and he realized that he was all alone, on a part of the mountain that was closed, where no one would find him. He tried to yell, but blackness swirled in front of his eyes and he had to fight to stay awake. He screamed before the darkness surrounded him again and this time, though he struggled, he passed out. His final conscious thought was that he was going to die. Alone.

Not that his parents would care. . . .

CHAPTER 2

VERONICA ANGLED HER skis, cutting the edges into the fresh snow as she glared up at the summit of Mount Echo, a jagged, craggy peak nearly concealed by the clouds that clung to its uppermost reaches. *A terrain of savage beauty,* one journalist had written. *Treacherous. Unforgiving. Cruel.* "Damn you," she whispered, then snapped her goggles over her eyes.

This is crazy, Ronni! You can't keep blaming the mountain for Hank's death! It's been four years. Enough time to heal. Time to move forward with your life.

Then why did she feel that she couldn't breathe sometimes, that the need to get back at someone or something was so great it suffocated her? She'd suffered through a grief support group, cried on her sister's shoulder, forced herself to smile for her child's sake, but had never completely come to terms with the fact that Hank was gone—irretrievably and forever.

"Get over it," she told herself, dismayed that she'd actually sworn at the mountain. Adjusting her straps, she turned her back to the wind that whistled above the timberline and planted her poles. Expertly she skied down a wide, tree-lined bowl. Most of the skiers seemed to be handling the gentle slope of North Alpine Run without much difficulty, though a few hotdoggers and snow boarders barreled at breakneck speeds past their more cautious counterparts.

Veering to the left, Ronni steered down a narrow cat track that headed into rougher territory, where the steeper grade of Redrock Canyon usually took its toll on less experienced skiers. As part of the rescue team, she patrolled the slopes, helping stranded or injured skiers get back to the lodge safely. Years ago, before the accident, she and Hank had worked the slopes together and after his death, she'd continued her association with the rescue team—helping the injured, vowing to prevent Echo from taking more victims, hoping to assuage the guilt that still kept her awake some nights. It was her personal quest—her vendetta against Mother Nature.

She spied a little girl in a pink ski outfit who seemed alone and lost. The child, around twelve, judging by her size, was standing on the edge of Jackpine Run, a trail that changed from softly rolling terrain to a steep mogul-filled slope. Veronica was about to see if the child needed help, when a man—probably the kid's father—swooshed up to her and together they tackled the difficult terrain.

All in all it had been a quiet day, thank God, but the temperature had dropped, the wind had picked up and on the east face even the groomed runs were icy. *Treacherous. Unforgiving.* She plunged her poles into the snow and started downhill. For years she'd told herself to give up this part-time job. Between managing her growing mail-order business and being both mother and father to Amy, she had her hands full. But she couldn't stop. It was as if she was compelled to tackle Mount Echo, to try to save lives, to help the injured, all the while spitting in the face of the mountain that she loved and hated.

She probably needed to see a psychiatrist, she thought, someone to help her quit blaming herself and the mountain for Hank's death.

Skiing down a final slope, she weaved easily through the throng that had collected around the base lodge. Skiers and snowboarders were moving in all directions, heading for the warmth of the lodge, the lift-ticket lines, the chairlifts, rope tow or parking lot. On the back deck of the lodge a crew was still barbecuing chicken. Black, fragrant smoke curled to the sky, and each time the lodge door opened, the sound of music added a throbbing backbeat to the general hubbub.

Maneuvering to the emergency hut, she was just

pushing out of her bindings when Bobby Sawyer threw open the door. "We've got two new ones, Ronni," he said as he stretched his fingers into his gloves. "Both on the north side. One on Double Spur, the other in Devil's Hollow."

"Let's go." She snapped off her skis, held them against her and together they climbed onto a waiting snowmobile. Bobby drove and Ronni tucked her head against the wind. The snowmobile roared up an icy cat track, away from the skiers.

Yelling to be heard over the noise of the engine, Bobby filled Veronica in on the details. "I'll go up to Double Spur, that's where a little girl slammed into a tree. There's a possible head injury and we may have to life-flight her."

Ronni's heart sank. No! No! No! This mountain couldn't claim another life, not that of a child.

"The other injury is a kid who was taking a jump off the rocks on Devil's Spine. I think he ended up tangling with a tree. From the reports it sounds like leg problems. Tim's already coming with the sled."

"When did it happen?"

"Someone saw him less than ten minutes ago."

"I thought the spine was closed today."

"Either the guy can't read or he ignored the warnings."

There was always some fool who didn't think the rules applied to him and took off on his own. Bobby dropped her off near the empty chairlift that linked the base lodge with all the runs shooting off Devil's Hollow and Veronica snapped on her skis. She sped under the lift, shot through a narrow trail that cut through the trees to the ridge of boulders and run that was known as Devil's Spine or just the spine. Icy and treacherous, the mountain wasn't giving an inch on this side. She caught a glimpse of the downed skier lying in the snow beneath the rocks. Both skis had been thrown off. One lay split near the protruding red boulders that formed the vertebrae of the spine; his other ski was tangled in the broken branches of a small fir tree.

"Hang in there, kid," Veronica said under her breath as she skied down to him. "Hey, you all right?" she said when she reached him.

He didn't move.

"Oh, God."

First-aid training swept through her mind.

She was out of her skis and next to him in an instant. "Hey, are you all right?" she repeated. "Can you hear me?"

Eyes, a startling blue, blinked open and focused. A good sign.

"How do you feel, hmm?" she asked, watching as consciousness slowly returned.

"Like hell," he finally whispered. He tried to move and winced.

"I'll bet that was quite a fall you took," she said, just talking to keep him awake. He lifted his head, then closed an eye.

"Just lie still."

"My leg," he whispered, blinking rapidly as the tears started to form in those incredible eyes.

"Shh. Let me look at it."

He tried to move again. "I can't get up," he said with an edge of panic to his voice.

"Don't worry about it. I'll take care of you. All you have to do is relax and don't move."

"It hurts," he said, then uttered an oath under his breath. He had the look in his eyes of a wounded, cornered dog and Veronica's heart went out to him.

"I'm sure it does," she said, offering him a smile. "Hang in there, we've got a basket coming and we'll get you down. Do you hurt anywhere else?" She was touching him gently, looking for signs of injury. He had a bruise forming on his chin, but thankfully there were no signs of other head injuries.

"No."

"No headache?"

"No."

"But you did pass out?"

"Yeah—" He looked around and blinked again. "I guess I did."

Aside from his leg, he didn't appear to have sustained any other injuries, but she had to check and the fact that he'd lost consciousness earlier wasn't a good sign. Either he'd hit his head or nearly scared himself to death. "How about your back, neck or arms?"

"Just my leg, okay?" he shouted, then clamped his mouth shut and looked guilty as sin. "Sorry."

"Don't worry about it," she said quickly, realizing how scared he was. He was big, five eight or nine and probably somewhere between the ages of twelve and fourteen, but he still resembled a little kid. "How long have you been here?"

"Don't know. Not long."

Good. He was dressed warmly, so he shouldn't have any frostbite. But he couldn't move his leg without biting hard on his lower lip. She glanced at the sky, ever-threatening, and noticed the wind was too fierce for any snow to collect on the branches of the surrounding trees.

"My skis—"

"We'll take them, too." *Or what's left of them.* "What's your name?"

"Bryan."

"Got a last name?" she asked, watching carefully for any signs of shock setting in. *Come on, Tim. Hurry up.*

"Keegan," he said.

"Okay, Bryan Keegan, I'm going to untangle you from this Douglas fir and if anything hurts too bad, you let me know, okay?"

" 'Kay." He didn't utter a sound as she worked him gently away from the branches of the trunk. Tears filled his eyes and he brushed the drops aside with the back of his gloved hand when he apparently thought she wasn't looking. She had seen the tears and the look of embarrassment on his face, and her heart went out to the hurt boy. Somewhere nearby, she heard a snowmobile rush by and in the distance was the wail of an ambulance. Above both sounds was the disturbing sound of a helicopter's rotor. The little girl on Double Spur hadn't been as lucky as Bryan.

Ronni thought of Amy and sent up a silent prayer for the injured child, then she looked at her new charge. "That's not for you," she assured him. "I think it's about time for formal introductions, don't you?" Before he could answer, she said, "My name's Ronni Walsh and, if you haven't guessed yet, I'm part of the ski patrol," she said, even though her red jacket and name tag said as much. "Are you skiing here alone or are you part of a group?"

"My dad. He's here somewhere. I, uh, was supposed to meet him at the lodge."

"Good." She hoped to sound reassuring. "We'll find him and let him know what's happened. That way he can meet you in the clinic. What's your father's name?"

"Travis."

"Keegan? Same as yours?" These days she didn't want to assume anything.

"Yeah."

"Okay." He was finally untangled from the tree and some of his color seemed to be returning. Rocking back on her heels, she asked, "What day is it?"

"Sunday."

"Do you know where you are?"

"Mount Echo. Devil's . . . Devil's Bowl?"

"Close enough." He didn't seem to have any kind of memory loss, which heartened her. "As soon as my partner gets here, we'll take you down to the lodge and find your dad. Sound like a plan?"

"I guess," he said warily, but offered her the faintest of smiles.

Tim Sether arrived pushing the basket-sled, which was shaped like a canoe with bicycle handles and runners. Together they helped Bryan into the sled, covering him with a plastic thermal blanket before strapping him in tightly. Kneeling beside the rig, Tim laid a comforting hand on the boy's shoulder and explained the procedure. "I'm gonna take you down the hill. Just relax and go along for the ride. I'll do all the work. Ronni, here, she'll try to find your dad. Okay?"

" 'Kay," the kid mumbled, his teeth chattering.

"Let's do it," Tim said to Veronica as he tugged on the edges of his knit cap.

The going was rough, the wind a blast of arctic air that blew across the snow. Veronica skied down first and Tim followed behind, never losing his grip on the sled as he guided it, plowlike, down the hill. At a path, they cut across the face of the mountain, back to the protected area and groomed runs. Within minutes they were at the basement of the lodge where the small emergency clinic was housed.

An ambulance, lights flashing, was already waiting at the double doors and a little girl wearing a cervical collar and strapped to a gurney was being hauled into the back.

"It's going to be okay, Jackie," a man in a black jumpsuit was saying as he leaned over the stretcher. His goggles hung around his neck, his face was ashen and his eyes were worried.

A middle-aged woman in a purple jumpsuit who was fighting tears cleared her throat. "That's right, honey, you just hang in there."

"Don't worry," the doctor, Syd Fletcher, was saying. "I've called Dr. Bowman in Portland. He's a good man, been to him myself. He'll be able to help you get back on your feet again, Jackie."

The woman blinked rapidly. "But a crushed pelvis—"

"It'll be fixed. Come on, let's go." They didn't have time to argue and the mother climbed into the back of the ambulance before an attendant slammed the door and the vehicle tore out of the parking lot.

Veronica stepped out of her bindings. "Are you all right?" she asked Jackie's father.

He was still standing where his family had left him, his eyes fixed on the brake lights of the disappearing ambulance.

"What? Oh, yeah. Yeah, fine," he said brusquely before letting his mask of bravado slip a bit. "It's just that Jackie's our only child and if anything happens to her . . ." Kneading the stocking cap he was holding, he let his voice trail off. "Damn it all, anyway." He shook his head and seemed to snap out of it. "I don't know what

I'm doing, standing around here like a dime-store dummy, I've got to get to the hospital."

"Maybe you should have a cup of coffee first—give yourself a little time to pull yourself together."

"No time," he said as he gathered skis and headed across the parking lot and disappeared behind a bus.

Dr. Fletcher turned his attention to the boy on the stretcher. "What have we got here?"

"Right leg—though the injury seems to be confined to the knee," Tim said. He'd already stepped out of his skis and was unstrapping Bryan from the sled. "Possible head injuries, he was knocked out, but he's stabilized, no sign of concussion."

Fletcher frowned. Bending down, he ran expert hands over Bryan's head, examined his eyes and asked him a few questions. Apparently satisfied that Bryan wasn't injured more seriously than Tim had said, he smiled at the boy and clicked off his penlight. "Knee, is it, son? Haven't had one of those today." Fletcher gave Bryan his famous relax-and-let-me-take-care-of-you smile, which people always said reminded them of an old-fashioned country doctor who made house calls. In truth, Syd Fletcher was a sought-after internist whose thriving practice in Portland was more than enough to keep him busy. A skiing enthusiast who spent every other Sunday working in the clinic, he spent as much free time as possible on the mountain. "You'll be my first this afternoon. Kind of an honor."

From the looks of him, Bryan didn't think so.

"What's your name?"

"Bryan . . . Bryan Keegan."

"His father is somewhere on the mountain," Veronica said to Fletcher, then smiled at the boy. "Okay, Bryan, hang on to Tim and me and we'll carry you inside to a wheelchair."

"'Kay." He didn't argue and within seconds they'd maneuvered him into a chair.

"Now, about your father. Any idea where I can find him?" Ronni asked.

"Probably in the lodge," Bryan said with a shrug, but beneath his nonchalance and the pain that caused his skin to be the color of chalk, there was a hint of guilt in his eyes as he avoided looking directly at her. "I, uh, was supposed to meet him."

"Don't worry, we'll find him."

The nurse on duty, Linda Knowlton, was a friend of Veronica's. With a "Well, what have we got here?" she wheeled Bryan through a maze of stainless-steel equipment, desks and occupied beds to an area behind a heavy door where an X-ray machine was located.

Once Bryan was out of sight, Veronica used the phone mounted on a wall near a cupboard containing first-aid equipment and called the information desk. She asked the receptionist to try to find a male skier by the name of Travis Keegan who might or might not be in the lodge. If located, Travis was to be sent to the clinic to pick up his son, who, though injured, wasn't in any medical danger.

Now all they could do was wait for the father to come looking for his missing boy.

After a few minutes with Linda in the X-ray room, Bryan was lying on one of a series of hospital beds that were crammed against one concrete wall of the small clinic. His boot was off, his leg in a brace. "Nothing's broken," Dr. Fletcher told his patient. "You were lucky this time."

"Don't feel lucky."

Fletcher chuckled. "Well, no, I imagine not."

Veronica felt a measure of relief for Bryan though she couldn't help remembering the little girl who had been rushed away by ambulance. The mountain had a way of taking its toll on young and old alike.

Unforgiving. Savage.

Gritting her teeth, she noticed the other patients. One woman in her sixties had twisted her ankle and seemed to think it was a snowboarder's fault for cutting her off and causing her to fall. "They shouldn't be allowed on the mountain," she asserted. "Dangerous, reckless wild kids who have no place on ski runs! I've been skiing for forty years and never seen the like. Rude. That's what they are. Should be barred!"

"Hey, I board and it's safer than skis," a teenage boy with long bleached hair and a splint on one arm chimed in.

A little girl wearing a thumb splint was waiting for her parents and a man in his twenties was being given pain relievers. His right arm was in a sling and the preliminary diagnosis was that his elbow was broken. An ambulance had already been called. "When's it gonna get here?" he demanded as Bryan stared at the ceiling.

There was something about the boy that tugged on Veronica's heart strings. Beneath his macho I-don't-give-a-damn attitude was a scared little kid. She could read it in his eyes whenever he glanced in her direction.

"Look, I've been here for half an hour," the twenty-year-old complained.

"The ambulance will be here soon," Fletcher remarked without looking up from the chart on which he was scribbling.

"I'm dying here."

"I don't think so."

"But there was already a vehicle."

"Which took away a little girl who was in worse shape than you," Fletcher snapped. "This isn't a cafeteria line where it's first come first served. Everything here is done by priority—the more serious the injury, the faster you get medical attention."

The patient rolled his eyes. "I'll never get out of here."

The nurse, Linda, a blond woman with a patient smile, said, "I know it feels like it, but it will be just—"

The doors burst open and two attendants stormed into the room. With a cold rush of air and the smell of exhaust was a glimpse of an ambulance, lights spinning eerily as it idled next to the clinic. "Here you go," Linda added, and without the least bit of wasted motion, the two attendants, dressed in ski coats and caps, hustled their charge into a wheelchair and out the door. Within seconds they were gone.

"Thank God," Linda muttered.

"So how're you doing?" Veronica asked Bryan.

"Fine," he mumbled and wouldn't look in her direction.

"You up here for the day?"

His gaze flattened as if he was bored. She could hear the words, *What's it to ya, lady? Buzz off!* though he hadn't uttered a sound.

"Well, good luck," she said. It was four o'clock and she was officially off duty. She could pick up Amy from the Snow Bunny area where the little girl had taken toddler ski lessons earlier. After the group lesson, Amy was fed lunch, then encouraged to nap on one of the cots placed around the play area. She spent what was left of the afternoon in a special day-care area of the lodge where she played with kids her age under supervised care.

Ronni had just started for the double doors when they flew open and banged against the wall. A tall man, mid-thirties from the looks of him, with harsh, chiseled features and dark hair dusted with snow, strode into the room as if he owned it. His mouth was turned down at the corners, his gray eyes dark with worry, his thick, unruly eyebrows slammed together in concern. "I'm looking for—" He stopped suddenly when he saw Bryan lying on one of the beds. "Thank God," he said, relief softening the hard angles of his face. His gloved hands opened and clenched in frustration. "Hell, Bryan, you gave me the scare of my life. I thought you might be dead or unconscious somewhere."

"May as well be," the boy responded. He glanced sullenly around the room, disdain radiating from him. "This place is about as lame as it gets."

"But you're okay?"

"He'll walk again." Syd extended his hand. "I'm Dr. Fletcher—"

The phone rang shrilly.

Linda answered it and waved to Fletcher. One hand over the receiver, she said, "It's Dr. Crenshaw. He wants information on the little girl who came in this morning with the injured spleen. Her name was—" She searched for a chart.

"Elissa, I remember. Excuse me for a second." Dr. Fletcher took the phone from the nurse's outstretched hand and turned his back on Bryan while he concentrated on the conversation. Meanwhile, Linda attended the older woman who was asking for a pain pill while she waited for her husband.

Keegan turned his attention to his son. "I thought I told you to meet me at the lodge."

Bryan scowled deeply. "I lost track of time."

"You've got a watch and the lifts have clocks at the bottom as well as the top."

"Yeah, I know, but I said I lost track of time," Bryan repeated sullenly.

Keegan rubbed a hand around the back of his neck in

frustration. "It doesn't matter. You're all right and that's what I really care about, but why don't you fill me in? Tell me what happened, how you ended up here."

"I caught a little air and landed wrong."

"Where were you?"

Bryan didn't answer.

Veronica thought she had to step in. She didn't want to get the kid into trouble with this large man who looked as if he was barely hanging on to his patience, but it was important that they both realize how dangerous it is to ski in closed areas, how lucky Bryan was not to be in worse shape.

"I found him on Devil's Spine," she said, stepping to the other side of Bryan's bed.

"Devil's Spine?" the man echoed, seeing her for the first time. His troubled gaze centered on her face, hesitated, then dropped for an instant to skim her chest where her name tag was pinned.

"I'm Veronica Walsh, one of the rescue team."

He was staring into her eyes again and she noticed just how intense his gaze was—flinty gray, the color of storm clouds gathering over an angry ocean. "*You* found Bryan?"

"Yes." She bristled slightly as she always did when she came up against someone who didn't seem to think a woman could handle the job. But she held on to her temper as she realized he was upset about his son. Maybe he wasn't a first-class chauvinist.

"Where on earth is Devil's Spine?"

"North canyon," Bryan said.

"That's right. Because of the windy and icy conditions today, parts of the north side weren't groomed and the area around the spine, which is an expert run, was closed today."

"Closed?" Keegan repeated and his son's face hardened.

Feeling like a rat, Ronni did her duty. "I think Bryan might have been jumping from the top of the spine to the bottom. That's a drop of nearly ten feet." She stared at the kid. "Am I right?"

Bryan shrugged.

Keegan's mouth thinned into an unforgiving line and Ronni couldn't help comparing him to the mountain. *Fierce, savage, challenging.* Keegan's fingers tightened over the rail of the hospital bed as he stared at his son. "For the love of God, Bryan, what were you thinking?"

"Look, Mr. Keegan, people do it all the time, but not when the run's closed," she said, trying to soften the blow. Bryan's father needed to know that his son had broken the rules, but she didn't want to get the boy into big trouble. She touched Bryan on the shoulder and he flinched. His gaze was hard and accused her of being a traitor. "It turned out all right," she added. "Bryan was lucky."

"Lucky?" Bryan grumbled under his breath. "Lucky?" He rolled his eyes. "Why does everyone keep saying that? I've been so *lucky* lately, I can barely stand myself."

"That's enough," Travis said, embarrassed by the

boy's lack of gratitude, even though this woman was getting under his skin a little. She was pretty, with all-American looks and a smile he found beguiling, but he didn't need her, or any woman, for that matter, messing with his mind. "The least you could do is thank these people for helping you," he said to his son. Then, despite his best efforts to hold his tongue, he added, "Geez, Bryan, what was going through your head? Why were you skiing where you shouldn't have been when you were supposed to meet me?"

A defiant light flared in his son's eyes and Travis gave himself a hard mental shake. The boy was hurting already and Travis needed to remember that Bryan was just a kid.

"Mr. Keegan?" a woman in a lab coat asked. Slightly overweight with short, straight, blond hair, she was sliding X rays into a large manila envelope.

"Yes?" His attention returned to the nurse.

"Hi, I'm Linda Knowlton and I've been working with Bryan." She grabbed a clipboard that hung suspended from the foot of Bryan's bed. "We have a few forms for you to fill out."

"Can I just get outta here?" Bryan complained.

"In a minute," Linda said patiently. Winking broadly, she clucked her tongue. "You're going to make me feel like you don't love us."

"I don't love . . . geez—" Bryan flopped back on the bed. "Nothin's busted. I don't see why we just can't leave."

"We will, once the doctor gives you the okay," Travis said, too relieved to be angry. When he'd split up from his son on the mountain a couple of hours ago, he hadn't panicked. Bryan was a good skier and they'd planned to meet at the lodge for a snack at two. He'd gotten in early, drunk a cup of coffee and when Bryan was late, Travis wasn't worried. Hell, the kid still let time slip away from him, but after an hour had passed, Travis had become concerned, and was on his way to the information desk when he'd been paged. His heart had nearly stopped. In his heavy ski boots, he'd sprinted through the carpeted hallways, shouldering past slower-moving people. In terrifying mind-numbing images, he'd imagined his son's broken and bent body, even his death.

Fletcher hung up the phone and walked back to Bryan's bed. "As I was saying, I'm Dr. Fletcher." Travis yanked off his ski glove and shook the shorter man's hand. About five-ten, Fletcher had lost a good amount of his hair. What remained was a clipped horseshoe of red blond strands which matched his thick moustache. "Your son's going to be fine, but I'm afraid he'll be laid up for a while." Quietly, while the nurse looked in on the patients in the other beds, Fletcher explained his concerns for Bryan's knee, the possible torn ligament and cartilage damage, though no bones appeared to be broken. "You might want to have an MRI on the knee and check with your orthopedic surgeon," he said. "If you don't have one, I recommend any one of these. . . ."

He opened the desk drawer, withdrew three business cards, including one of his own, and offered them to Travis. "I have a clinic in town myself." Winking at Bryan, he added. "I just moonlight up here."

"Thanks." Travis took the cards, then noticed Ronni stepping away from the bed.

She patted the top rail. "I'll see ya, Bryan." Smiling, she waved to the other people in the room. "Linda . . . Syd . . . that's it for me for the day. Someone else will have to bring you your next victims." Winding her rope of braided hair onto the crown of her head, she tugged on a ski hat. "See you next weekend."

"Not me, Ronni, I'm off, till after Christmas," the nurse, who was placing a plastic cover on a thermometer, said. "Nancy and Cal are rotating through the holidays, so the only way you'll see me is if I need help getting down the mountain or medical assistance."

"Don't tell me you're going to spend your honeymoon back here?"

Linda shook her head and for an instant her eyes, behind her oversize glasses, gleamed. "Nope. Ben and I are going to Vegas and then spending a week at Timberline on Mount Hood, in the old lodge."

Ronni couldn't help smiling at the blush of romance in her friend's cheeks. Linda was forty-five, her children grown, her first husband a man who had walked out on her and the kids when they were still toddlers. Linda hadn't dated much over the years. All her time and energy had been devoted to her kids. But two years ago, she'd met Ben through a mutual friend. Now they were going to run away and get married. It almost made a person believe in romance again. Almost.

"So, if you're patrolling on Hood next weekend and see a downed skier in a hot-pink jumpsuit and a wedding veil—"

"Don't even think it," Ronni said, zipping up her jacket. "I guess I should say merry Christmas, as well as congratulations." She was tugging on her gloves.

"You, too. I hope little Amy gets everything she wants."

Ronni's smile faltered slightly before she managed to pin it back into place. "She wants a puppy. I think I'm doomed."

"I know someone who's got a litter. Blue Heeler and spaniel, I think. Call me if you're interested."

"I'm not, but Amy is. Give my best to Ben. Tell him he's lucky to have you for a bride."

"I remind him every day," Linda assured her before being summoned by the woman who was complaining about snowboarders ruining the runs for the skiers.

Ronni tossed a look to the boy with the sad eyes. "You, too, Bryan, have a good Christmas, and the next time you're up here, be sure to check the signs so you know which runs are open and which are closed." She glanced at the kid's father, an imposing man if she'd ever seen one. She'd give ten to one odds that he was a corporate big shot—all take-charge energy and impatience. An out-of-towner, coming to the mountain to unwind. Now, with his son injured, he was rattled. "Have a great holiday."

"It's not starting out so great, is it?" he asked, motioning to Bryan.

"Then it's bound to get better, right?" She offered him a smile that Linda had once told her could melt ice.

"Let's hope."

" 'Bye."

Travis watched her leave. There was something about her that he found damnably fascinating. He, a man who had sworn off women. He, who had been through a gutwrenching divorce that he still found painful. He, who didn't trust any female.

Suddenly hot, he unzipped his jacket and found his son staring up at him. "You want to tell me why you were skiing on a closed run?"

Bryan lifted a shoulder. "Not really."

"I'd like to know."

With a grunt, Bryan moved on the bed then winced. "What's the big deal?"

"It was unsafe. As you found out. The only reason they close a run is—"

"Yeah, I know, it's dangerous. I already heard the lecture. From her." He jutted his chin toward the empty spot where Ronni had stood only moments before.

"Fine." This was no place for an argument. From the corner of his eye, Travis watched Ronni shoulder her way through the double doors that swung slowly closed as she passed through. She didn't bother looking over her shoulder as she found her skis and poles, which had been propped against the outside of the building. Then the doors swung shut.

"How are you doing?" Dr. Fletcher, looking harried, was back at Bryan's bedside.

Shrugging, Bryan mumbled, "Okay, I guess."

"I've prescribed some pain pills, just enough for the next couple of days. You might not even need them." He looked at Travis. "Bryan's young and strong. This will slow him down for a while, but he'll be up and around and probably be able to ski by next season."

"Next year?" Bryan said, closing his eyes in disappointment. "Oh, man."

"And you might be prescribed a special brace to wear when you're involved in sports."

"No way!"

Fletcher grinned. "They're not too bad, really. I wear one myself."

Glowering, Bryan's eyes silently accused the doctor of having to resort to such a device because Fletcher was old.

Fletcher didn't seem to notice. "Let's not jump the gun. Wait and see what your orthopedic doctor suggests."

Bryan swallowed and blinked.

"Feelin' rough?" Travis asked, laying a hand on his son's head.

"Like sh— horrible." Bryan slid away from his touch.

"It'll get better."

Suddenly, the doors swung open and a woman, dressed in a silky aqua jumpsuit, hurried into the clinic. Her nose wrinkled in disgust at the concrete floor and tight quarters. "I'm Wanda Tamarack. Is my daughter, Justice—"

"Mommy!" The girl nursing her sprained thumb sent up a wail loud enough to wake the dead in another continent.

"Dear God." Wanda hurried past the desk and around a curtain to spy her daughter stretched out on one of the beds. "Oh, honey, what happened?" Wanda asked.

"Sprained thumb," the nurse replied. "I have some forms you'll have to—"

"We've got to get you to a specialist. Oh, baby, does it hurt?" The woman went on and on, and her daughter, under control a few minutes before, began to fall apart. Her lower lip quivered and tears drizzled down her cheeks. "Oh, sweetheart, don't cry. Mommy's here and we'll get you out of this awful place." The woman's diamond earrings flashed in the wavering light from the fluorescent tubes mounted high on the ceiling.

Bryan rolled his eyes at the woman's flair for the dramatic—so like Sylvia, his mother.

"See, it could be worse," Travis whispered into his son's ear. "Wanda could be taking you home with her."

"Ugh!" Bryan almost cracked a smile before he tried to move his leg and sucked in his breath in a hiss of pain.

"We'll take care of that," Travis promised. "You'll be okay."

"You think so?" Bryan retorted. Scowling down at the brace surrounding his knee, Bryan gritted his teeth. "No matter what you say, Travis, this Christmas is going to be the pits!"

CHAPTER 3

"WATCH OUT, MOMMY." Amy gave the toy tugboat a push and it plowed through the high mounds of bubbles surrounding Veronica as she soaked her tired muscles. Amy was standing on tiptoe on the bath mat, leaning over the side of the tub, precariously close to falling face first into the suds and drenching herself all over again.

"*You* watch out," Ronni warned.

Already bathed, her hair still damp from her recent shampoo, her body snug in red-and-white elf pajamas that Ronni had found on sale, Amy was happily splashing the warm water.

"You're getting soaked!"

Amy giggled.

"Come on, let's get out of the bathroom." So much for the relaxing bath. "How about a hot cup of lemonade?"

"With strawberries?"

Ronni plopped a mound of suds onto Amy's tiny nose. "If that's what you want."

Amy's impish grin stretched wide. "Hurry, Mommy, get out!" Amy cried, already scampering into the living room, the red-and-blue tugboat forgotten.

Ronni pulled the plug and reached for a towel. She rubbed the water and suds from her body and called after her daughter, "First the lemonade, then will you read me a bedtime story?"

Footsteps echoed from the hallway and Amy stuck her head around the corner. "You're silly, Mommy."

"And so are you." Rotating the kinks from her neck, she dropped her towel into the hamper and stepped into a thick terry-cloth bathrobe. Amy was off again and Ronni heard the distinctive click of the refrigerator door opening.

"Wait for me," she called as she cinched the belt of her robe. Barefoot, she followed Amy's trail of forgotten and dripping toys. Scooping up each sodden piece of plastic, she smiled. Amy was so innocent; such a joy. Ronni couldn't imagine her growing up and developing into a teenager with an attitude like the boy, Bryan, who'd been injured today. Not that he was all bad. Veronica had seen through his bravado and witnessed the pain in his eyes, the fear contorting his features when she'd helped him off the mountain.

His father was a different sort, she thought as she

lifted her hair away from her neck and tied it with the ribbon she kept in the pocket of her robe. It was clear he'd been torn between anger with Bryan for his rude remarks and relief that the kid was in one piece. There was something about him that nagged at her and it wasn't just the fact that he was so sensually masculine. Though she'd tried to deny it earlier, she couldn't lie to herself. He was tall and lean, with wide shoulders, thick neck and blade-thin lips. His hair, unruly from a stocking cap, was a deep brown and straight, his nose slightly crooked, his eyebrows thick and harsh over intense eyes. Handsome, yes. Sexy, undeniably. And trouble of the worst order. He looked like the kind of man who barked out orders to underlings.

But he did care about his kid. That much was obvious and that won him points with Ronni. Big points. Not that she'd ever see him again. So what was it about him that was so disturbing, so fascinating, if that was the right word? For what had remained of the afternoon, she'd thought about him, unable to shake his image from the corners of her mind. Had she seen him before somewhere? Certainly she would have remembered such a take-charge individual. What was it about him? "Stupid woman," she muttered. What did she care?

"Who's a stupid woman?" Amy asked, her cheeks flushed as she made the drawers into stair steps and climbed onto the counter.

"Your mama, she's the stupid woman, but only sometimes. Hey, you know you're not supposed to do that. I'll get the lemonade." She reached for the tin and spooned healthy tablespoons into a couple of mugs before adding water and placing both cups into the microwave.

Travis Keegan had been all business, worried about his son and seeming a bit lost with this aspect of fathering, as if he was more at home at the head of a boardroom table than dealing with a teenage boy.

She plucked a couple of last year's strawberries from a bag in the freezer and, once the lemonade had heated, dropped the frozen berries into the now-steaming cups. "I'll carry," she said to her daughter. "You go pick out the book."

Amy was off, sorting through a basket of toys and books as Ronni settled into a corner of the couch. She placed the lemonade on the coffee table as Amy returned dragging five of her favorite bedtime stories.

"We don't have the tree decorated yet," Amy complained as she stood on the couch and pressed her nose to the windowpane. The tree they'd picked out from a local stand was propped against the rail of the porch. Amy's breath fogged the glass as she peered at it.

"I know. We'll do it tomorrow."

"Now."

"Not now. I just got clean from taking care of the horses. If I started fooling around with the tree, I'd probably get pitch all over me, and so would you. Besides, you wanted some strawberry lemonade."

Amy wasn't really listening. Once she got an idea in her head, that particular notion was set in concrete. "Katie Pendergrass's daddy did theirs after church on Sunday."

"Do you think he'd come and help me with ours?" Veronica teased, touching her daughter on her crown of silky curls.

"Why not?"

Veronica laughed, then sipped from her cup. "He probably has a dozen reasons."

"You could call him."

"No way, José. Tomorrow we'll put up the tree and we'll manage alone."

Amy's face fell in on itself and a sly look came into her round eyes. Veronica braced herself. Though not yet five, Amy had already learned about feminine wiles and how to wheedle to get what she wanted. It was annoying—being manipulated by a four-year-old. "But I want a tree."

"You'll have one. That one." Veronica tapped on the window with her fingernail and pointed at the rugged little fir. She couldn't help noticing that the lights were on in the Johnson place again and she wondered if she had permanent neighbors or people who were just hanging out at the old lodge for the holidays. She still thought they might be trespassers, people camping out and gaining free rent. *Or maybe they're here to stay.*

"I want one today," Amy insisted, drawing Ronni back to the conversation about the Christmas tree. She picked up her lemonade, took a sip and lost interest again.

"Tomorrow," Veronica said firmly. "I'll tell you what, though, we can put up the stockings tonight."

"Can we?" The storm clouds in her daughter's eyes suddenly disappeared.

"Mmm. See if you can find them."

"In one of the boxes?" Amy said, already squirming from the couch, her feet in motion as they hit the floor.

"That's right."

Amy started rummaging through the old cardboard crates. Ronni took a final sip from her cup, then stepped into her slippers and cinched the robe a little tighter around her middle. By the time she crossed the room, there were ornaments, tinsel, strings of lights and tissue paper all over the floor.

"Hey, slow down," she admonished, eyeing the decorations and frowning. "I know they were in a white box with—"

"Here they are!" Amy yanked two stockings out of a box and held them up proudly. One was red with felt-and-sequin angels, holly and hearts on it, the other green and decorated with a miniature baseball bat and glove, Santa face and reindeer.

Veronica's heart wrenched painfully. Memories assailed her and she remembered Hank had worked overtime for two months each evening that first fall after they had married. While dinner was simmering on the stove and she was waiting up for him, she'd spent her evenings watching television and working on her secret projects, lovingly sewing the felt pieces and sequins together by hand. The red stocking was hers, the green had belonged to Hank. She'd never had the heart to throw his away. "Oh, honey . . . well, isn't there another one—white, I think?"

Amy dropped the first two on the floor and tossed out the Christmas-tree skirt before discovering the third stocking—white felt decorated with a rocking horse, teddy bear and mistletoe. Sequins glittered under the lights. "Here's mine!" Amy cried, waving the stocking like a banner while Veronica picked up the scattered decorations.

"Let's hang yours and mine on the mantel," Veronica suggested, her voice thick as she placed Hank's stocking back into the box. She closed the lid and her memories of their first Christmas with Amy, who, barely able to sit up, had stared at the lighted tree with wide, wondrous eyes.

Together, Veronica and Amy draped the stockings from the nails that were permanently driven into the mortar just below the mantel and Veronica tried not to notice that one nail was vacant, a reminder that their family was no longer three.

She tucked a damp curl behind her ear. Maybe Amy was right. They could get a puppy this Christmas and in the coming year she could construct the dog's own stocking so that it wouldn't be quite so obvious that there was a void in their lives.

"They're beautiful, Mommy," Amy said proudly as she gazed at the glittery socks, their toes nearly touching the curved top of the fireplace screen.

"And think how nice they'll look when we put the fir boughs and holly on the mantel. Come on, now, time for bed."

Amy went through her ablutions, standing on a stool while brushing her teeth, wiping her face and extra toothpaste onto a wet towel, then climbing the stairs to the loft. At her bed, she fell to her knees and began to pray, saying the usual "God Blesses" for Aunt Shelly, Uncle Vic, her twin cousins and Veronica. She paused a moment, then added, "And please, God, bring me a puppy for Christmas and a new daddy so my mommy won't be so sad. Amen." Scrambling off her knees, she climbed into bed and slid between the covers.

Veronica didn't move. Her heart felt like lead in her chest. "Oh, honey," she whispered around a lump of tears caught in her throat. "Mommy's not sad. I've got you."

"But you miss Daddy."

"I'll always miss him," she said, kissing Amy's crown of dark curls, "but that's okay. Besides, you remind me of him every day. Aren't we happy together?"

"Happy," Amy repeated around a yawn as she threw an arm around her one-eyed stuffed tiger.

"I'll see you in the morning." Veronica smoothed a hair away from Amy's face and sighed. It was time to stop grieving, time to let go. Hank was gone, his life lost on the slopes of Mount Echo, and for the past few years Ronni had held her grief and anger inside, blaming herself, blaming the mountain, blaming the company who'd sent him the new bindings and demo skis, trying to find a reason that her husband, not yet thirty years old, had been stolen from her.

Determined to start over and push the pain of losing Hank into a dark, locked part of her heart, she walked down the stairs from the loft and eyed the pile of paperwork on her desk. Letters to be answered, orders to be filled, invoices to be paid. She should be thrilled, she supposed; her cottage business was taking off. Ronni did most of the legwork finding new items, putting together the catalog, locating new outlets, while her sister Shelly handled the day-to-day business of boxing and filling orders. Between the business, her part-time job at the mountain and Amy, Ronni didn't have time to house-train a new puppy, let alone search for a new man. Not that she needed one. She could be both mother and father to her little girl.

Then why was Amy praying for a new daddy?

"He'll be okay," Travis said, assuring his ex-wife that their son was still in one piece. He'd made the call from the first phone booth he'd found near the hamburger joint where they'd had dinner. "The doctor on the mountain thought the injury was more serious than it was, but the specialist we saw tonight in Portland is more optimistic. Bryan will be laid up a week or so because the tendons are stretched and there's some damage to the ligament, but it's hanging together and the cartilage damage doesn't look as bad as was originally thought."

"You're not just trying to make me feel better?" Sylvia asked in her pouty, accusing voice.

Travis closed his eyes and didn't give in to the urge to ask her why a woman who'd walked out on her son and husband years before would feel guilty or bad about the kid's latest injury. "No. I just thought you'd want to know." God, what time was it in France? Why was she still up?

"Why didn't you call earlier? The accident happened, what—sometime yesterday?"

"I didn't want to worry you. Besides, we didn't really know how laid up he'd be."

"So you wait until the middle of the night?" she said around a yawn.

"Sorry." Travis glanced to the dark sky. He couldn't explain that he'd been too busy to call. Things had changed since Bryan's injury; the old "fixer-upper" lodge was no longer quaint. He'd spent hours with contractors and movers, making the house as livable as possible.

"Can I talk to him?" Sylvia asked.

Rain pounded on the small, open telephone booth. Travis gauged the distance to the Jeep and nearly laughed. "Not right now. I'm in a phone booth and he's in the car, but I'll have him call you as soon as the phones are installed at the house."

"Tell him I love him," Sylvia ordered.

"Will do." Travis hung up and sighed. Ducking his head against an icy gust of wind, he strode to the Jeep and climbed inside where the radio was blasting some bass-throbbing hard-rock song. Bryan sat slumped against the passenger window and was staring through the glass. Traffic roared by, splashing water and dirt into the parking lot of the fast-food restaurant where they'd stopped for burgers after a lengthy session with the orthopedic surgeon. Though he would have to take it easy for a few weeks, Bryan would heal quickly. Things were looking up—or should have been, though Bryan had slipped back into his sullen you-can't-make-me-care-about-anything mood.

"Okay, cowboy, let's go," Travis said, turning the volume-control dial of the radio so that the riff of an electric guitar didn't threaten to burst his eardrums. Twisting in his seat, he watched for other traffic as he backed the vehicle out of the lot. Shifting into first, he nosed the Jeep into the steady stream of cars, trucks and buses heading east toward the ridge of mountains that weren't visible in the dark. "Your mom sends her love."

Bryan made a sound of disgust in the back of his throat.

"She wants you to call her when the phone's hooked up."

"She can call me."

"Bryan—"

"She took off. Not me," he charged angrily.

"It's ancient history," Travis said, but didn't add anything else. Obviously, Bryan still felt abandoned, though his perspective wasn't quite on the money. True, Sylvia had packed up and moved to Paris, but she still cared about her son—in her own, odd way.

"And I'm not a cowboy," Bryan grumbled.

Travis wasn't about to argue as he concentrated on the drive. Red beams of taillights smeared through the wet windshield as the traffic cruised along, steadily climbing through the forested foothills and across bridges spanning icy rivers. They drove through several small towns along the way and eventually the rain turned to snow that stuck to the pavement and gave a white glow to the otherwise black night.

Traffic thinned as vehicles pulled off at two ski areas that were lit up like proverbial Christmas trees. Night skiers were racing down the slopes, one of which was visible from the highway.

Soon they were nearly alone on the road. The quiet, snow-blanketed hills were soothing to Travis and he wondered why he'd clung to big-city life for so long, why chasing the dollar had been so damned important to him? When, exactly, had he lost touch with what was really meaningful in life?

"Tell me about the woman who helped you down the mountain," he said, wondering why he'd thought about her several times in the past couple of days.

"What about her?"

"Her name is Veronica, right?"

Bryan scowled. "Ronni." He reached for the volume-control dial, but a sharp look from Travis caused him to settle back against the cushions. A permanent scowl was etched across his face. "Why do you want to know?"

"I think I owe her a thank-you."

"So send her a card."

"I'd like to talk to her."

"Oh, brother. Why?"

Good question. One that had been bothering him ever since she'd flashed that blinding smile of hers in his direction. "Just curious, I guess."

"Don't tell me you've got a thing for her."

"A thing?" Travis couldn't help the amusement in his voice.

"She's not your type," Bryan muttered.

"My type?" Travis grinned in the darkness of the Jeep. "Who's my type?"

Bryan glared through the glass, watching as snow-flakes were batted away by the wipers. "You know,

Dad, I don't really think you have a type. Or maybe you shouldn't. Your track record with women isn't all that great."

Travis couldn't argue the point. The few dates he'd had since his divorce from Sylvia could only be described as nightmares. But then, he wasn't looking for a woman to go out with. He just wanted to tell Ronni Whatever-her-name-was that he appreciated her helping his injured son. That was all there was to it. Nothing else and certainly nothing romantic.

He'd learned long ago that romance, if it existed at all, wasn't for him. No woman, not even one as intriguing as Veronica, with the thick rope of dark hair and a smile as warm as morning sunshine, could change that one simple inalienable fact.

"So we can count on you and Amy for Christmas?" Shelly asked as she shoved the final box into the back of her battered old station wagon. She and Veronica had spent the past twelve hours packing the last of the orders to be shipped for Christmas, while Amy had "helped" packing stuff into boxes, coloring or playing in the snow-covered yard between the house and garage warehouse.

"Sure," Veronica said. "Why not?"

"Because you hate the holidays," her sister said as she searched in her purse and pulled out a heavy ring of keys. Three inches shorter and twenty pounds heavier than her sister, Shelly was blessed with the same dark hair and eyes, but a more rounded, softer face, larger breasts and more than the start of a belly that she'd never lost after her pregnancy with the twins, who were now six and hell on wheels.

"I love Christmas," Ronni argued.

"Sure you do. That's why you're always vowing to go to Mexico or Brazil or the Bahamas every year."

"Idle threats."

"I know, but I just wanted to make sure you'd be around. Vic and I are counting on you, and the boys would die if Amy wasn't coming."

"Sure. I'll bring the rum cake and spiced cider and molded salad."

Shelly grinned. "Just bring Amy. And maybe a date."

"A date?" Veronica laughed at the absurdity of it. Just like Shelly to suggest something so silly. "On Christmas Eve? Oh, sure. Just let me check my little black book."

"Come on, Ronni." Shelly slammed the tailgate and climbed into the front seat. "You must meet lots of cute, eligible bachelor types up on the mountain."

"I do. But they're usually wearing casts and using crutches," Veronica teased.

"Think about it."

"Oh, right. Long and hard," Veronica said as Shelly buckled her seat belt and closed the door.

Shelly twisted the key in the ignition. The old car

wheezed, sputtered and died. Pumping the gas several times, Shelly winked at her sister and tried again. A plume of blue smoke shot from the exhaust and Shelly rolled down the window. She patted the dashboard fondly. "Hasn't let me down yet."

"Knock on wood."

"See ya tomorrow." Shelly shifted into first and was off, the station wagon gently coasting along the lane that wound through the trees.

A date? Trust Shelly to come up with some lame-brained idea. Veronica smiled as she watched the blue car disappear past a thicket of fir trees. No matter what her troubles, Shelly always looked on the bright side of life. Though her husband, Victor, who had been a sawyer for a mill that had shut down last winter, was still unemployed, Shelly refused to worry. Victor managed to make a little money doing odd jobs. He chopped and hauled firewood or helped out at the gas station in town when the crew was shorthanded. Right now he spent his time down at the D&E Christmas Tree Lot, helping Delmer and Edwin Reese sell natural, flocked and even some artificial trees. Shelly just wasn't one to dwell on her troubles. "As long as there's bread on the table and gas in the tank, we don't need much more," Shelly was fond of saying. "The Lord has a way of providing for everyone."

Ronni crossed her fingers and hoped Shelly was right. She spied Amy drawing in the snow with a stick.

"Come on, let's go feed Lucy and Sam," she said, motioning in the direction of the barn. Both horses were standing outside, their winter coats thick and shaggy, their ears turned back as they stood beneath one of the fir trees in the paddock.

"Can't we make a snowman first?" Amy said, her little face crumpling in disappointment. "You promised."

"That I did," Veronica said, even though she was dead-tired.

"And put up the tree?"

"Another promise that won't be broken." If only she had her daughter's seemingly endless supply of energy. "Come on, we'd better get started."

They spent the next half hour rolling snowballs, piling them on top of each other and sculpting Mr. Snowman's face and belly. The result was a decent enough Frosty, especially when he was given a stocking cap, carrot nose and stones for eyes.

Setting up the tree proved more difficult. After the horses were locked into the barn and fed and watered, Ronni and Amy struggled with the little fir tree. Veronica had to keep biting her tongue to keep from swearing as she tried to adjust the trunk in the stand while attempting to keep the tree standing as close to straight as possible. "You know, when Uncle Vic sold us this tree, I thought it was straight," she grumbled. "I don't know what happened." When she was finally finished, she decided to prop the tree in a corner so that it wasn't so obvious that it still listed.

For dinner they ate home-baked pizza and after the dishes were done, Ronni took a quick shower. Amy helped her string lights, popcorn and ornaments. The red tinsel that Amy had used as a boa a few nights earlier was draped in the appropriate places. But there was no star or angel for the top of the tree. "We'll find one at the bazaar." Veronica promised as she turned out all the overhead lights. Amy was sitting in the big wooden rocker—the one Hank had built before his daughter was born—and staring at the tree as Veronica plugged in the electrical cord. Hundreds of miniature lights sparked to life.

"Oooh," Amy breathed, clapping her hands together. "It's *sooo* pretty." Her face glowed in the reflection of the tree lights.

"That it is. You did a good job."

The doorbell chimed and Veronica nearly jumped out of her skin. "Who in the world . . . ?" she asked, glancing out the window to the porch. Travis Keegan, holding a bag, one shoulder propped against the door frame stood under the porch light. Snowflakes clung to his hair and the shoulders of his battered aviator jacket, and his expression was set, grim and determined, no hint of a smile in his beard-shadowed jaw. For a second she thought that something was wrong, that something must have happened to his injured son and her heart leaped to her throat. That poor kid—then Keegan's gaze touched hers through the glass and her heart jolted. His eyes were intense and bright and his expression softened a bit.

"Who is it, Mommy?"

"A man I met last Sunday."

Amy scampered across the room but Ronni barely paid attention. She was struck by the same feeling of power in him that she'd recognized in the clinic. His features were large, chiseled, all male, and the tiny lines near the corners of his mouth indicated he'd frowned too many times in the past few years and a deep-seated harshness had developed. Yet there was something in his eyes that suggested a kinder man who wanted to learn how to smile again. Never, since Hank's death, had she been attracted to another man. Travis Keegan seemed about to change all that. She couldn't help but notice the way his faded jeans hugged his hips, the wayward lock of hair that fell forward over his forehead or the tiny scar near the corner of one eye.

So what was he doing on her porch?

There was only one way to find out. Bracing herself, she yanked open the door. Wind, cold and raw, swept into the room.

"Is something wrong?" she asked.

"Wrong? No." Black eyebrows slanted together.

"But—" She sounded like a ninny. "Then why are you here?"

For the first time, a hint of a smile pulled at the corner of his mouth. "Everything's fine, it's just that I thought I owed you a thank-you . . . or something for seeing that Bryan got down the mountain safely. Everything happened so quickly, I didn't have a chance earlier." He hesitated, shook his head and smiled.

So he did have a kinder side.

A blush climbed up his neck and Ronni swallowed a smile of her own. Keegan didn't look like the kind of man to show any kind of embarrassment. "Now, to tell you the truth, I feel like a damned fool," he said.

"That makes two of us. No one ever stops by here at night, and when I saw you, I thought that something might have happened to your son, though why you'd be on my porch—" She tossed back her head and laughed. "Forgive me. I've been accused of being a pessimist, worrywart, you name it." She stepped out of the doorway, "Come in, we were just admiring our work." Still holding the door, she motioned to the little tree with her chin. "And before you say anything, the Christmas tree is straight, it's the house that's crooked."

By this time, Amy, curiosity being one of her primary personality traits, was hiding behind her mother like a skittish foal, while peeking around her legs and sizing up Travis, who was still standing on the other side of the threshold.

"So who are you?" Keegan said, bending a knee so that he could look Amy square in the eye.

"Who are *you?*" Amy repeated, refusing to answer.

"I guess it's time for formal introductions," Ronni said. "Travis Keegan, this is my daughter, Amy. And Amy, this is Mr. Keegan. He has a son, Bryan, who was hurt on the mountain a couple of days ago. I helped take Bryan to the clinic."

"You can call me Travis."

Amy's eyebrows drew together in concentration and cold air swirled into the house. "Where's Bryan?"

"At home," Travis replied as he straightened and his gaze touched Ronni's again.

"Come on in before we all freeze." She stood aside to let him pass, only then noticing that there was no truck or car parked anywhere nearby, though the snow was broken by a steady path of footprints leading into the woods. For the first time, she felt a drip of fear slide down her spine.

Still on the porch, he stomped the snow from his boots while Veronica kicked herself for asking a total stranger into the house, one who'd appeared on her doorstep like a vagabond, one whom she knew nothing about other than he had a son, could afford to go skiing and wore expensive jeans.

"You walked here?" she asked before softly closing the door. Surely she could trust him. If not, there was Hank's old deer rifle. But it was unloaded and locked in a crate in the attic. Not too handy. But then, Veronica didn't believe in owning a gun. She just hadn't been able to sell any of Hank's beloved personal belongings, including the rifle his father had bought him for his sixteenth birthday.

"It didn't seem to make much sense to drive," Keegan said. He opened the bag and withdrew a chilled bottle of wine—chardonnay—which he handed her. "To say thanks," he explained. "And to get better acquainted, I guess. We're neighbors."

"Neighbors? I don't understand, where do you . . . ?" she asked, but a sense of dread told her she already knew the answer.

"I bought Cyrus Johnson's old place a few weeks ago. Signed the papers and picked up the keys on the tenth and Bryan and I moved in just last week."

CHAPTER 4

TRAVIS WATCHED AS Ronni's face drained of color.

"Ick!" the little girl, Amy, said, staring up at him with round, horrified eyes. "It's creepy there!"

"Creepy?" Travis smothered a smile because the imp was so vehement in her appraisal of his new home.

"Shh!" Ronni sent her daughter a glance meant to hold the girl's tongue, but it didn't work. The precocious kid had to get in her two cents' worth.

"It's scary. Gots bugs and snakes and—"

"Amy! Please." Forcing a tentative smile, Ronni shook her head as Amy rambled on.

"Probably ghosts, too."

Some of Travis's doubts about hiking over here disappeared. He'd argued with himself long and hard about visiting the intriguing woman who had helped save his boy, and in the end rational thought had lost to curiosity and a desire to get to know more about her. No woman had interested him, really interested him, in a long, long while. "Ghosts?" he repeated, raising his eyebrows. "At my house?"

Wide-eyed Amy nodded with the heartfelt conviction of the young. "Lots of 'em!"

Keegan winked at her. "Haven't seen any yet."

"So you bought the old Johnson place," Ronni said, and he imagined a note of discouragement in her voice.

Amy made a big production of rolling her eyes. "You'll see," she predicted.

"There are no ghosts!" Ronni said as she set the bottle of wine on a side table in the cozy little house.

"It doesn't matter if the house is haunted or not," Travis said as he stuffed his gloves into his jacket pocket. "Even if there was a battalion of ghosts and goblins, Bryan's in such a black mood these days, he's probably scared them off." Frowning to himself, he unzipped his jacket.

"Mommy said no one would buy the old lodge 'cause it was too 'spensive."

Ronni let out a little gasp, then in an effort to change the subject, said, "Why don't you tell me how you found me since I don't remember giving out my address to anyone?"

He felt a grin tug at the corners of his mouth. "That required all of my detective skills, I'm afraid. It took hours, and I finally was forced to take drastic measures. I had to look you up in the telephone directory."

Chuckling, she tightened the belt of her robe around

her slim waist. "Sometimes I think this town's too small." She was nervous and he didn't blame her. Aside from having to deal with the little girl, she had to make small talk with a virtual stranger who had trudged through the snow and appeared on her doorstep. Walking over here tonight was a mistake, a half-baked idea that had entered his head and wouldn't be dislodged, no matter how hard he'd tried to talk himself out of it. From the moment he'd seen her leave the clinic, he'd hoped to meet her again. And he wasn't the kind of man to sit idly by while time slipped away. He was and always had been a man of action.

"I think I should apologize for my daughter," she said as Amy played with some ornaments on the tree and yawned loudly.

"Why?"

She gazed fondly at the little girl. "Sometimes Amy is a little forward, if you didn't notice."

"She's just a kid," he observed. "Remember, I've got a teenage son." He offered her a knowing smile. "Believe me, it only gets worse."

"Great!" she said sarcastically. "And I was hoping with maturity, things would improve."

"Not for a long, long time." He eyed her speculatively. Her hair, piled onto her head, was damp and curling around her face, her skin flushed as if she'd just stepped out of the shower. The thought of her naked body caused a tightening deep in his gut and he shifted his gaze away from her face and the wicked turn of his mind. "But if I were you, I wouldn't do too much apologizing for that one." He motioned toward Amy. "I'd rather meet a kid who wasn't afraid to talk to adults, to ask questions, to speak his or her mind. It's the quiet ones I wonder about."

The little girl yawned again and Ronni took her cue.

"Just let me put her to bed and we can have a glass of wine or, if you'd prefer, hot strawberry lemonade—Amy's favorite."

"I'm not tired," Amy complained, her heavy-lidded eyes belying her words.

"You never are. Come on, I'll read you a quick story."

"No night-night." Amy started to scramble away, but Veronica scooped her up and carried her, protesting loudly, up the stairs. He heard voices, Ronni's calm and even, the little girl's louder and more insistent as he removed his boots and jacket. His conscience pricked at him because he knew he was disturbing their nighttime ritual that Ronni, dressed in the soft bathrobe, was ready to settle in for the evening rather than entertain. But he hadn't been able to keep himself away, especially when he'd learned they were neighbors.

Within minutes, she was hurrying down the stairs, but she'd taken the time to replace her robe with a sweater and pair of black jeans. "You didn't have to change," he said, feeling even more like an intruder.

"No problem. I was just being lazy because I took my shower so early. Come on, I'll get a couple of glasses and we'll have a drink by the fire." With a fleeting smile, she padded barefoot into the kitchen area where she searched in a drawer and muttered to herself. "I know it's in here somewhere. Ah— *Voilà!* I've captured the elusive beast!" With a flourish, she held up the corkscrew. Dark eyes assessed him and her full mouth curved into an easy, heart-stopping smile. "Half the battle is won. You can do the honors while I find glasses." She tossed him the corkscrew.

As he uncorked the bottle, he wondered if this is what his subconscious had planned when he'd stopped by the little deli down the road and bought the wine.

"I guess I should explain about my daughter's comments earlier," Ronni said as he worked the cork free. "Amy and I walked over to the lake last summer and Amy didn't think much of the lodge. She let her imagination run away with her."

"The house does need a lot of work."

"Mmm, but it's beautiful over there. I remember when the Johnsons lived there. My dad was the caretaker for a while." Was there a touch of regret in her voice? She stood on tiptoe while trying to reach the wineglasses gathering dust on an upper shelf. "We lived in the cottage on the south side of the lake. It's still there, but in worse shape than the main house."

"Here, I'll get those." He was close enough to smell

the scent of soap clinging to her and noticed the way her sweater hugged her breasts as she reached her hands over her head to pluck the glasses from the shelf. Clearing his throat, he handed her two glasses, which she rinsed quickly in the sink and then dried with a clean cloth.

"I, um, haven't used these in a while." A trace of wistfulness crossed her features and he caught her coffee brown gaze in his. Quickly glancing away, she poured the wine, then touched the rim of her glass to his. "To new neighbors?" she asked.

He nodded. "And no more skiing accidents."

"Amen." Again that note of muted misery.

As he sipped, he took stock of the house. A tipsy Christmas tree glowed with the colored lights strung through its boughs, and stockings—two of them—hung from the mantel. A fire warmed the grate and Travis, while drinking his wine, looked for signs of a man on the premises. But the coatrack held only two ski jackets— one for a woman of Ronni's size, the other for a small child. The same was true of the skis mounted near the back door. No oversize male boots warming by the fire, no magazines targeted for men spread on the coffee table, no hunting trophies displayed on the wall or baseball bats or other sporting equipment tucked in any corners, no newspaper lying open to the sports page.

If there was a Mr. Walsh, he'd definitely made himself scarce.

Feeling out of place, Travis sat in an old rocker and she settled into a corner of the couch. "So, you've lived here, I mean in Cascadia, a long time," he remarked, remembering her comment about the caretaker's house.

"Born and bred here. I'm a native and so's Amy."

"Family nearby?"

If she thought his questions were too personal, she didn't show it. "Just my sister, Shelly. She lives closer to town with her husband, Victor, and their two boys. Twins, a couple of years older than Amy. They keep Shelly hopping." Leaning back, her dark hair falling in restless tangles that tumbled over her shoulder and curled over the swell of her breast, she studied the wine in her glass as if it held the secrets of the universe. "My folks are both gone," she said sadly as she twirled the stem of her glass between long, ringless fingers. "Dad had a heart attack years ago and didn't survive. Mom eventually remarried, moved to California and died a few years later. Breast cancer."

"I'm sorry."

"So am I," she said, growing contemplative. "So am I."

"What about Amy's father?"

She started, then stared at him as if he'd trespassed on private property. "Hank?" Sighing softly, she glanced up to the mantel where a photograph was mounted. Captured by the camera's eye, a handsome blond man in a plaid shirt, worn jeans and hiking boots was holding an infant and grinning proudly as he stood back-dropped by snow-laden fir trees.

"He died." Amy's voice floated down from her hiding spot on the landing. Clutching a beat-up stuffed animal that might have—considering the yellow-and-black stripes—once been a tiger, she peered through the rails.

"What are you doing up?" Veronica asked, her voice firm as she cleared her throat and seemed to chase away the melancholy thoughts that had gathered around her at the mention of her husband. But the sight of her child caused her eyes to twinkle and Travis suspected that the imp could get away with murder.

"He asked about Daddy."

"I know," Ronni said quickly.

Amy pointed a chubby finger in Travis's general direction. "Mommy misses Daddy. She cries sometimes—"

"Amy!" Horrified, Ronni set her glass on the table. "It's way past your bedtime. Tell Mr. Keegan goodnight." Her cheeks burned bright and she blinked rapidly as she hurried up the stairs. Amy scrambled ahead of her and Travis was left with a half-full glass of wine and an inkling that he'd stepped over an invisible and very private line, one he should never have crossed.

"I don't want to sleep!" Amy cried, her voice trailing down the stairs.

"I know, but it's time. Settle down, honey."

Restless, Travis climbed to his feet. He walked to the

tree, lit so brightly and decorated with unique ornaments that were, for the most part, hand-crafted. Strings of popcorn and cranberries were woven between the branches, so unlike the trees they'd had in Seattle.

Sylvia had always called an interior decorating company that had supplied the tree—usually a gargantuan noble fir decorated with a theme and sporting shiny ornaments, metallic bows and glittery tinsel. One year, every decoration had been gold on a white flocked tree; the next year had been red balls and ribbons on snow-dusted bows. But the most memorable had been a flocked blue tree with navy and silver ornaments that had fascinated Bryan when he was about six. He'd played with the ornaments until several broke and then he wasn't allowed in the living room until Christmas morning, after the annual office staff party where everyone from the company was invited to their house to ooh and aah over the elaborate decor and pick at catered trays of hors d'oeuvres and fill their rented glasses from fountains of champagne.

As Travis thought about it now, he cringed. The holidays had come and gone but they'd held no soul. Christmas had been a time for spending a lot of money and putting on a show. New Year's Eve had been a day to hand out bonuses and party long into the night. All that was about to change. This year was going to be different. In the extreme.

Veronica, blowing her bangs from her eyes, hurried

down the stairs. "It's official. Amy's down for the night. Exhaustion won over curiosity, thank God."

"I should probably get a move on, anyway." Standing, he reached for his jacket. "I don't want to leave Bryan alone too long."

She didn't argue, just walked him to the door. "Thanks for the wine," she said after he'd slid into his boots and zipped his jacket. "It wasn't necessary."

"I know, but, to tell you the truth, I wanted to see you again."

"You did? Why?"

He stared at her a moment and her brown eyes seemed to reach into his and search past his soul. "I wish I knew," he admitted with a shake of his head. "I wish to God I knew." He grabbed hold of the doorknob, then hesitated. "Stop by sometime. I'll give you the grand tour and maybe then we'll be able to show Amy that the lodge isn't haunted."

She laughed softly. "I don't think that's possible."

"Wrong, Veronica," he said, thrusting open the door. "Haven't you learned yet that anything's possible?"

"Keegan? Travis Keegan?" She shook her head. "You know, that name sounds familiar . . . but . . . no, I've never heard of him." Shelly said as she poured another cup of coffee from the pot on Ronni's counter. This morning they'd shipped out a few late orders that had to be rushed to the nearest express mail company and were taking a break at the kitchen table.

"He's not from around here." Ronni straightened the napkin holder and salt and pepper shakers—Christmas elves in honor of the season.

"Oh." Shelly eyed her sister skeptically. "You—and a new guy?"

"Don't get any ideas. He's just someone I met and you'll get to meet him, too. He bought the Johnson place."

"*Bought* it? But I thought you were interested."

"I was."

"Wasn't the real estate agent supposed to call you if anyone had a serious offer?"

"Taffy told me she would, but it's not like I could have bought it if I'd known anyone was interested. I couldn't scrape up a down payment if my life depended upon it."

"Still, she should have phoned. Taffy LeMar was always a flake. A flirt and a flake. Even in high school. I never liked her much."

"She wasn't obligated to let me know about the house selling, she was just going to call as a favor. Besides, it was probably just a pipe dream, anyway."

"I believe in pipe dreams." Shelly walked to the refrigerator, pulled out a carton of cream and added a thin stream to her cup. "But then, I guess I have to." Biting her lower lip, she shoved the carton back onto the shelf and closed the fridge door. "I have some news of my own."

"Good or bad?" Ronni asked, puzzled by her sister's change in attitude. Shelly was always so happy-go-lucky, a person who was known to fly by the seat of her pants and somehow make everything turn out right. Now her brown eyes were dark and serious.

"Depends upon who you ask. Me or Vic."

Ronni's stomach knotted in apprehension. "What?"

Resting a hip against the counter, Shelly watched the clouds of cream roll in her dark brew.

"Uh-oh. Shelly?"

Blowing across the top of her cup, Shelly stared at her sister. "I'm pregnant."

"What?" Thunderstruck, Ronni nearly dropped her mug. *Pregnant?* "But—"

"I know, I know, I don't need a lecture." Tears starred Shelly's lashes and she blinked rapidly. "This couldn't have come at a worse time with Vic's being out of work and all, but you know something, Ronni, I'm happy about it. We've always wanted another baby and I guess we're going to have one." She was smiling despite the tears drizzling from her eyes.

How in the world were they ever going to make it? Financially strapped as they were, another mouth to feed was the last thing they needed. On the other hand, the thought of a new baby was invigorating and uplifting. Maybe a new member of their family was just what they needed.

"I think this calls for a celebration!" Ronni said,

though she was stunned. Not only was Vic out of work but Shelly was already run ragged. Between working for Ronni and dealing with the twins, Shelly barely had a minute to herself. How could she squeeze in any extra time for an infant?

"Vic doesn't think so." Shelly wiped her eyes with the back of her hand, smearing streaks of mascara that were already running down her cheeks. "He—well, he's in a state." When she read the horror on her sister's face, she held up a hand. "Don't get me wrong, he doesn't want me to do anything to jeopardize the pregnancy, but—"

"But he's not happy."

"And he blames me."

"Didn't a wise man once say that it takes two to tango?"

Shelly laughed a little and dabbed at her eyes with a napkin. "He knows that, but he's just having a little trouble adjusting. He'll get used to the idea."

"He'd better," Ronni said, her hackles up a bit. She liked Victor, he was a great guy, but he had a tendency to place blame and come up with excuses when things didn't go exactly as he planned. Though Ronni didn't doubt for a minute that he'd be as good a father to this new baby as he was to the boys, another child was a burden as well as a joy.

"Vic's worried, and, really, I don't blame him. We don't have insurance, you know, and if there are any complications, like last time with the twins and the C section . . . it could be devastating." Taking a deep breath, she straightened her shoulders. "Look, I didn't mean to bring you down, I just wanted you to know that you're going to be an aunt again."

"And I'm thrilled," Ronni said from the bottom of her heart. Sliding out of her chair, she crossed the room and hugged her sister fiercely. "There's nothing so special as a new little person."

"I knew you'd feel that way," Shelly said, her eyes filling with tears once more. A broken little sob escaped her throat. "Oh, look at me, blubbering and going on. You know how emotional pregnant women are."

"So when's the blessed event going to occur?"

"Middle of July. I suspected that I might be pregnant last month, even took one of those in-home tests, but I didn't want to say anything until I'd seen the doctor."

Ronni was disappointed; while growing up, and even as adults she and Shelly had shared their deepest secrets. "I don't blame you," she lied. "And really, you couldn't have chosen a better time of year to have the baby. No worry about not being able to get to the hospital because of the weather in July." She squeezed her sister's shoulders again. "Well, come on. We just have time for me to take you to lunch before I have to pick up Amy."

"But we should work."

"Nah. The shipping's done for the day and I can clean up tomorrow. I'm closing down the shop at the beginning of the week anyway and I think we"—she glanced pointedly at her sister's belly—"all three of us, need a break. Come on, get your jacket. Hamburgers on me."

Shelly brightened. "Okay, but just this once. The doctor's already worried about my weight."

Ronni grinned. "Good. Then I get your fries."

Shelly took a look at her sister's slim figure. "You're disgusting," she said with a grin.

"Yeah, but I work hard at it." Ronni tossed Shelly's thick jacket to her. "You know, Shell, I think this is the best news I've heard in weeks."

Ronni wrapped a scarf around her neck as they trudged through the snow to her van. The snowman was still standing, looking a little heavier with a fresh layer of snow dusting his features, and the tracks where she and Amy had rolled the snowballs were covered with white again.

The old Ford started without a fuss and as they drove passed the turnoff to the old Johnson place—now the Keegan lodge—Ronni bit her lip. She'd envisioned the huge old lodge as a bed-and-breakfast inn that she'd own and manage, and Shelly and Vic could move into the caretaker's house and out of their small duplex in town.

Snapping on the radio, she heard the first strains of "White Christmas." She'd had a lot of silly dreams, she realized, but they'd all changed in the past few days. All because of Travis Keegan.

* * *

"Come on, come on," Travis growled, glaring at the fax machine and waiting for a report that was supposed to have been transmitted. For the most part, everything was working correctly. He'd had to call an electrician whose crew had worked the better part of a week rewiring the old house, bringing it up to code, making sure that there was enough power to accept the strain of the additional equipment such as the microwave, satellite dish, three televisions, extra telephone lines, computer, modem, fax machine, printer and on and on.

He'd converted a small first-floor bedroom with a bay window overlooking the lake for his private office, which was linked electronically to the factory and home office just northeast of Seattle. His vice president, Wendall Holmes, was in charge of operations. When Travis had decided to move to Oregon, he and Wendall had worked a deal and now Wendall was buying shares of the sporting goods company. Eventually, if everything worked out over the long haul, he and Travis would be equal partners in TRK, Inc., which was the umbrella corporation for all his businesses.

For his part, Travis was glad to be this far away from the rat race.

The fax finally whirred and pages started spewing forth, a memo from Wendall and sales reports, accounting information, employee reviews, everything. Satisfied that the electronic linkup was working properly, Travis began reading through the latest proposal from the advertising firm handling his company's accounts, the newest marketing strategy to sell more skateboards, snowboards and ski equipment. The new line of apparel called Rough Riders was selling well in the Northwest and as far south as Sacramento. Yes, Wendall was doing a more than respectable job and this setup hundreds of miles away was working.

He worried a little because just two days ago this room was cold enough for ice to sheet on the inside of the windows. He'd contacted a local contractor who'd helped him with some preliminary remodeling and revamping of the place. Storm windows had been added and a new furnace and duct work were scheduled to be installed at the beginning of next week. A plumber had already given his estimate to replace the ancient pipes and fixtures. Some walls would have to be broken into and it looked as if there was no chance of a simple remodeling job, but maybe that was good. Travis had envisioned Bryan working with him to restore the old lodge. Trouble was, Bryan wasn't interested. He was still grousing about missing his friends in Seattle and now that he was laid up, the father-and-son bonding would have to wait for other projects.

At that moment, he heard his son hitching himself across the huge room they'd designated as the living area. A few seconds later, the rubber tips of Bryan's crutches came into view and he was leaning against the door frame.

"I called Marty today."

"Did you?"

"So that he would have my new number."

"Good idea." Travis tried not to show any sign of emotion though he didn't trust Marty Sinclair, a friend of Bryan's from Seattle. The kid had been in and out of trouble for the past six or seven years, his latest stint involving driving under the influence of alcohol with a suspended license. There had been another incident with stolen compact discs and then the trouble with vandalism. Bryan had been in on that one. All these "incidents" and Martin was barely sixteen. He'd only escaped being sent to a juvenile center because his old man had money and a bevy of lawyers at his command. "What did Martin want?"

"For me to fly up and spend the weekend with him."

This was the part he hated. Saying no. It was harder than any kid could ever imagine. "I think you'd better stick around. You've got another appointment with the doctor on Monday and sooner or later we've got to register you for school."

"Yeah at Backwoods High. What do they teach here— whittling, tobacco spitting and log rolling?"

"Those are just electives," Travis replied, managing to keep a straight face while consternation crossed his son's features. Obviously, Bryan was in no mood for jokes.

"Sure, Dad. Look, I don't see what going back home would hurt. It's just a couple of days," he whined.

"This is home now. Marty can come and visit."

"Here?" Bryan gestured broadly, taking in the entire lodge with its rough cedar walls and sparse furniture.

"Sure, he could think of it as camping, you know, roughing it."

"Travis, get serious!"

"I am."

"This is *Nowhere*, USA. Marty's not going to want to come here."

"He would if he's a good friend."

"Yeah, and if I were a good friend, I'd go up there."

"The answer is no."

"You hate all my friends."

"No, Bry, not true." Travis snapped out the lights in the den and walked down the short hall to the living room with its dying fire and tall windows, all of which would be eventually replaced with double panes. Bryan followed after him, his crutches moving jerkily over the old wooden floors. "I like all your friends, including Marty. But I don't think he's a very good influence right now," Travis said.

"Just 'cause we got caught ripping off a couple of hood ornaments."

"Right. Stealing and vandalism all wrapped up together."

"The car belonged to Marty's uncle. The guy's a jerk."

Travis raised a hand. "Good thing he wasn't enough of a jerk to swear out a complaint against you. Do you realize how lucky you were that he let you pay for the damage and get off without dealing with the police?" Bryan had spent four weekends stacking boxes in Travis's sporting goods company's warehouse in order to earn the money to pay off his debt. "Look, call Marty back and invite him to come spend some time over the holiday break, but don't count on going to Seattle."

Bryan wanted to argue; Travis saw all the classic signs, defiant light in his eyes, chin thrust forward belligerently, fists opening then closing over the handholds of his crutches, but he didn't argue. With a sound of disgust, the boy turned and headed back to his room on the first floor. It was small, originally some kind of servants' quarters, Travis suspected, but until the remodeling was finished and Bryan could mount the stairs, there was no reason to move him to the second floor.

Bryan's door slammed, the noise echoing through the high-ceiling rooms.

He'll get over it, Travis told himself. He looked around the big, empty lodge and thought of Ronni's cozy cabin just down the lane. With a lumpy snowman standing guard and a string of lights on the front porch, the little cottage seemed more like home than this cold, empty behemoth. But all that would change—he'd see to it.

Walking along the hallway to Bryan's room, he

called loudly, "Come on, Bryan, I'll buy you dinner, then we can pick out a Christmas tree."

No answer. Just the pounding sound of rock music.

Travis rapped sharply with his knuckles, and pushed open the door. "I said, let's find ourselves a tree."

"Can't you have one delivered?" Bryan was lying on his makeshift bed, his hands stacked behind his head as he stared through the window to the moonlit night. Some hard rocker was screaming through the speakers of the stereo.

"I suppose, but we can pick one out."

"Oh, sure. Next I suppose you'll want to pull a Paul Bunyan routine and chop down your own!" He slid his father an ungrateful look. "If only I could remember where I put my ax and blue ox. Get real, Travis."

"Lose the attitude."

"I don't have an attitude, I'm just bored."

"Well, it's time to change all that." Travis snatched a pullover from a wrinkled pile and tossed it onto his son. "Let's go, Bry. I'll buy you a pizza and a rootbeer, too, but not one more word about going north for any part of the holidays."

"You just don't know what it's like," Bryan grumbled as he struggled into a sitting position and reached for the hooded sweatshirt. "This is a big adventure for you. Throw away the suit and tie, put on flannel shirts and jeans and move to Oregon. Play Dad for a while. Don't you know that I don't know anyone here—not one stupid person? How do you think I'm gonna feel walking into that school the day after New Year's, huh? You know how embarrassing it will be to be introduced to each class—to have the principal or the teachers tell the kids to welcome me, that we all should become fast friends?" He blinked against tears blurring his vision. "It's gonna be hell, Travis," he said, swallowing hard. Jerking to his feet, he sniffed loudly. "Good thing I know just who to blame."

CHAPTER 5

RONNI SLID HER skis into the back of the van and slammed the back doors. She was tired. It had been a long, hard day on the mountain. Strong winds and whiteout conditions had closed down the upper lifts and she'd had to deal with lost skiers and too many injuries. Finally, the storm had abated and the sun had dared to peek through the dark clouds, even as a few final flakes floated to the ground. But the damage had already been done. Rubbing the kinks from her neck and finding her keys in her pocket, Ronni was thankful the day was over. She envisioned a hot cup of tea and a warm bath.

Then she spied Travis Keegan leaning against the driver's door of her van, his arms folded over his chest as if standing in the middle of the parking lot of Mount Echo's base lodge was the most natural thing in the world. Wearing aviator sunglasses, old jeans and a rawhide jacket, he managed a thin replica of a smile when he saw her.

"Fancy meeting you here," she quipped, yanking off her cap and shaking out her hair.

"I was looking for you."

She couldn't help the silly little jump in her pulse when his gaze, hidden though it was, sought hers. "Why?"

"I think I need your help." Sunlight refracted against his dark lenses and he scowled as if the admission was difficult. It probably was. Keegan didn't appear to be the kind of man who asked for assistance. While everyone else was wearing down coats and parkas, ski pants and woolen hats, he stood bareheaded, snow catching in the dark strands of his hair, the arms of his jacket shoved up to his elbows, his big hands bare.

A horn honked as a four-wheeled pickup roared past. Ronni waved to Tim and his son before turning her attention to Travis and quieting the unsettling feeling that played with her mind whenever he was around. There was something about him that put her on edge, made her restless, though she didn't know why.

Because he's attractive, sexy and a take-charge kind of guy, the first man who's interested you since Hank. Oh, God. She nudged that wayward thought back into a dark corner of her mind where it belonged.

"What kind of help?"

"I need your expertise," he admitted.

Laughing, she said, "My expertise? Let me guess— how to tie a four-year-old's shoelaces?"

"Nothing quite so complicated," he drawled and behind his tinted lenses his eyes sparked. "Why don't you let me buy you a cup of coffee or a drink while I plead my case?"

Tilting her head to the side and sizing him up, she decided it wouldn't hurt. Hadn't everyone she knew told her it was time to start meeting people again, time to start letting go of the past? "Why not?" She checked her watch. "I have to pick up Amy in about forty-five minutes, but until then, I'm free." The errands she was going to run before she stopped at Shelly's to collect her daughter could wait until later.

Travis Keegan interested her and it had been long, too long probably, since she'd spent any time alone with a man. Maybe Amy was right. Maybe she was lonely. No, she told herself as they walked carefully over the icy ruts of the parking lot and climbed the metal-grate steps to the lodge, she just missed Hank.

They found an unoccupied booth near the window of the café where they each ordered cups of Irish coffee. Floor-to-ceiling windows provided a panorama of white snow, tall evergreen trees and skiers racing down the runs.

"How long have you been a part of the team?" he asked, motioning to her red jacket with its patch proclaiming her part of the ski patrol.

"Ever since I was eighteen," she admitted with a smile. "*Years* ago."

"You must be quite a skier."

"My dad had my sister and me up on skis about the time we learned to walk," she admitted. "He was part of the patrol and a ski instructor part-time, so it was pretty natural that Shelly and I would follow in his footsteps—or ski tracks, I guess."

"Shelly—your sister?"

"Yeah. She still lives in town, too."

"You're close?"

"Best friends." Ronni nodded as the waitress brought glass cups filled with coffee and topped with whipped cream. A drizzle of green crème de menthe added a bright spot of color that melted into the cream. "You said something about needing my expertise," she prodded, expecting him to ask her to teach Bryan the finer points of skiing. She was wrong.

Travis scowled and took a swig from his mug. "I can't believe I'm here doing this."

"What? Doing what?"

"Asking you to help me organize the house for Christmas . . . I realize it might be an imposition, and believe me, if you don't want to help, I'd understand. And I'd pay you for your time—"

"What time? What are you talking about?"

"The tree. Some garlands. A strand or two of lights, I guess." He leaned closer and took off his sunglasses. "Look, I can't believe I even care about anything as trivial as Christmas decorations, but after I stopped by your place the other night, I decided that drafty old lodge could use some sprucing up for the holidays. This is

Bryan's first Christmas away from his friends and . . . well, he's apart from his mother and laid up and I thought . . . hell, I don't know what I thought," he admitted, looking up at the high cedar ceiling in frustration. "This is all fairly new to me—this single-parenting business and you're so good with your daughter. I tried to talk Bryan into picking out a tree with me the other night and you would've thought I'd asked him to rip off his toenails. Anyway, it didn't happen, but I think . . . well, some kind of decoration would help make the place feel more like home."

She stared at him in wonder. "You want *me* to help *you* organize your house for the holidays?"

"Something like that." Shaking his head as if he was disgusted with himself, he lowered his eyes so that his gaze touched hers. In that single heart-stopping moment, she felt a spark, a connection, as if his soul was reaching for hers . . . but that was silly. Good Lord, what was wrong with her? He rimmed the top of his mug with one finger. "To tell you the truth," he told her, "I haven't been much of a father to Bryan. Too many years spent in the office, at meetings, trying to make a bigger profit, expand the company, make more money." He spewed out the words as if they tasted bad. Another swallow from his mug. "I missed a lot, didn't spend as much time with Bryan as I should have and I'm now trying to . . . ."

"Make up for lost time?"

"So to speak."

She stirred the cream into foam that melted into her coffee. "And you think throwing up a few lights and strings of tinsel will change all that?"

"No," he admitted with a sound of disgust. "I can't change the past. That's the way we lived our lives, like it or not. I made a helluva lot of mistakes, so did my ex-wife, but I'm trying to make it up to Bryan now."

"And be a real father rather than an absentee?" she said, unable to keep her tongue from being harsh. She'd seen a lot of men who didn't have time for their families, who were so concerned about chasing after the dollar or other women that they ignored and neglected their wives and children. Oftentimes, they ended up divorced, with a new, younger wife and no relationship with their kids whatsoever. And then there were men like Hank, a man who would have done anything for his newborn baby. A man who was snatched from life far too young. Bitterness climbed up the back of her throat. "You can't make up fourteen years in one Christmas."

His jaw tightened. "I know that."

"And you can't hire a stranger to come in and expect her to toss some glitter around the house, throw up a Christmas tree and hang a few sprigs of mistletoe in the hopes that the spirit of Christmas will see fit to touch your home."

"I'm just trying to get started on the right foot," he said, his voice rising in pitch. "Look, I was hoping you and Amy would come over and we'd . . . I don't know, have a tree-trimming party or whatever you want to call it."

"And you would pay me?" she asked, sick inside.

"Right."

It all seemed so callous, so unfeeling, so crass and commercial. So *un*Christmassy. "No thanks." She stood, reached into her wallet and found a couple of dollars, which she slapped onto the table.

"I offended you." He seemed surprised.

"Bingo." She placed both hands flat on the table's surface and leaned forward so that her nose was close to his. Staring deep into his eyes, she noticed the varying shades of gray and the thick spiky lashes that refused to blink. "Look, Keegan, I know you're used to the city, to the boardroom, to giving orders and expecting everyone to hop to them. You're one of those corporate executives who flies around in a private jet, sleeps at the best hotels and thinks that he can buy anything he pleases, including a merry Christmas for his son, but you're wrong. Christmas, real Christmas, comes from the heart, not the pocketbook.

"Now, whether you want to hear it or not, I'm going to give you some advice," she continued, holding his stare, feeling the heat radiate from him, sensing the anger that caused his chin to tighten and his nostrils to flare. "Cascadia is a small town, the people are close-knit, they help one another because they want to, not because they feel obligated or because they expect to be paid. That's why it's so special here. That's why I live here and that's why big-wheels from the city sometimes have trouble fitting in.

"Goodbye, Mr. Keegan. Thanks for the company."

She turned to leave but he caught her wrist in a quick motion. On his feet in an instant, he pulled her body close enough that her breasts nearly brushed his chest. Almost—but not quite. "Look, lady, I didn't mean to insult you."

"Well, you did."

"I—"

"Leave it alone, Keegan," she said, yanking her hand from his. "We're just neighbors, we don't have to like each other." Spinning on her heel, she walked stiff-backed out of the café and sensed him watching her every move.

"You did what?" Shelly said, dipping her French fry into a pool of catsup in the paper-lined burger basket. They were sitting in a booth at a local hamburger den and an old song from the Righteous Brothers was play-ing over the sound of the loudspeaker for the drive-up, the rattle of French fry baskets, orders being yelled to the cooks and the scrape of spatulas on the grill.

The restaurant, a hangout for teenagers ever since Ronni and Shelly had been adolescents, was about half-full. Their children were in the next booth arguing over how Santa could possibly finish his rounds and slide down everyone in the world's chimney on Christmas Eve.

Ronni swirled her straw in her soda. "I guess I told him to get lost. Not in so many words, maybe, but he got the message."

"Are you out of your mind? Why?" Shelly snapped up her French fry and munched blissfully.

"I didn't like his attitude."

Rolling her eyes, Shelly wiped the salt and oil from her fingers on a paper napkin. "The most interesting bachelor to show up in town in years—at least that's the way Taffy LeMar describes him—and you tell him to get lost? You know, Ronni, sometimes I think you should have your head examined."

"So you talked to Taffy?" Ronni said, still disappointed that her friend hadn't let her know that the old Johnson place was going to be the new Keegan estate. As many times as she reminded herself that there was no way she could have bought the land and the old, rambling lodge on it, she wished she'd had the chance to put some kind of deal together. *With what?* She'd saved twenty-five thousand dollars from the insurance money when Hank had died, but that money was earmarked for Amy's education and so far she hadn't touched a dime of it. Not that it would have helped all that much.

"Yeah, I talked to Taffy and she was lit up like the proverbial Christmas tree, all atwitter about Keegan, saying he's tall, dark, handsome and single." Shelly slid a glance toward her boys, then said, "I reminded Taffy that you were interested in the place and she mumbled something about being sorry but that this guy just swept into the real estate office, told them what he wanted, how much he wanted to spend and within twenty-four hours the deal was done."

"That sounds like Keegan," Ronni said.

"How would you know?"

"As I said, it's the man's attitude."

"Men," Shelly said, shaking her head as her eyes clouded over. "Sometimes . . ." Her voice faded off.

"How's Vic these days?"

Shelly sighed and leaned an elbow on the table. "Trying to buck up, I think. He says he's excited about the baby, but he's worried. I can tell. He's started talking about moving to California again. His brother would hire him, but what does Vic know about computers?"

"He could learn," Ronni suggested. "Vic's only what—thirty-five?"

"I know, I know, but he hates to be cooped up. An office job would kill him." She frowned, then heard the boys' voices begin to rise. "Kurt, Kent, hold it down," she ordered.

"But he stole one of my chicken nuggets," Kurt complained.

"Don't you each have your own?"

The thought of Shelly moving away was depressing, but Ronni would never show it. She and Shelly had been best friends all their lives except for a period in high school when they'd pretended not to know each other. Now they saw each other every day and Amy thought of the twins more as brothers than cousins. Shelly had been Ronni's strongest support when Hank had been killed and the thought that she might be moving away was devastating.

"Has it really come to that—to leaving?" Ronni asked.

Shelly's eyes were dark with worry. "I hope not," she said, "but Vic needs to find work, permanent work, to make him feel good again." As quickly as the concern had crossed her features, she chased it away with a smile. "I tell him not to worry—things always have a way of working out, but you know Victor. If he didn't have something to fret about, he wouldn't be happy."

Ronni laughed, because that much was true. Ever since Ronni had known him, Victor Pederson had been a guy who stewed about the future, while the wife he'd chosen barely looked past the end of the week.

"You know, Shelly, if things are bad, I've got money—"

"Amy's inheritance? Forget it. We've been over this before, Ronni." She picked up the tray. "Now, forget about me for a second and think about your new neighbor. The way I see it, the man just asked for a favor. He needs help decorating for Christmas, so he offered to pay you. Is that such a crime?" She turned her head and shot out of her chair. "Kurt, stop it! Now." Kurt had his

brother in some kind of headlock and Kent was screaming. "I think it's time we took off," Shelly said as the
boys, red faced and hurling insults, squared off. "I'll call
you later. Come on, boys, let's go. Now!" She grabbed
each one by a tight, grimy little fist and shepherded
them out of the restaurant.

"Come on, Amy," Ronni said, gathering up the
trash. "I think it's time we left, too."

"Why do they do that?" Amy asked, her little face a
knot of vexation as she stared through the swinging
glass doors to the parking lot where her cousins were
climbing into Shelly's big car.

"What? Oh, you mean the boys? Why they fight? It's
just natural, I guess. Aunt Shelly and I used to fight."

"No!"

"All the time. It drove Grandma nuts." She tossed
the trash into one of the containers near the door, then
paused to help Amy zip her jacket.

"You don't fight anymore."

"Oh, but we did, like cats and dogs, even though we
were really each other's best friend. I know it sounds
silly, but it's true. Kurt and Kent will get over it, too. But
not for a long, long time."

"It's a pain," Amy said as Ronni tied her hood in
place.

"I'll second that."

"If I had a sister, I'd never fight with her."

Ronni laughed as she searched for her car keys.

"So why don't I?" her daughter demanded.

"Have a sister?" Ronni asked as she pushed open the door. "I thought you wanted a puppy."

"I do!" Amy said with a grin, her attention derailed from the subject of a sibling, a painful subject that came up every once in a while. Long ago, Ronni had promised herself she'd never have an only child, that because of her close relationship with her sister, she'd want Amy to have a brother or sister. Hank had agreed, for the opposite reason. He'd had no brothers or sisters and thought he'd missed out.

But then fate had stepped in and taken him and any plans for another baby.

"Come on," Ronni said, refusing to dwell on the past. She planned to make it her New Year's resolution that she'd start living her life for the future, not for the past. And she didn't have to wait until New Year's—she could make that resolution today, even though there were several weeks of this year left.

They stepped into the parking lot just as Shelly's car eased into traffic. Ronni tried to envision her sister with another baby and she smiled. Shelly was cut out to be a mother—she was right, things would work out. "Have faith," she told herself.

"What?" Amy screwed up her face and stared up at her.

"Nothing, sweetheart. Hey, let's go see what they've got in there," she said, pointing across the street to the variety store that had stood on the corner of Main Street and Douglas Avenue for as long as she could remember. The display window was filled with Christmas decor—lights, ribbon, tinsel, everything a person would need to decorate their house . . . or an old hunting lodge. Ronnie held on to her daughter's hand and walked briskly to the cross walk. Shelly's words followed after her, accusing her of misinterpreting Keegan's offer, and Ronni decided there was no time like the present to right a wrong. Or to eat humble pie. Gritting her teeth, she pushed open the door of the little shop and heard Jake, the owner's parakeet, whistle out a throaty, "Come in, come in."

"Ronni and Amy!" Ada Hampton, the proprietor, grinned, showing, perfect, if false, teeth. A woman with wide hips and a wider smile, she'd stood behind the same cash register since her husband died thirty years ago. "What a nice surprise." Wearing a crisp red apron, she waddled through a narrow opening in the counter. "What can I do for you?"

"I wish I knew," Ronni replied, not really knowing where to start.

Ada reached into a voluminous pocket and pulled out a green sucker. "This is for you," she said to Amy. "You know, I used to give suckers to your mother and her sister when they were about your age," she said. "But that was a long time ago."

Jake, hopping from one perch to the other, whistled out a sharp, "Hey, honey, what'cha doin'?"

"What're you doin'?" Amy responded, licking on her sucker and staring up at the green-and-yellow bird.

"Come in. Come in," Jake said.

"Silly bird!" But Amy giggled and Jake bobbed his little head wildly.

Ada chuckled and reached for a tissue. Dabbing eyes that were always running from her allergies, she said, "Now, is there anything special you want today?"

"Lights, ribbon, garlands, the works," she replied, wondering if she was out of her mind. She only had a vague notion of what she planned to do, but it included landing on Travis Keegan's doorstep with a small fortune in Christmas decor. She only hoped he still wanted it. After their last conversation, there was a good chance she might end up with a door slammed in her face. "Do you have anything on sale—like last year's stuff?" she asked while mentally calculating what she had in stock at home and in the warehouse. Most of her mail-order Christmas inventory had been sold, but there were still a few garlands, bells and spools of ribbon. She could cut boughs of holly and cedar from some trees in her backyard. With a little money, a lot of imagination and some work, she could make the old lodge look like a Christmas picture postcard.

"I've still got a few things," Ada said, leading her to a sale table where most of the items had already been picked over. "Not much left, I'm afraid, but what's here is at bargain-basement prices."

"I think I can find what I need." Ronni picked up a

large spool of red-and-white gingham ribbon that had been marked down to half price. "This'll do just fine."

Over the thrumming beat of hard rock, Travis heard a buzzing. He listened, heard the noise again and put down his screwdriver. He'd been trying to fix the bathroom door as it wouldn't latch, and pieces of the lock were strewn across the counter. "What the devil?"

The noise quit again and suddenly there was a loud pounding on the front door. The doorbell! Of course. Something was wrong with it and the chimes were reduced to a static-laden, irritating buzz.

Thinking one of the contractors had returned to pick up a forgotten tool, he threw open the door and found Ronni and her daughter on the front porch. Involuntarily, his throat tightened at the sight of her. Wearing oven mitts, Ronni was holding a white pan, covered in aluminum foil. The scents of tomato sauce and cheese seeped out in the steam rising from a slit in the foil. "I, uh, think I owe you an apology," Ronni said quickly. "I didn't mean to come unglued this afternoon when you asked me to help you, you just kind of blindsided me and . . . I overreacted. I brought a peace offering." She held up the pan and more tantalizing odors wafted from the dish.

"So you're here to . . . ?"

"Boy, I wish I knew," she said, shaking her head. "How about to eat a little crow?"

"Crow?" Amy, bundled in a yellow snowsuit, wrinkled her nose and acted as if Ronni had lost her mind. "It's lasagna, Mommy."

"That it is." She winked at her daughter. "I guess I forgot." She took in a long breath and squared her shoulders. "Look, you can't imagine how awkward I feel—this is really not my style, but here goes . . ." Meeting his gaze squarely, she said, "I thought we should start over and I'm going to try and be more neighborly, so Amy and I brought dinner and some Christmas decorations and if the invitation's still on, we'll have that tree-trimming party you wanted."

He couldn't stop the smile that crept from one side of his mouth to the other.

"Unless you've already eaten or have other plans," she added hastily.

"No plans and we're starved." Thoughtfully rubbing his chin, he pinned her with a stare he knew was sometimes disturbing. "You know, Ms. Walsh," he drawled, "I don't know what to say."

"'Come in' would be nice or 'Gee, thanks. Apology accepted' would do. I'd even go for, 'Woman, I'm starving. Thank God you showed up!'"

Travis laughed. Seeing her standing on the porch with her face upturned, her cheeks rosy with the cold, he felt an unlikely stirring deep in his heart that was completely out of line. She was here offering food, for crying out loud. "Okay, here goes. Woman, I'm starving. Thank God you showed up."

"That's much better." As he stepped out of the way, she strode into the house. Amy wasn't going to be left on the porch, and clutching a bag full of some kind of tinsel, she followed her mother.

"Can I help?" he asked Ronni, a little bewildered by her change of heart. Why was it he felt as if he'd just won a major battle?

"I thought you'd never ask," she teased. "The van needs to be unloaded."

"You brought more things?"

"A few," she said, then laughed lightly and the sound seemed to echo through the house. Her dark eyes sparkled and she shook the snow from her hair. "When Amy and I are asked to trim a tree, we come prepared, don't we?"

Amy nodded, but stuck close to her mother, eyeing the high ceilings and mantel as if she expected ghosts, goblins and an assortment of demons to fly down the chimney and, cackling evilly, snatch her away.

"You've done a lot with the place," Ronni said as she stopped at the step leading down to the living area and gazed across the polished floors to the bank of windows stretching along the back wall. Beyond the glass, the lake, dark and serene, was visible through snow-dusted strands of hemlock and fir trees.

"We've still got a long way to go, though. I'd like to restore it the way the original architect would have liked it—well, as much as possible, and still bring it up to the local building code. But that's going to take a while and now that Bryan's laid up, all those father-son projects have become just father jobs."

Her eyes seemed to search every nook and cranny, exploring the floor-to-ceiling bookcase, now empty, each stone of the large fireplace and every exposed beam in the ceiling. "It really is beautiful," she said, placing her warm pan down on a small table and using an oven mitt as a pot holder. Running a finger along the time-smoothed banister leading to the second floor, she gazed up at the railing of the reading loft. "I remember when there used to be huge parties thrown here and my sister and I would hide in the shrubbery and watch expensive cars line the driveway." She walked to the windows and stared into the chilly darkness where soft moon glow played upon the inky waters of the lake. "Sometimes the Johnsons would hire a singer, other times a piano player or a band and they always strung Japanese lanterns down the path and along the dock to the lake."

"Dock?"

"It's gone now," she said. "No one's brought a boat in here in years." She cleared her throat, but a trace of sadness seemed to linger in her eyes. "Oh, well, ancient history." She managed a smile as she grabbed the steaming pan again. "I'd better take this down to the kitchen or it'll get cold."

"I guess I'll unload the van," he offered, wondering what she had brought and feeling guilty that she had obviously spent not only time but money in her attempt to apologize and be neighborly. Somehow he'd have to make it up to her, but he doubted, from her reaction in the ski lodge earlier, that she'd take a check. "The kitchen's down that hallway and through—"

But she was already on her way, walking swiftly along the corridor as if she was as familiar with this drafty old lodge as she was with her own snug little cabin. Her daughter was right on her heels, never letting Ronni out of her sight and sometimes glancing nervously behind her.

Travis stood at the door a second, watching her swing down the hall. Black jeans hugged her hips and a red vest and white blouse peeked out from beneath a short woolen jacket. A scarf was wound around her neck and her black hair bounced and gleamed beneath the lights. Her back was ramrod straight, her footsteps determined—a no-nonsense lady with a vulnerability that she tried so hard to hide. He wondered what it was about her that he found so very fascinating?

A cold gust of wind reminded him that he was standing in the middle of the hallway, gaping and practically drooling, like some sex-crazed adolescent with a bad crush. "Damn it all," he muttered, not bothering with a jacket as he broke a trail through the snow to her van.

He was used to attractive, aggressive women. He'd met them in the workplace. Usually trim and sleek, always well-groomed and well-spoken, they could be bold and brash, or quiet and sedate, but they were all determined and came with their own agendas—hidden or otherwise. He'd dealt with them on a daily basis before and after his divorce. Some of the women were aggressive not only in their jobs but in their personal relationships, as well.

He'd been chased, propositioned and almost seduced by strong-willed women who, beautiful though they had been, hadn't interested him. Nor had he been attracted to the few homebodies he'd met through mutual friends, often desperate women who looked at him as if he were an answer to their prayers—a wealthy man who could help them quit chasing after deadbeat ex-husbands for child support, a means to get rid of their boring jobs.

He'd never been tempted, hadn't even started an affair that he knew would only end badly. In fact, he'd convinced himself that he was now a confirmed bachelor.

Until now.

Until he'd seen Veronica Walsh deal with his injured boy.

Until he'd seen how she handled her imp of a daughter.

Until he'd looked into those dark, knowing eyes that could penetrate all his defenses or twinkle with laughter.

She'd started to change his mind about women because she'd been so different. Strong, yet vulnerable, with a quick tongue and sharp wit. But there was something more, something deeper—a sadness—that touched him and made him feel as if he wanted to fold her into his arms and tell her everything would be all right. Hell, he was losing it. He didn't even know her, for crying out loud, and here he was fantasizing about her.

The back of the van was stacked with boxes and sacks. For the love of Saint Peter, she must have spent a small fortune. His guilt started eating at him. She was a single mother and she couldn't afford whatever it was she'd come up with.

Gritting his teeth, he carried in two boxes, then returned for four more sacks, which he set in the living room. He paused once to knock on Bryan's door and let himself in. While the beat of some grunge band was throbbing through the room, Bryan was lying on his back lifting weights.

His son slid a glance his way when he turned the volume of the stereo down several decibels.

"Hey!" Bryan complained.

"You're going to go deaf with this so loud."

"Who gives a rip?" Bryan was still giving him the cold shoulder and hoping to back Travis into a corner of guilt so that he'd break down and let him spend some of the holidays in Seattle.

"We've got company."

Bryan tried hard to keep his gaze flat and his expression bored, but he couldn't quite hide the curiosity that rose to the surface.

"Ronni Walsh and her daughter."

"The *three-year-old* you told me about?" Bryan pulled a face and pushed the weights off his chest.

"Actually, I think she's four."

"No difference. Still a little kid." He lowered the bar.

Travis wasn't going to argue with him. "Just put on a clean shirt, wash your hands and come into the kitchen. Ronni brought dinner."

"Why?"

"I asked her to help us decorate the house."

"Oh pleeease, Travis. You didn't." Again he lifted the bar and weights away from his body, his muscles straining.

"I did and it's going to be fun."

"Yeah, a blast," Bryan grumbled.

"I'll see you in five minutes," Travis said and closed the door behind him. He could only hope that Bryan's appetite, which had been phenomenal of late, would force him to comply so that they wouldn't have to get into another one of their knock-down-and-drag-out arguments.

Delicious aromas drifted from the kitchen and as Travis pushed open the swinging doors, he found Ronni tossing a salad and Amy standing on a chair beside her. The table was already set. Two candles were already lit and dripping wax down the sides of old wine bottles. The flames reflected in dozens of flickering lights upon the mullioned windows surrounding the table.

"I *hate* cucumbers," the little girl was saying.

Ronni wasn't intimidated. "Too bad, I like 'em."

"And I *hate* tomatoes."

"Not tomatoes. These are red peppers, and they're good for you."

"Then I *hate* red peppers."

"Fine, pick around them."

"I *hate* salad."

"I know, I know, but I don't really care. You're going to eat some, anyway." Ronni blew her bangs out of her eyes but looked up when the door creaked shut. With an exasperated smile, she said, "We're in a negative mood tonight. Sorry."

"Don't be. I'm used to it. Negativity seems to be a way of life around here these days. Remember, I told you it doesn't get any better."

"Thanks for reminding me." She sprinkled an oil-and-vinegar dressing over the salad greens and he was taken with how natural it seemed for her to be bustling around the kitchen. "I assume Bryan's joining us?"

"He is if he doesn't want to be grounded for the rest of his life."

"I'm here," Bryan announced as he hitched himself through the swinging doors and scowled at the crowded room.

"Good. How're you feeling?" Ronni asked.

"Compared to what?"

"Well, compared to, 'Gee, I feel great, I think I could run a marathon,' that's a ten—"

He snorted derisively.

"Or 'I feel so crummy—like I've been run over by a

steam roller and I think I'll curl up and die,' that's a zero."

"About a minus six, okay?" he grumbled and Travis felt the familiar tensing of his jaw.

Ronni's eyes glittered merrily. "Funny, you don't look near death's door, but then it's been said that looks can be deceiving. I was going to ask you if you wanted to come over and exercise my horses, but, if you're too sore—"

"Horses?" Bryan's head snapped up.

"Mmm. Quarter horses. Loose Change—we call her Lucy—and Sam," she said and Travis noticed the boy's bored expression changed slightly. "Amy and I ride them whenever we get the chance, but it would be nice if someone came over on a regular basis. It doesn't have to be right away, we're doing fine, but in the spring when your knee's healed and the doctor says it's okay, it would help me out."

Bryan glanced at his father, then rolled out his lower lip as if he didn't really care. "It's up to you," Travis said.

"I'd pay you, of course." She shot Travis a knowing look. "You could ride them around the lake over here, if your dad doesn't mind."

"Fine with me," Travis said. "As long as the doctor agrees." He could barely believe the transformation in his son. Try as he might, Bryan couldn't hide his interest. Somehow, Ronni had known how to get through to the kid when no one else—teachers, school counselors and certainly not he—could pierce Bryan's emotional armor.

Ronni screwed the cap back on the vinegar bottle. "We've got time, just think about it. Now, Amy, why don't you show Bryan what we brought?"

The little girl scrambled off her chair and rushed to the refrigerator where she found a bottle of sparkling cider and hoisted it proudly into the air over her head.

Ronni placed the salad bowl on the table between the two candles. "We usually save this for special occasions like birthdays, Christmas and New Year's, but I figured this was close enough since it's the holiday season."

"You like it?" Amy asked the teenager, her eyes round with anticipation.

"It's okay." A dismissive shoulder raised.

"Let's open it," Ronni suggested. "Bryan, why don't you do the honors? And Travis, I brought a bottle of Chianti, it's—"

"Got it," Travis said, spying the green bottle resting on the counter and scrambling through the top drawer where he thought he'd placed his corkscrew. He pushed aside spatulas, spoons, a potato peeler and a wire whisk before he located the opener. "Here we go." As Ronni placed the pan of lasagna and a basket of garlic bread on the table, he poured them each a glass. "It looks great," he said and she grinned under the compliment.

"Let's just hope it tastes as good as it looks!"

She didn't have to worry. Everyone appeared to be

hungry, and by the time the dishes were carried to the sink, most of the food had been devoured. Even Bryan, though trying to maintain an image of being cool and disdainful, ate as if he hadn't seen food in a week. When they were finished, some of the tension had eased and Amy seemed to have forgotten that the house was supposed to be haunted and inhabited by all manner of creepy-crawlies.

"Bryan and I will tackle the dishes," Travis announced and the boy didn't bother hiding his shocked look.

"Women's work," he grumbled.

"You think so?" Ronni asked, amused.

"In Seattle, we had a maid—"

"I hate to be the one to tell you, kid, but we're not in Kansas . . . er, Washington anymore."

"What?" Bryan looked at his father as if he thought Travis had lost his mind.

"An old joke, comes from the movie *The Wizard Of Oz,* I think. Never mind, you're too young, but the point is, as many of us males have learned rather painfully over the past twenty years or so, there is no such thing as women's work versus men's."

"There should be," Bryan argued.

Travis picked up his dish and carried it to the sink. "Okay, I'll grant you that men and women are different, physically, mentally and emotionally, and there have been some heated debates on the subject, lots of tempers flared, but I believe deep in my heart that men, if they wanted to, could clean the dinner dishes just as well as their wives. If only someone would give them the chance," he said.

His son rolled his eyes to the ceiling. "Oh, Travis. But maybe they don't want to."

Ronni couldn't leave it alone. "Okay, okay, you two, bring out the white flags and declare a truce. Tonight I'm going to do you a favor, Bryan. Since you're on crutches, I'll cut you a break. You show Amy around and I'll handle the pots and pans." She glanced at Travis, half expecting him to argue with her, but this time he held his tongue, and Bryan, after looking at Amy and sizing her up, made good his escape, moving out of the kitchen faster than any person on crutches should. Amy, realizing she was about to be dumped, hurried after him.

"If he thinks he can outrun her, he's got another think coming," Ronni said fondly.

"Where did you learn to handle teenage boys?" Travis asked, studying her so intently that she wanted to squirm.

"I gave ski lessons for years. Dealt with all kinds." She carried the plates and stacked them in the sink. "You're worried about him, aren't you?"

Deep furrows etched the skin between his eyebrows and he glanced at the door to the kitchen, still swinging slightly. "You know, there was a time I thought I could do anything. Didn't matter what it was. Form a company, hit a baseball, climb Mount Everest if I wanted to. I guess

I was a little full of myself." Smiling in self-mockery, he shook his head and closed his eyes. "Damn but I was wrong. I never realized how trying teenagers could be."

"You'll work it out," she predicted, turning on the faucets and listening as the old pipes squeaked and groaned.

"I hope you're right," he said, unconvinced.

The phone rang and Travis snatched the receiver. After a short pause, he grimaced, glanced at his watch and swore under his breath. "What time is it over there?" he demanded, then said, "I don't think I even want to know." He paused and listened, all the while his fingers clenching the receiver in a death grip. "No, no, he's fine, Sylvia. Better every day. I told him to call . . . oh, please, don't cry."

Ronni recognized Travis's ex-wife's name and wished there was a way she could graciously back out of the room. She didn't need to be a part of the emotional turmoil that was suddenly reeling through the room like a tornado.

"Pull yourself together, okay? I'll get him. Hang on."

All the animation had left his face. Turning on the heel of his boot, Travis stormed through the swinging doors and within minutes Bryan hobbled back through the room. His lips were pursed and his jaw tight. Before he could pick up the receiver, Ronni decided she didn't want to eavesdrop on a private conversation. Turning off the taps and grabbing a towel for her hands in one swift motion, she pushed open the swinging doors with her hips and nearly collided with Travis striding back to the kitchen.

"Oh . . . look, maybe this is a bad time. Amy and I can come back later."

"No!" he nearly yelled, then let out his breath slowly. Touching her lightly on the arm, he said, "It's just Sylvia. She's into theatrics, and right now she's ticked at me because I haven't called her every day with a progress report on Bryan."

"At least she cares—"

He cut her off with a look that silently called her a fool. "When it's convenient, that's when Sylvia cares." He opened his mouth as if to say something more, then, seeming to think better of it, snapped his teeth together. "Forget the dishes, I'll handle them later. Let's start in on the rest of the project."

"Okay, uh, I guess we should begin with a tree. You said that you and Bryan went out looking for one, but that—"

"It was a bust. A major bust. We ate dinner and by the time we were finished, it was too late. The lot was closed. Which was just as well, considering both of our moods."

"Uncle Vic will help you," Amy said.

One of Travis's dark eyebrows quirked. "Who's Uncle Vic?"

"My sister's husband. He works at a lot in downtown Cascadia for a couple of his friends."

"Then that's where we'll go." He started for his

jacket just as Bryan appeared in the doorway. His face was red, his gaze distant as he leaned on his crutches.

"I think you'd better call Mom in the morning, Travis," he said, biting his lower lip.

"Why?"

Bryan's jaw tightened in a younger whisker-free imitation of his father's. "Because she wants me to come to France."

"What? For the holidays?" Travis muttered something under his breath. "That woman doesn't know what she wants."

"No, Travis," he said and his voice quivered slightly. "You're wrong. I think this time she's serious. She says she wants me to come and live with her. And not just for a few weeks. She's talking about marrying Jean Pierre and she wants me to move in with them. Permanently."

CHAPTER 6

"DAMN THAT WOMAN," Travis said, shoving one hand through his already-rumpled hair. "Why can't she make up her mind?" Then as if suddenly realizing he had an audience, he shook his head. "She's going to marry Jean Pierre?"

"What's it to you?" Bryan wondered.

"Nothing. Nothing. She can marry whomever she pleases, but when it affects you, then I care."

Bryan's fingers clenched nervously over the smooth metal of his crutches. "Maybe it wouldn't be so bad."

"You *want* to live with your mother?" Travis demanded, pinning his son with a gaze that would make a grown man shudder. "In Paris?"

With the aid of his crutches, Bryan stood his ground and elevated his chin. "Don't know."

"You don't even speak the language."

"Couldn't be much worse than here," the boy said,

his eyes slitting in anger. "You won't even let me go up and see my friends, so what does it matter if I live in Podunk, Oregon, or Paris, France?"

"I told you Martin could come visit."

"That's not what I asked for, though, was it?" Bryan threw a scathing look around the room and started for the door. "Mom said to call her tomorrow and let her know what I want to do."

"She wasn't going to talk to me?"

"She's ticked at you," Bryan yelled over his shoulder.

"Why?"

"Because of these." He lifted one crutch. "She thinks that if you were keeping better track of me, I wouldn't have gotten hurt."

Travis's neck burned red with rage but he didn't answer, and Ronni, feeling like an outsider, said, "Maybe Amy and I should come back another time."

"No!" Travis was vehement. "Bryan, we'll talk about this later, okay?" When the boy didn't reply, Travis repeated, "Okay?"

"Yeah. Fine. Okay," he agreed, obviously none too pleased as he managed his way across the room to stand at the tall windows and stare outside at the serene waters of the lake. His shoulders were slumped and Ronni's heart went out to the boy. Though both parents loved him, he was obviously torn and missed his mother. The rebellion he aimed so pointedly at his father was in direct response to Travis's authority, though Bryan probably didn't realize it.

"Okay, so what now?" He motioned to the boxes and sacks and Ronni tried to turn her attention away from Sylvia—the mystery woman who lived half a world away from her son and ex-husband—to tackle the job at hand, a job she now wished she hadn't started. She and Amy didn't belong here in this tense room, intruding on a family with problems they needed to solve between themselves.

"I thought you didn't have a tree, from what you'd said at the ski lodge, but I didn't pick one out for you." She began unpacking the sacks and boxes. "I think choosing the tree is a personal decision."

"Who cares?" Bryan said from the corner of his mouth. "It's just a stupid tree."

"It's not stupid!" Amy planted her little fists on her hips.

"Of course it's not," Travis said. "Bryan—"

"So let's go down to the lot," Ronni cut in, trying to forestall an argument that seemed ready to explode again between father and son. "I told Vic we'd stop by, so he's expecting us."

"Can't I just stay here?" Bryan complained. "It's such a hassle with the crutches and everyone stares at me."

Travis looked about to disagree, but didn't. "Yeah, fine. Whatever," he said.

She saw the father, frustration etched across his features, and the son, a look of defiance across his, and her heart went out to them both.

*   *   *

They drove into town in Travis's Jeep. Cascadia was deep in the throes of Christmas. Nativity scenes were on display at both churches, lighted candy canes were supported by lampposts and the D & E Christmas Tree Lot was doing a banner business. Cars and trucks were wedged into the few parking spaces surrounding the rows of trees. Colored lights, suspended around the perimeter of the lot, bounced in the wind, and the smell of fresh-cut cedar and pine mingled with the tantalizing scents of coffee and cinnamon. Everyone who walked onto the lot was given a free cup of coffee or spiced cider and entire families strolled through the rows of newly-hewn trees while sipping from paper cups.

Vic, in his plaid jacket and hunter's cap, was ready to haul the chosen tree, chop off any unwanted branches and bind it to a car, or offer advice to potential customers. He was a big, rugged man, blond and blue-eyed, evidence of his Danish ancestry. He'd been raised in Molalla, a small logging community in the foothills of the mountains, and had moved to Cascadia when he was in high school. He'd worked in the sawmill from the time he was seventeen until recently when the local mill had shut down and he'd been forced to look for another means to support his family. Reduced to scavenging for odd jobs, his once-carefree face had begun to line and weather, his honey-gold hair showed strands of gray.

"Ronni!" He spied her and clapped her on the back. "I was beginning to think that you'd stood me up."

"No way."

Amy scampered through the trees and Vic caught her, spinning her off her feet. "How's my favorite niece?" he said and she giggled. It didn't matter to her that he had no other nieces, Victor Pederson was the only father figure she'd ever known. He plopped her back to the ground and said, "I think I've got just the animal you want."

"A Christmas tree isn't an animal!" Amy said, giggling again.

"Isn't it? Well, I guess you're right." After quick introductions, Vic showed them a fourteen-foot noble fir, so large it was propped against the side of the next building—a vacant warehouse. "If you want this one, I'll tie it to the back of the pickup and bring it over," he offered. "No delivery charge."

Travis gave a curt nod. "Can't beat a deal like that. How about a stand? You sell 'em?"

"Absolutely!" Vic said. "Over here." In a lean-to tent he showed a couple of different styles of tree stands that could support a large tree. Within minutes, the decision was made and the men shook hands. "I'm off in half an hour. I'll bring tree, stand, the whole ball of wax, over to the Johnson place then."

"Can I ride with you?" Amy asked, clinging to her uncle and showing him her dimples.

Victor was easy. "You bet, pumpkin. If it's okay with your ma."

Ronni wasn't convinced. Amy, if the mood struck her, could be more than a handful and Victor was already busy. "You sure you want her?"

"Heck, yes, I'm sure. When do I ever get a little girl to spoil?"

"All right," Ronni said, caving in to her daughter's wishes yet again. "But Amy, you be good, do just what Uncle Vic says."

"I will," she called brightly as she dashed off through the rows of trees propped against lines of sawhorses.

"She'll probably get you fired," Ronni said worriedly.

"Not a chance. Delmer and Edwin think I'm the god of Christmas-tree sales." Laughing, he adjusted the brim of his hunting hat. "Now, don't worry about Amygal. She and I will get along just fine."

Ronni believed him and secretly prayed that Shelly's unborn baby was a little girl for Vic to spoil and love. Travis paid for the tree and shook Victor's hand once more. He helped Ronni into the Jeep, then climbed behind the wheel.

"Seems like a nice guy."

"Vic? Yeah, he is," she agreed as the Jeep lunged forward, rocking over potholes in the old, cracked pavement. She tried not to think about the fact that she was alone with Travis, or that his knee was only inches from hers and his hand on the gearshift knob was near enough that his fingers could easily graze her thigh. She shifted slightly, huddling closer to the passenger door even though she told herself she wasn't intimidated, that just because he was more purely animal male than she'd been around in a long time, she had no reason for the nest of butterflies that seemed to roll and flutter in her stomach.

The silence stretched between them and she blocked her mind to his scent, a mixture of soap and leather, and refused to notice the way his lips compressed in a sexy, blade-thin line. She didn't want to be reminded of how starkly male he was. He was a complicated man, she decided, and right now she didn't need or want any complications in her life.

"What do you do when you're not rescuing idiots who get lost on the mountain?" he asked, shifting down to take a corner as the streetlight changed from green to amber. They passed the old theater building, built like a World War II Quonset hut and now boarded over. "You have some kind of shop on your property, don't you?"

"It's a warehouse, really. A few years ago, I started advertising in some magazines about items unique to Oregon—items I sold through mail order. I got a handful of orders, found some new inventory, advertised again and each year I sold a little more."

"More what?"

A service station, its lights dimmed for the night,

flashed by and then they were on the outskirts of town where the once-thriving sawmill was now shut down. The gates of the fence were chained and padlocked shut and a single tall security lamp gave off an eerie blue glow. Her brother-in-law had spent most of his adult life working at this very mill and now it seemed, with the restrictions on old-growth timber, environmental concerns and forest depletion, the sawmill would never re-open. And Victor would take Shelly and the boys and move away.

She realized then that Travis was waiting for an answer. "Oh. What do I sell?" she said, shaking away her case of melancholy. "A little of this and that, odds and ends that I think are difficult to find anywhere else. Myrtle wood, that's big here and hard to get in other places. And specialty jams and jellies made from native fruits. Books on Oregon. Some Native American art—mainly from Northwest tribes, jewelry, handcrafted pieces, even chain-saw sculpture and kits for tying fishing flies indigenous to Oregon. It's all kind of a hodge-podge. Some of the Christmas decorations I brought over are last year's stock."

"Sounds like a big operation."

"Bigger by the year. I hired my sister to do the secretarial stuff and handle some of the orders and when it really gets busy, I call a temporary agency in Portland. It's not a huge operation by any means, but it's grown so that I make enough money to support myself and Amy without having to worry too much."

"But you're still part of the ski patrol and search-and-rescue team?" The town had given way to the forest and only a few lights from hidden cabins sparkled warmly through the thick stands of fir and hemlock.

"Have been for a long time," she admitted, looking out the window and touching the fogging glass with a finger. She wondered how much she should tell him, or if she should bother explaining at all.

"You must love it."

Sighing, she glanced over to him and his gaze touched hers for just an instant. Even though she knew little about him, she sensed that he was trustworthy, a man who cared. "My husband, Hank, was killed on Mount Echo nearly four years ago—a few months after Amy was born."

His jaw tightened. "I didn't know."

A pang of the same old sadness stole into her heart and she felt as if the temperature in the Jeep had dropped twenty degrees.

"I'm sorry."

"Oh, God, so am I," she admitted. "So am I." She focused past the front end of the car and the dual splashes of light offered by the headlights. "He and a partner, Rick, were up on the ridge, setting off charges to make the mountain avalanche-safe before the runs were opened. But something went wrong. A charge went off early, though no one can tell me why. Hank and Rick tried to outrace the snow but Hank's bindings failed. It didn't really matter anyway; Hank and Rick were both killed, buried in the snow." She shuddered at the thought.

"I'm sorry," he said as if he meant it.

"It's not your fault."

He wheeled into the long tree-lined driveway of the old lodge. "It sounds like it was no one's fault, that it was a freak accident."

"Maybe." She closed her eyes a second, trying to dispel the horrid image of Hank, her beloved Hank, caught in the rage and terror of thousands of pounds of snow.

"There's something else," he said as if reading her mind. They passed through the open gate to the lodge. Snow was beginning to fall again, sticking to the windshield before melting. Through the trees, from the windows of the lodge, soft, golden patches of light welcomed them.

"Hank shouldn't have died that day," she said, her throat closing.

"Of course he shouldn't have."

"No, you don't understand," she said, feeling that painful gnawing in her insides, that raw scraping of guilt. "I mean, he wasn't supposed to be on duty that morning." She rubbed a drop of condensation from the window as he parked in front of a dilapidated garage. Swallowing hard, she said, "It was my shift. I was the one that was supposed to be up there that day."

She felt rather than saw him move, and when his

hand reached forward and his finger hooked beneath her jaw, she didn't fight him, just turned her head to look into dark, caring eyes. "You've been blaming yourself," he said, shaking his head, his breath whispering across her face.

"No, not just myself. I spread the blame around."

"But deep inside, you think you were at fault."

"Yes."

"And do you also think you should have been the one to die?"

She nodded, feeling the heat of his curled finger on the soft skin near her chin.

"You can't beat yourself up over an accident you couldn't have prevented." Travis stared at her long and hard. "I didn't know your husband, but I'm willing to bet that he wouldn't have traded places with you."

Squeezing her eyes shut, she tried not to think of Hank or the pain.

"Let it go," Travis advised, and when she opened her eyes, his face was nearly touching hers and the fog clouding the inside glass of the idling Jeep seemed to cut them off from the rest of the world. His fingers slid around her neck to her nape and with just a little pressure, he drew her close. "It's over, Ronni." His eyes searched her face. "He's gone and he wouldn't have wanted you to shroud yourself in guilt and grief forever."

His words were a soft balm on her old scarred wounds. "What do you know about it?" she asked, her voice hoarse.

But he didn't answer. Instead, his lips brushed over hers in a feathery kiss that brought goose bumps to her skin and an ache to her heart. She didn't want him to kiss her, or so she told herself, but she was unable to resist the sweet, delicious pressure of his mouth when it found hers again. Her breath was lost somewhere deep in her lungs and her heart was knocking wildly against her ribs.

She should stop, she should break away, but when his arms surrounded her, she felt her body yield and soften against him and she sighed willingly, opening her mouth against the touch of his tongue.

How long had it been? Years. Since Hank. Tears were hot against the back of her eyes and her throat clogged.

When he lifted his head, he brushed a strand of hair off her cheek. He looked about to say something, seemed to think better of it and switched off the ignition.

Ronni's fingers scrambled for the door handle. She needed to put some distance between herself and this man. "I, uh, think we'd better go inside. Vic will be here with the tree soon."

Travis stared at her a second, then pocketed his keys. "Right."

Opening the passenger door, she slid to the ground

and silently called herself a fool. What had come over her? She hadn't kissed a man since Hank, never once wanted another man to get close, and yet in the Jeep, she'd felt the old stirring of lust and longing that she thought she'd buried along with her husband.

He caught up with her at the porch and his fingers curved over the crook in her arm. "Ronni—"

"What?" She turned and his arms wrapped around her. As she gasped, he kissed her again, this time with more urgency, his lips hard and strong, hers soft and pliant. Her pulse thundered and her legs seemed to turn to liquid.

His tongue slid into her open mouth and she felt a thrill of anticipation spread through her bloodstream, warming her from the inside out, creating a hunger she'd thought she would never again experience. With a groan, he leaned closer, the kiss deepened and his hands tangled in her hair. "Ronni," he whispered hoarsely when he finally lifted his head.

He tucked her against him and she felt the strength of his arms surrounding her, the tickle of his breath as it swept over her crown. Her heart was pounding like a jackhammer.

"I—I can't get involved with anyone," she said, cringing at the breathy tone of her voice.

"Me neither." Tipping her chin with one hand, he stared into her eyes. "But if I could . . ."

"Don't even think about it, Keegan," she teased,

even though her own thoughts were racing ahead to what it would feel like to make love to him, to sleep in his bed, to wrap her arms around him and wake up in the morning smelling his scent. She bit down on her lip at the wayward turn of her mind. She was a woman who had no interest in a relationship, a person who had pledged her life to her child, someone who had tried to defy gender by being both mother and father to Amy.

"You can't blame yourself forever," he said.

"Why not?"

"And you can't go on punishing yourself."

"I don't!" she snapped. She was too sane, had her feet planted too firmly on the ground to fall into the trap. Or did she? "So who do you think you are? Sigmund Freud?"

"It was just an observation."

"What do you care?" she asked and the question hung between them like ice crystals gathering in the cold night air.

"I wish I knew," he said, holding her close. "I wish to God that I knew."

Headlights flashed and Vic's old half-ton pickup rolled into the driveway. Travis dropped his arms, and Ronni, embarrassed though she didn't really understand why, stepped away from him. She thought she saw a movement inside the house, a flutter of a curtain, but it could have been a trick of light combining with her hyperactive imagination.

Amy flew out of the truck, while Vic, careful of a bad

knee he'd injured hauling wood a few years back, was a little slower. While Ronni carried in the stand, the two men wrestled with the tree and finally managed to get it upright without its leaning much. Bryan, though clearly loathe to admit he was interested, hobbled out of his room to watch the endeavor.

Spying his son, Travis said, "Don't we have some fishing wire around here—heavy-duty stuff like twenty-pound test? Why don't you see if you can find it, Bryan?"

"I'll help," Amy piped in.

Bryan, an unfriendly scowl set on his features, took off in the direction of the kitchen with Amy scampering after him. Travis located a ladder in a closet under the stairs and by the time the ladder was snapped open, Amy was dashing back, a spool of clear plastic fishing line in one hand. "We found it," she announced and Bryan hobbled back into the room.

Vic steadied the ladder while Travis drove nails into the wall and anchored the uppermost branches. Ronni helped Vic hold the tree steady and noticed the way Travis's sweater stretched upward as he pounded, allowing a glimpse of his flat abdominal muscles above the waistband of his jeans. He jammed the hammer into a back pocket and the faded denim slid lower. Ronni's stomach tightened and she bit her lip. Hard, lean muscles moved as he pulled the fishing line taut.

Realizing she was staring, she dragged her gaze away only to find Bryan's suspicious eyes fixed on her.

"You got Nintendo?" Amy was asking, obviously fascinated with him.

He didn't bother to answer even when she repeated the question.

"That should do it," Vic said, testing the stability of the tree. "I think one of Ronni's fool horses could come stampeding through here, hit the tree and the thing would still stand."

"Oh, right," Ronni said, grinning.

"Good." Travis hopped to the floor.

"I'd better be shoving off." Vic eyed the tree and nodded to himself. "Shelly will be startin' to worry."

"Let me pay you for your trouble," Travis offered and was rewarded by a sharp look from Shelly's husband.

"It was part of the deal."

"Then, how about a drink? Or a cup of coffee."

"Another time, maybe, but now I'd better get home before the twins are in bed." He squared his hat upon his head and Travis extended his hand.

"Thanks."

"Don't mention it."

"I think we should be leaving, too," Ronni interjected as she caught her daughter, still pestering Bryan as she tried to hide a yawn.

"Nooo!" Amy protested. "We gots to put the lights on the tree."

"Not tonight, kiddo. It's waaaay past your bedtime."

And Ronni didn't want to spend any more time close to Travis. Not until she'd sorted out the jumble of emotions that being around him evoked.

"But we have to—"

"She could sleep in one of the guest rooms," Travis offered, his eyes suddenly dark and serious, his voice soft as a caress. Ronni's heart kicked into third gear.

"But I'm not tired!" Amy said.

"I think it would be better to get her home." *For her, for Bryan and especially for me,* she added silently as she searched for her purse and jacket.

"So you're abandoning us to this mess?"

"We'll come back and help," she said, finding her leather bag near the fireplace.

"We can handle it." Bryan was still glaring at her as if she were the embodiment of all things evil. She didn't have to ask why he'd suddenly turned on her; obviously, he had watched his father kissing her on the porch. No one else had been home and the curtains had moved. So Bryan had seen them embracing, which was difficult for any teenager, and Bryan was going through a rough enough time as it was. Between the move and his mother's demands, the last thing he needed was his father to be distracted by another woman.

Travis didn't seem to hear his son. "How about tomorrow evening?" he suggested. "And this time, Bryan and I will cook dinner."

"Oh, brother," Bryan said, rolling his eyes.

"Can we?" Amy, finally accepting the fact that her mother wasn't about to budge on her decision to return home, jumped all over the suggestion.

Ronni hesitated for a second, but when her eyes found Travis's again, she managed a smile. "Sure," she replied. "Why not?"

There had to be a million reasons—a million good, sound reasons—but at that moment, staring into Travis's eyes, Ronni couldn't think of one.

CHAPTER 7

"OH, JANICE, THEY'RE adorable," Ronni said, stepping closer to the pen and eyeing seven wiggling puppies. Six weeks old with bright eyes, wagging tails and high-pitched yips, they scrambled over one another in an eager attempt to reach her. Some brown, others black, still others with gray-and-white markings on their fuzzy coats, they staggered on unsure legs across old news-papers that had been spread across the floor of the Petrocellis' garage.

"We're not really sure what they are exactly," Janice admitted, running fingers through her spiky blond hair. As she moved her hand, her bracelets jangled, causing more excited yips. "I'm afraid they may have had more than one dad—that's possible, you know." A heater in the corner kept the shell of a room warm enough for the inhabitants of the huge pen. "Our Fangette, here," she said, motioning to the tired-looking mother dog, "she's part German shepherd, Lab and golden retriever, and a sweetheart, aren't you, baby?"

She patted Fangette's wide head and was rewarded with a sloppy pink tongue washing her palm. "She escaped once while she was in heat and this is the result. Seven of 'em, five males and two females. Near as I can tell, some of them look like they have some husky blood in them—see the ones with the curly tails and white markings—and the others could be anything. I don't think Fangette was particularly discriminating—kind of like some women I've met." She chuckled to herself.

"Well, she certainly ended up with some beguiling pups," Ronni said.

"Her first and last litter, believe me. We're going to get Fangette fixed pronto. It's not easy finding homes for these little guys."

Ronni petted all the eager, upturned faces, watching little curly tails whip with excitement. One brown puppy with black-tipped ears was the most playful of the bunch. She growled and lunged at her brothers and sister and the spark of devilment in her eyes touched Ronni. "This one," she said, picking up the wiggling bundle of fur. "Will you keep her until Christmas Eve? She'll be a surprise for my daughter."

"Will do." Janice seemed relieved to have found an owner. "Just hold her there a minute." She walked to a cabinet, opened the cupboard door, and amidst the fertilizer, insect spray and camping equipment, found a bottle of red nail polish. "I'll paint her toenail so that we don't give her away to anyone else by mistake."

The puppy licked the underside of Ronni's chin.

"Hold her still." Janice applied a dab of quick-drying polish and then blew on the tiny foot. "There ya go, darlin'," she said to the pup, and reluctantly, Ronni placed the little dog back in the pen with her brothers and sister. "One down, six to go. If you hear of anyone else interested in a puppy, please tell them about Fangette's litter."

"I will," Ronni promised and cast one last look at the puppy who was happily chewing on one of her brothers' ears. Smiling, she headed to the van. Amy would be in seventh heaven when she found the furry little pup under the tree on Christmas morning.

Travis had cut his teeth on tough negotiations. When he was expanding his business, buying out smaller corporations, dealing with union officials, talking to lawyers, accountants and sales representatives from all walks of life, he'd prided himself on his ability to usually, through minimal concessions, get his way.

But bargaining with Bryan was more difficult than anything he'd ever been through. Because his heart was involved. Because he cared. Because if he messed up with his son's life, he would never get a second chance. And the kid seemed to sense it.

They sat on the floor of Bryan's room amidst the clutter of compact discs, magazines, baseball cards and

clothes, staring at each other as if they were mortal ene-
mies. Travis leaned against the bed for support, Bryan
sat cross-legged and was sorting through a stack of baseball cards that he hadn't looked at in over two years.

"Okay, let me get this straight," Travis said, feeling
manipulated by his own adolescent son. "You're willing
to give up this idea of moving to France if you can
spend a weekend with Martin in Seattle?"

"That's it." Bryan's defiant eyes met his father's. Dar-
ing. Challenging.

"One weekend for the rest of your life."

"Yeah." He shoved the baseball cards aside.

"I don't think so."

"Fine." Stretching out on the floor and leaning on
one elbow, he said, "Then I'm going to live with Mom."

"In a pig's eye. You'd no sooner get over there and
you'd be on the phone to come home. You tried living
with your mother once before, remember?"

"That was different."

"Yeah, she still lived in Seattle and you could see
your friends anytime you wanted. You went to the old
school, lived in our house. It still didn't work out."

"Thing's have changed," Bryan argued glumly.

"That's right." Travis drove the point home, even
though it was bound to hurt a little. "Now your mother's
in a foreign country and you wouldn't know anyone
there. You'd be isolated in some American school, if you
were lucky, and get to hobnob with the sons and daugh-

ters of diplomats and the like. You think life here is hard, just you wait."

Bryan's lips rolled over his teeth and he stared at the floor. Travis gambled. "But if it's what you really want, if you think you'd be happier in Paris, then go. With my blessing. Just remember two things."

"What?"

"First and foremost, I don't want you to go. I want you to live with me." He stared at his son long and hard. "I love you, Bryan, and even if it's not a guy thing to say, I want you to know it."

A growl of disbelief.

"Now the second thing, and it's important, too." He folded his arms over his chest. "If you decide to go to France, then you can't come back until summer. You've got to learn to commit, sport, and if you want to live with Sylvia, then you can't play this same game over there that you're playing with me now. You can't use me, or living with me, as a bargaining chip to get what you want from her, because even though your mother might buy into that kind of blackmail, I don't."

Bryan drew his finger in a circle on the faded carpet. "Then you're a liar, right. If you really loved me—"

"I'd do exactly what I'm doing because it's the best thing for you and that's what matters."

"Bull!"

"I guess you don't understand, Bry. When you love someone, really care for them, you don't use that love as a weapon, or a wedge, or a trump card. You don't use it against them at all. It's a gift."

"Geez, Travis, listen to yourself! Talk about sounding hokey! All you need is a pulpit and you could open your own church." His finger quit moving on the carpet. "You never were this way before."

"I know." Travis picked up a barbell and wrapped his fingers around the cool metal. "I'm trying to fix that."

"If you ask me, you're getting weird. What happened to you?"

"I looked in the mirror one day and didn't like what I saw." Travis lifted the weight over his head.

"Oh, sure. It didn't have anything to do with Mom deciding to 'find herself' or whatever it is she thinks she's doing."

"It happened about the same time."

Bryan chewed on his lower lip a second, then he raised his eyes and pinned his father in his troubled gaze. "You ever gonna get married again?"

"Me? No," he said quickly. Then the image of Ronni's upturned face, her lips parted, her brown eyes warm and inviting chased through his mind, and for the first time in years, he doubted himself. "At least I don't have any immediate plans."

"You're sure?"

"Why?"

"No reason," he said quickly, then added, "Me neither. I'm *never* getting married!"

"You're a little young to be saying that."

"Yeah, but girls are trouble."

"I think that's what makes them so damned fascinating." He transferred the barbell to his other hand and started a series of repetitions.

"What about you and that Ronni?" Bryan asked, his eyes narrowing suspiciously.

The muscles in the back of Travis's neck tensed. "What about us?"

"She seems to like you a lot."

"We're friends." *Liar! It's more than that. Much more. Even Bryan's picked up on it.* "I barely know her."

"Her kid's a pain."

"Amy?"

"Yeah. Always askin' questions and gettin' into my stuff! Messin' it up."

"How can you tell?" Travis asked, eyeballing the clutter that was strewn everywhere. Bryan's bedroom looked like a cyclone had stormed through, turned around, decided enough damage hadn't been done and swept back the way it had come. But Travis wasn't riding him about the mess. At least not yet. There were bigger, more important issues to deal with. Until his son was off crutches, in school, had made some new friends and felt more comfortable living in Cascadia, Travis had decided not to sweat the little things, such as a messy room.

"I can tell, okay? The kid was only here a few hours and most of the time stayed out of my way, but boy, when she was in here, she trashed the place. She bugs me."

"She's only four."

"Well, she can be four someplace else."

"Not tonight. They're coming over. We're cooking."

"*You and me?* I thought that was just a joke."

Travis rolled his eyes to the ceiling, then lifted his hand solemnly, as if he were about to take the most important oath of his life. "I swear on my honor. It's the truth."

With a sound of disgust, Bryan flopped onto the floor and stared at the ceiling. "Well, that's great, Dad. Just . . . just great."

"You don't know the half of it. We're going to barbecue."

"What?" Bryan glanced to the window where snow was settling against the lower panes. "It's freezing outside."

"We've got pretty big porches."

"But—but you barbecue for the Fourth of July or . . . what's wrong with you?" Bryan stared at his father as if he'd completely lost his mind, and Travis couldn't really blame him. The idea of a barbecue had just popped into his head.

"I don't even think you can do it in the winter," Bryan said. "It must be against the law or somethin'."

"They cook outside up at the lodge on Mount Echo all the time."

Bryan leveled his father a look that silently called him a lunatic, but he held his tongue.

"It's going to be fun," Travis assured him.

"Since when do you care about fun?"

Good question. For years he'd avoided any activity that wasn't business-related, including seeking out a good time. He'd been single-minded and with only serious purposes in mind. "Since I decided that living inside a boardroom was a waste of time—mine and yours. So this is the start, and we're going to do a lot of fun things in the future."

"Like what?"

"Camping, trail riding, fly fishing, maybe even mountain climbing." Travis set the weight down and climbed to his feet. "Now, I'd better go locate some charcoal and a grill in the middle of winter in Cascadia."

"While you're at it, you might try to find the rest of your brain," Bryan said, but there was a twinkle in his eye that Travis hadn't seen for weeks.

"Very funny. You coming?"

"I don't know why," Bryan grumbled, but grabbed his crutches, propped them against the bed and struggled to his feet. He followed his father to the hallway and as Travis checked to make sure he had his keys, his son asked, "Hey, Dad, what are the symptoms of a guy who's going through a second childhood?"

"I don't want to be a wise man," Kurt announced, crossing his arms over his chest as Ronni, on her knees

148   *Lisa Jackson*

in the dining area of her house, tried to adjust the hem of his costume. "They're dorks."

"Stand still," Shelly ordered around a mouth of pins. "And remember that the wise men were *not* dorks. They were very important kings. That's right, isn't it?" she asked Ronni. "Kings, right?"

"I think so."

"Well, dressing in towels is dorky," Kurt stated emphatically. The costume, cut from two old striped beach blankets, draped over his body and touched the floor.

"How about sheets?" Kent twirled, sending his shepherd outfit of muslin billowing. "That's dorky, too."

"They didn't have malls back then, or big department stores," Shelly said as she made a final tuck in one sleeve. "This will have to do."

"I hate the pageant," Kurt muttered under his breath.

"Don't they go to church to learn how *not* to hate?" Ronni asked her sister.

"That's the way it's supposed to work."

"I hate church, too."

"Stop it, Kurt, you do not."

"Do, too."

Shelly rolled her eyes to the ceiling as if searching for God and hoping that He would intervene. "The pageant will be fun. Now, come on, boys, settle down, we're just about done."

Amy fluttered through in the garb of an angel. "I like being an angel," she said, her tinsel halo bobbing as she talked, her wings stiff.

"You would," Kurt observed.

"I was an angel last year," Kent said.

"Yeah, who ever heard of a boy angel?"

"How about Gabriel?" Shelly asked. "He's a man, right?" Again she looked at her sister. "Maybe I'd better brush up on my Bible study."

"Who cares?" Kurt complained.

Ronni stood and dusted her hands. "Okay, that does it. Take off your costume—carefully, now," she added when Kurt began to rip off the offensive robe. "You three can play outside for a while, if you want, run off some of that restless energy."

Towel-robes, sheets, wings and halo went flying as the kids grabbed their jackets and headed out the front door. Ronni had to help Amy with her zipper, hat and boots, but the little girl was out the door in a flash, chasing after her older cousins. From the window, Ronni watched Kurt hurl a snowball that smashed against the back of Kent's jacket. With a squeal, Kent scooped up a handful of snow and the fight was on.

"Victor told me about helping set up a tree for you over at the old lodge," Shelly observed as she draped the shepherd's outfit over the end of the ironing board.

"It wasn't really for me. I'm just helping decorate it."

"For Keegan?"

"Mmm." Ronni nodded and adjusted the pins on the sleeves of Kurt's costume.

"How does the old place look?"

"Good," Ronni admitted, despising the wistful tone

that stole into her voice. "The lodge is still pretty drafty and there's lots more work to be done, but what he's done so far is nice and he's trying to refurbish it rather than remodel it." She snapped the pin box closed and stretched her arms over her head. "He didn't say too much about it, but it seems as if he's not going to do anything as stupid as modernize it—except for the needed repairs and necessary updates to bring it up to code."

"Did you ever talk to Taffy—ask her why she didn't tell you someone was interested in buying the place?"

"Nah." Ronni wound measuring tape between her fingers and frowned at the mention of her old school friend turned real estate agent. "What would have been the point? I couldn't have afforded the place anyway."

"I know the feeling," Shelly said. "I'm afraid it's going to have to be a spiritual Christmas this year."

"That's the best kind."

"I think so, too, but tell it to a couple of six-year-olds who want everything they see on television. Kent's list is two pages and he keeps coming up with more ideas."

"How about a puppy?" Ronni suggested. "I know where there's a great litter."

"We rent, remember? No dogs allowed. And if we have to move—"

"You're not moving. Don't even talk like that," Ronni said, but saw the worry in her sister's eye before Shelly changed the subject back to Travis.

"So tell me about your new neighbor."

"Not much to say."

"Oh, come on. Vic wouldn't say a word, just that he seemed like an okay, regular kind of Joe. I told him that was crazy. Regular guys don't buy old lodges and lakes and hundreds of acres of woods. The guy's got to be loaded."

"Or in debt."

"Nah. The banks only loan money to you if you don't need it. Believe me, I know." She placed her hand near the bottom plate of the iron, decided it was hot enough and started pressing the wrinkles out of Kent's shepherd costume. "So what does Keegan do?"

"He's never really said." Ronni, glancing through the window over the sink to make sure the kids were okay, reached for the coffeepot and turned on the water while watching Kurt climb onto the fence and try to lure the horses to the side of the paddock with a handful of oats. The animals, standing in the shelter of a fir tree, pricked their ears forward and flicked their tails, but weren't enticed. Loose Change, nicknamed Lucy, snorted in disdain and her tail flicked over her rounded belly.

"Well, he must earn a living some way, or else—God forbid," she mocked, "he's independently wealthy."

Ronni chuckled as she rinsed the glass pot and scooped coffee into the maker. "I think he owns some sporting goods company in Seattle and it runs itself or he has a manager who does all the legwork. I don't know." She looked up at her sister and noticed a gleam in Shelly's eye as she leaned across the counter. "Why?"

"You seem to be spending a lot of time with him."

"Not a lot."

"So come on, tell me, what's he like, what's he look like . . . ? Vic wouldn't fill me in on the details."

Coffee started to drizzle through the filter and the scent filled the room. "What's he like?" Ronni said, pulling down cups and saucers from an open cupboard. "Well, he's in his mid-thirties, I'd guess, and he's tall, about the same size as Vic, but he's got dark hair and gray eyes and . . . a great smile, very sexy, but he hardly ever shows it off." She set the sugar bowl on the table along with a small creamer filled with half-and-half. "Oh, and he's got a son. Fourteen going on twenty-five."

"You don't like his boy?"

"No, that's not the problem," Ronni said, watching Loose Change finally deign to amble through the snow and nuzzle Kurt's mittened hand in search of grain. "He doesn't like me."

"Oops."

"Yeah. He's a little mixed up and needs to settle in with his dad before he should have to deal with a woman . . ." She let the words trail away. What was she thinking? Bryan would never have to deal with her, not permanently. She was just Travis's neighbor, potentially a friend. *Who are you trying to fool?* a tiny voice in her mind nagged. *Do you tell your neighbors your darkest secrets? Fantasize about them? Stay awake all night remembering what it felt like to kiss them?*

"So you're interested," Shelly said with a match-making glimmer in her eye.

"Not really."

"Sure you are. Look, he's new in town, doesn't know anyone and lives up in that rambling old place with just his son. Why don't you invite him to have Christmas dinner with us?"

The coffeemaker sputtered. "Christmas?" Ronni repeated.

"Why not?"

"Look, Shelly, don't start with this, okay? It's not like we're dating or anything. I'm just having dinner with him—"

"Twice." Shelly held up two fingers and wiggled them before she turned off the iron and hung up Kent's costume. "When's the last time you went to dinner with a man, hmm?"

"I'm not inviting him to Christmas dinner," Ronni said firmly as she poured them each a cup of coffee and they settled into their usual chairs at the table.

"We'll see," Shelly murmured, undeterred.

"Don't do anything stupid, Shell."

"*Moi?* Of course not."

"Don't you go around my back and invite him."

"Wouldn't dream of it." But a sly smile curved her lips, and before Ronni could say another word, the door burst open. Kent, holding his mouth, ran into the room. He was crying and sobbing and slipped on the floor.

Shelly was on her feet in an instant and scooping him up. "What is it, honey?" she asked.

"K-Kurt, he tagged me—"

Shelly pulled his hand away from his mouth. Blood was smeared on the lower half of his face and his glove. He let out a terrified howl of pain. Shelly's face drained of color.

"I'll handle this," Ronni said. "Let's see." Kent clung to his mother as Amy and Kurt, looking sheepish, slid into the room. "Close the door," Ronni ordered while taking a clean cloth from a drawer, soaking it in warm water and washing Kent's tear-streaked and blood-soaked face. "I think you'll live," she said as she studied the scratches around his mouth and looked inside where one of his front teeth wobbled precariously and blood still ran. "You'll probably beat your brother in the tooth-loss department, though. My guess is the tooth fairy might come before Santa Claus this year."

"Really?" Kent blinked against the tears standing in his eyes.

"No way!" Kurt complained. He'd been born ten minutes before his younger brother and seemed to think, as eldest son, he had all sorts of privileges.

"Really. Here, let me get a mirror and you can see for yourself. Amy—" But her daughter was already dashing through the dining and living area, her boots squishing as she left a trail of water on her way to the bathroom.

"Got it," she cried. Back in an instant with a hand mirror, she nearly stumbled in her attempt to hand it to a sniffing Kent. "Lookie," she said as the boy tried his best to eye his injuries.

Shelly's color returned. "Now, since no one has to be placed permanently on the injured reserve list, what happened?"

They all started talking at once, but near as Ronni could tell, Kurt, bored with petting Lucy's soft nose, had packed a snowball with pieces of ice he'd picked up from the frozen mud puddles. He'd hurled the icy snowball at Kent, whose back was turned, but a second before the moment of impact, Kent had turned and the hard-packed missile had caught him in the face.

"I think I'd better take my warriors home before anyone else gets hurt in battle," Shelly said. She glanced longingly at her cooling cup of coffee. "I'll see you tomorrow. Come on, boys." Kent refused to walk—Shelly had to pack him into the car—and Kurt hung his head, probably because he knew that during the drive home, he was sure to receive a long lecture on playing safely.

"Kurt wanted to hurt Kent," Amy announced as she watched the boys struggle with their seat belts.

"No—"

"Yes, he did, Mommy. Kurt's mean."

"Just rambunctious."

"'Bunctious and mean." Amy flounced back into the house and Ronni hesitated on the front porch. Dusk was just beginning to settle and the forest seemed dark and gloomy, but through the trees she caught a glimpse of colored lights at the old Johnson place and her heart warmed. What was wrong with her these days? she wondered as she closed the door and looked forward to an evening with a man she barely knew and a boy who seemed to hate her.

Bryan, obviously coached by his father, was on his best behavior. Beneath the surface was the same sullen boy, but he was outwardly friendly. After a meal of grilled steaks, salad and baked potatoes, they finished decorating the tree. Travis had already strung lights through the branches, so most of the hard work was done. The ladder was necessary again and when the last ornament was hung and the final length of tinsel draped, they lit candles, turned out the lights and plugged in the tree.

Amy gasped as hundreds of tiny, winking lights blazed, lending the huge room a cozy glow. "It's beautiful," she breathed, her eyes shining in wonder. "But it needs a star."

Ronni shrugged. "We've got the same problem and thought we might find a homemade star or angel at the church bazaar."

"Church bazaar?" Bryan snorted. "Don't tell me, there's a Christmas pageant, too."

"Are you coming?" Amy asked eagerly and Bryan rolled his eyes.

"No."

"Why not?"

"A dumb pageant?"

"It's not dumb," Amy said, her lower lip trembling. "I'm an angel."

"Then it will be great!" Travis said, bending on a knee so he could look her squarely in the eye. "We'll be in the front row."

"No way!" All of Bryan's pretenses shattered and fell away. "I'm not going to some stupid show about Jesus getting born. I've seen it a hundred times."

"We'll be there," Travis said, rumpling Amy's hair and shooting his son a look that brooked no argument.

Bryan grabbed his crutches and hitched himself out of the room. A second later, the door to his bedroom slammed shut.

"Why did he say it was dumb?" Amy asked, wounded.

"Because he's fourteen," Travis said, "and sometimes he has a hard time remembering to be polite."

Amy started off in the direction of Travis's room, but Ronni caught her by the shoulder. "Why don't you give him a few minutes to cool off, honey? He'll probably change his mind."

"No doubt about it," Travis said, his jaw set.

Amy fell asleep on the couch watching a Christmas special and Ronni covered her with a hand-pieced quilt Travis found. "This looks like an antique," she said, tucking the faded blue squares beneath Amy's chin.

"My grandmother's. I think her great-grandmother made it—or maybe it was her great-great-grandmother, I can't remember. Anyway, the story is that it came over on the wagon train—Oregon Trail—and then when the family moved north a generation or so later, it traveled along with them.

"My grandmother thought I should have it and so now it's back in Oregon. Come on." He took her arm and guided her back to the kitchen where he made hot coffee, infusing it with a shot of brandy. They put on their jackets, walked to the back porch and watched as lacy snowflakes fell, powdering the boughs of trees and collecting on the ground.

"So you have a lot of family in the Seattle area?"

"Some. A sister, a few cousins and my folks, but my parents live in Arizona in the winter."

Funny, she'd never imagined him as part of an extended family. He seemed like such a loner, a man who was used to doing things for and by himself. "Is your sister coming down for Christmas?"

Frowning, he gave a curt shake of his head. "Nah. I don't see much of her."

"Oh." She didn't want to pry and yet there was so much she wanted to learn about him.

"She resents me." A simple statement of fact. No emotions tangling it down.

"Why?"

"I don't really blame her," he admitted with a crooked, humorless smile. "She was firstborn and smart as a whip. Excelled in school, studied abroad, a real academic."

She watched the steam rise from her coffee cup and blew across the cup, waiting for him to continue.

Leaning a hip against the top railing, he said, "I, on the other hand, was a screwup. Always in trouble. Never studied, barely passed, hated school. Despite all the grief I gave them, my parents, both of them, treated me as if I were the golden child. I was the boy, my father's only son, the last Keegan of his line. My sister, no matter how hard she tried, was always second best. It wasn't that they didn't love her in their own way, it was the fact that I was supposed to excel, be the best." He took a long swallow. "My sister never forgave me."

"But that wasn't your fault," she protested, trying to reconcile the image of the rebel teenager with that of the successful man staring into the winter-dark night.

"Maybe not, but when you're hurting, you try and hurt back. When she couldn't gain my folks' attention through achievement, she found other means, married someone they disapproved of and moved to L.A. She's divorced now, no kids and barely speaks to me." He shrugged, then drained his cup. "The ironic part was, about the time she started rebelling, I'd finally grown up, finished college and started working for a computer software company. A couple of years later, I was married, a father and had moved into sporting goods and equipment. All of a sudden, I had to live up to my parents' expectations, and by the time I stopped to take a breath, my marriage was falling apart and my son was a stranger who was starting to get into some of the same kind of trouble I got into as a teenager. I decided to change things."

"So you moved here."

His smile flashed in the darkness. "Sounds like I was running away, doesn't it?"

"No, just making a change."

He made a sound of disgust in the back of his throat. "Let's just hope it was for the best."

She set her cup on the windowsill and he linked his fingers through hers. Snow crunched beneath their shoes as he, tugging on her hand, led her through a copse of trees to the lake. Inky water lapped at the shore where ice had formed between the rocks.

At the edge of the lake, he turned to face her, his features in shadows, his eyes as dark as the night. Ronni felt that new feeling, the sizzle in her blood, the anticipation in the beat of her heart. With snow drifting around them, he pulled her against him and his mouth found hers in the darkness. He tasted of coffee and his lips were firm and hot, demanding. The feminine part of herself she'd buried so long ago responded and she linked her hands behind his neck. A cool winter breeze caught in her hair and lifted it from her nape. Snowflakes drifted from the sky.

Ronni felt her insides quiver as the kiss deepened. Her heart pounded so loudly she was certain he could hear it. Slowly he lifted his head and touched his forehead to hers. "Who are you, Veronica Walsh, and what are you doing to me?" he whispered.

"I—I was going to ask you the same thing." She swallowed hard, trying to get a grip on her equilibrium, but his lips claimed hers again, slashing across her mouth with enough force to shatter all thoughts of resistance.

Inside she shuddered. It was she who knew nothing about him—just a few comments about a sister and parents and a grandmother's quilt, about a troubled son and complicated ex-wife. But still he was a stranger, a man she'd only recently met, a man she didn't know well enough to trust.

Not that he was part of some sinister plot—that was silly—but the way he made her skin quiver when he kissed her, the power of emotions swirling and fighting in her being, the racing beat of her heart, all were signs that she needed to know more about him. He wasn't like Hank, a boy she'd grown up with and trusted, a man she'd loved, a husband she'd adored and been faithful to.

His hands slid beneath her jacket and farther, past the hem of her sweater to her skin. She sucked in a breath as his fingers grazed the stitching of her bra, moving sensually over the cup, heating her flesh beneath the thin layer of silk and lace.

Warning bells clanged in her mind. *Stop! Ronni, use*

your head! You don't love this man. You barely know him. Think!

But it had been so long. So very long. Endless, restless, sleepless nights had stretched from that time she'd last felt a man's touch, last realized what it was like to be wanted. His hand lowered, settling at the curve of her waist, fingers warm and supple.

His tongue touched hers, delving, retracting, toying with her until a dark warmth curled slowly in her belly. Liquid heat radiated from deep inside.

She felt the jacket being stripped from her, heard the soft thud of denim sinking into the snow. A breath of wind touched her flesh as he lifted her sweater over her head and her long hair fell back on her bare skin. Slowly he unhooked her bra, letting the scrap of lace fall into the white powder at their feet as he watched snowflakes melt against her skin.

She was breathing with difficulty, all too aware of the tightening of her nipples, the dark points high and proud and aching. His eyes touched hers and she licked her lips nervously as he traced one long finger along the cleft of her breasts and lower to hook on the waistband of her jeans.

"Veronica," he whispered across her open mouth. "Let me . . ."

"W-what?"

"Love you."

She squeezed her eyes shut.

"No, darlin'," he said, his breath tantalizing her ear.

"We both go into this with our eyes open or we don't go at all."

Swallowing with difficulty, she forced her eyes open. His hands moved up her rib cage slowly, achingly, until they reached her breasts and then he cupped them both, rubbing his thumbs across her nipples, staring into her eyes and kissing her lips. She didn't resist as he dragged her onto the snow, pulling her on top of him as he kissed one dark, proud point. Icy snowflakes settled against her back as he licked and teased, tasted and toyed. She moaned, arching her back, settling her hips against his and he suckled wildly, one hand lowering to grab her buttock and hold her firmly against him as he pleasured her.

Old sensations, new emotions, a storm of heat and fire and passion swept through her blood and she lost control, moving against him, her flesh yearning for his. All thought of restraint was caught by the passing wind and carried away. She wanted more of him, of his magic touch.

His mouth was moist and warm and wondrous and when he kissed her abdomen, she trembled with want. Her zipper slid down with a quiet hiss promising more and her body was on fire.

Don't think, just feel, her wanton mind cried.

"Oh, Ronni, no!" Suddenly he stopped. His hands quit moving and his entire body tensed. "No," he said, his words muffled against her skin. "Hell, no."

"Travis?"

Strong arms wrapped around her, holding her close for a second before he rolled over and still embracing her, swept a long dark strand of hair from her shoulder. "I . . . I . . . Look, Ronni, I think we should slow down."

Her laugh was brittle. So he thought she was easy—that it was common practice for her to fall willingly and naked into a man's arms. A hot blush climbed up her back as she tried to scramble away. What could she say? She hadn't acted like this for years. Not since Hank. Oh, what had she been thinking? "You're right," she agreed, trying to break away. "I don't know what got into me."

"Into us."

"I feel like a fool."

"Why?"

"Why?" She stared at his eyes, deep gray in the darkness, and shook her head in frustration. "Because, believe it or not, despite what just happened between us, it's not my usual practice to try and seduce a near stranger in the middle of a snowstorm—"

"We're not strangers."

"Nonetheless."

"And I was the one doing the seducing." His voice was tinged with self-condemnation and he cast an angry glance at the moonless sky. "I lose my head when I'm with you."

"Don't blame yourself." She extracted herself and, suddenly self-conscious, reached for her sweater.

"I'm not blaming anyone."

"Sounded like it to me." She jerked her sweater over

her head, then scooped up her jacket, shaking the snow from the folds of the denim. "Look, let's just call it a mistake and move on."

"Is that what you think?" he asked, his mouth tightening. "That being with me was a mistake?"

"Wasn't it?"

"No." He grabbed her arm. "Look, Ronni, I don't know what's happening between us and to be honest it scares me, but I don't believe for a second that it's wrong."

She tried to step away, but he held her fast, his fingers tightening possessively. "I just don't want you to get the wrong impression," she said.

"Have I?"

"I—I haven't dated much since my husband died and I've never even kissed another man since—" At his shocked expression, she added, "I know, it sounds unbelievable, but I wasn't . . . I mean, I'm not ready for any kind of relationship. I never expected anything like what happened between us and I think it would be best if we . . . Oh, Lord, I can't believe I'm having this conversation, but I think it would be best if we didn't . . . "

"Didn't what?"

"Get too involved."

"And what does that mean?" he asked, his eyes narrowing in the shadows. "That we shouldn't see each other?"

"No, not that, but—"

"That I shouldn't kiss you."

"Probably."

His laugh was harsh. "A few minutes ago, you were just about to—"

"I know what I was about to do and we both realize it would have been a mistake," she said, stung, her cheeks flaming in the darkness. "But nothing happened."

"Yet. Nothing's happened yet," he told her. "Look, things were heating up too fast for both of us, but that doesn't mean we shouldn't still see each other. We'll just take things slower."

"I think it's time for us to leave," she said, stuffing an arm down one sleeve of her jacket. "I'll just pack up Amy and—"

"Don't," he said, his voice a soft command.

"Don't what?"

"Don't leave angry."

"I'm not—" She clamped her mouth shut and silently counted to five. "I'm not angry with you."

"No, you're angry with yourself."

"So now you're a psychiatrist." She started for the house, half expecting him to try to stop her, but he followed after her at a slower pace and she was inside the kitchen by the time he'd caught up with her. He didn't say a word, just leaned one hip against a battle-worn butcher-block counter.

"So where do we go from here?"

"I don't know," she admitted, confused by the conflicting emotions that tore at her soul. "This is . . . it's all new to me . . . well, new the second time around."

"Since your husband?" he asked, his eyebrows drawing together.

"Yes."

"But you've dated."

"Look, I'm not trying to play the virgin's role here. I was married and have a child, but it's been . . . it's been a long time since Hank and—"

"Since Hank?"

She was startled by the accusation in his voice. "My husband."

"I know who he was," he snapped, the corners of his mouth tight. "But you're a young, vibrant woman. You don't expect me to believe that in the what?—nearly four years since his death, you haven't been involved with another man."

She inched her chin up a notch. "I don't care what you believe."

"But—"

"I was in love with my husband, Travis, and just because he died doesn't mean that my feelings for him disappeared, that I was ready to jump right back into the dating scene. Thanks . . . thanks for tonight," she added and pushed through the swinging doors and down the hall to the living room where Amy, in the glow of the Christmas tree, was still sleeping soundly.

Without a word, Travis helped her gather her purse

and, over Ronni's protests, wrapped Amy in the old quilt that his grandmother had given him.

Bryan, at his father's insistence, stumbled out of his room. Earphones surrounding his neck, he managed to mumble a quick good-night before Ronni strapped Amy into the van and drove the short distance home. In her sideview mirror, she caught a glimpse of Travis, legs apart, arm folded over his chest, watching her leave as the colored lights strung across the roof of the porch winked cheerily.

She waved despite the small hole she felt tearing her inside. "Don't be a fool," she muttered aloud. He was her neighbor—no more than a casual friend.

She worried her lip as she drove through the ice-spangled gates of the his newly acquired estate and reminded herself that casual friends didn't nearly make love on the snow-covered shores of a winter-dark lake.

CHAPTER 8

TRAVIS DIDN'T CALL. Not the first night, nor the second, nor the third. Not that he should, Ronni told herself as she waxed her skis in a lean-to area off the back porch of her house. Pink shavings littered the concrete floor beneath the sawhorses that Hank had set up years ago for just this purpose. His skis hung on an interior wall and in their upstairs closet she'd kept his boots, jumpsuit and poles.

She hadn't realized how many reminders of her husband she'd kept around the house and wondered for the first time in nearly four years if she was clinging to the past, unable or unwilling to let go. She'd told herself that it was important for Amy to know who her father was, to have some tangible evidence of the man he'd been, but now she considered the very real possibility that she'd never come to terms with his death. Not that she'd spent the past few years moping around, drinking wine and sighing over could-have-beens, but there was a part of her that hadn't been able to face the heartrending truth and the pain.

Stiffening her spine, she told herself that a new year was coming and no matter what else happened, Ronni Walsh vowed that she was going to put the past behind her, once and for all.

Through the open door to the house she heard the phone ring and her heart jump-started. *Travis!* "Oh, for the love of Saint Mary, Ronni, you're acting like you're sixteen again!" she reprimanded herself as she climbed the two steps into the kitchen and accepted the receiver from Amy's outstretched hand. "Hello?"

"Ronni?" Shelly asked, her voice sounding oddly strangled. "Do you think you could watch the boys this afternoon?"

"Sure, Shell, what's up?"

"Vic's going to run me to the clinic and I, um, think it would be best if the twins were with you."

"The clinic?" Ronni repeated, dread drizzling through her blood.

"Yeah. To see Dr. Sprick. It's, um, probably nothing but . . . well, I'm spotting a little and I think it should be checked out."

"Oh, Shelly," Ronni said, leaning back against the refrigerator and closing her eyes. "Sure. I can come and get the boys in fifteen minutes."

"No—we'll bring them by. Vic's already warming up the car."

A hard lump settled in the pit of Ronni's stomach and when she heard the rumble of Shelly's old station wagon, she dashed across the yard. The twins, more subdued than usual, clambered out of the backseat and ran into the house, but Ronni paused at the open passenger window.

"You're going to be all right," she said, managing a smile.

"I know it." Shelly's voice didn't have its usual lilt and Vic stared through the windshield, barely glancing in her direction.

"Don't worry about the boys. If they have to spend the night, it's no big deal."

"It shouldn't be that long," Vic said, and for the first time Ronni noticed the cigarette burning between his fingers. Victor had given up smoking seven years ago, before the twins had been born, and to Ronni's knowledge hadn't lit up since. Until today. He avoided her eyes.

"Okay, well . . . I'll see you later."

Shelly's chin wobbled and tears glazed her eyes. "Yeah." As Ronni patted the car door and stepped away from the time-worn station wagon, Victor slipped it into gear. They drove away in a cloud of blue exhaust, and Ronni, sending up a prayer for her sister, hurried into the house. "Come on, you guys," she said to the kids who were already jockeying for favored positions as they huddled around a cartoon show on television, "let's bake Christmas cookies." She touched her nephews on their shoulders, hoping to lift their spirits. Even though Shelly probably hadn't told them what was wrong, they'd obviously picked up that there was some kind of problem. "By the time your mom and dad get back, we'll have a plate just for them."

"Can we?" Amy was on her feet and dashing into the kitchen without a second thought to the cartoons.

Kent followed after her but Kurt rolled his eyes. "I don't cook. Dad says it's women's work."

"Now where have I heard that before?" she said, thinking of Bryan. "There must be some new macho conspiracy that I don't know about. Come on, Rambo." Sometimes, God love him, Vic could be such a throwback to some unenlightened generation.

"I don't wanna."

"Hey, sport, think about it. You've been into the bakery a million times."

"Yeah?" He continued to stare blankly at the television.

"And you've met Mr. Schmidt."

"So?"

"He's the baker, isn't he?"

Kurt scowled and scratched his head. "Maybe he's a sissy."

"I wouldn't tell him that, if I were you," she said with a smile. "Someone told me he was a pro wrestler for a while and he can outski me, so you'd better be careful what you say about him. Anyway"—she rumpled her wayward nephew's hair—"you decide what you want to do, but the rest of us are going to cut out cookies and decorate them."

Pasting a smile on her face, she went into the kitchen and tried not to concentrate on Shelly or stare at the clock and wonder what was happening to her sister. After all, as Shelly had told her dozens of times, worrying wouldn't help anything. Ronni went through the motions of mixing butter, sugar and flour, rolling out the dough and even cutting out shapes of Santas, reindeer and Christmas trees. Kurt, after only a few stubborn minutes, joined his cousin and brother at the table, and despite the flour and sugar spread over every inch of tabletop, counters and floor, the crisp results were soon cooling on a rack, ready to be frosted.

In the middle of the melee, Travis and Bryan appeared at the front door, and Ronni, sugar and flour dusting her apron, hair and face, felt as if a great burden had been lifted from her shoulders. The sensation was ridiculous, of course, but she couldn't help the rush of relief at the sight of him. "Come in, come in," she said, standing out of the doorway so they could join the general chaos.

"Want a cookie?" Amy asked. She was standing on a chair and placing red heart candies and green sprinkles on several works in process.

"Nah," Bryan said, then catching a pointed look from his father, looked at the floor and muttered, "Sure, why not?"

"They're Christmas trees," Amy exclaimed as if he

couldn't see the obvious. With a flourish she handed him a finished cookie and found a second for Travis.

Untying her apron, Ronni quickly introduced the boys who, tired of standing at the table, had resumed their positions in front of the TV. Kent was creating some kind of fort with plastic snap-together blocks, and Kurt, one eye on the television, was fashioning a weapon with them.

"Why've you got crutches?" Kurt asked, obviously in awe of the other boy.

"Fell down skiing. On the mountain."

"Can I try 'em?" Kurt was on his feet in an instant, the plastic blocks forgotten.

Bryan glanced at Ronni and his father with the worried look of someone who's looking for a means—any means—of escape. "A teenage boy's nightmare," Ronni said, watching the exchange. Even Amy gave up decorating cookies and scurried into the living room where she planted herself near Bryan, as if staking her claim.

"How about some coffee?" Ronni offered.

"I can only stay a minute."

"Oh?"

"Bryan and I were talking. He'd like to take some skiing lessons or . . . snowboarding lessons, either alone or with a group of kids his age when he gets better probably next season unfortunately—and I suggested you or someone you know."

"I don't know how good I am with a board," she admitted. "I've only tried it a couple of times and I wasn't that great, but I can get him in touch with someone up on the mountain who's worked with kids and could place him in the right class."

"Would you?" Travis said, seeming relieved. "I'd like him to meet some boys his age."

"No problem."

"Thanks." He shifted restlessly from one foot to the other and then, casting a look at the kids to see that they were all occupied, he grabbed Ronni by the crook of the elbow and shepherded her onto the back porch. The horses were huddled together near the fence line and a solitary hawk swooped through the sky, but otherwise the day was still. "Look," he said once they were alone outside, "I know I blew it the other night. I pushed too hard. I thought—er, I was hoping . . . oh, hell, I don't even know what I'm trying to say here." Frowning, his eyebrows beetling over his steady eyes, he cleared his throat. "I thought maybe there was a chance that we could start over."

"Start over?" she repeated, curling her hands over the railing and staring at the snow-covered remains of her vegetable garden. A soft mist gathered in the trees and a few solitary flakes fell from the darkening sky. "You mean, go back to square one?"

"I wish I knew what I meant." Impatiently, he shoved a hand through his hair and muttered something unintelligible.

"Let me guess," she suggested, unable to resist goading him. "You want to be friends? You know, wave when we meet at the mail box, feed each other's pets when one of us is out of town, work out the fence line and . . . oooh!"

He yanked her close to him and this time she knew she'd pushed him too far. His mouth was razor thin, his speech clipped with a patience that seemed to forever elude him. "What I want, lady," he said, the intensity of his stare laser bright, the fingers of his hand curved over her forearm in a white-knuckled grip, "is downright indecent. If you want to know the truth, what I want is to kiss you until you can't think straight and then carry you to bed so that I can make love to you all night long." His expression was stark with strain, his skin stretched tight over high, bladed cheekbones and there was a desperation in his voice that he failed to hide. "What I want, very simply put, is you. All of you."

Ronni's throat went dry and she tried to back away, but he caught her and squeezed her up against the door. "Ever since I first laid eyes on you, I've wanted you and I've tried to be patient and play the game, be the friendly neighbor, but it's just not my nature and"—he gazed at her lips so hard that she licked them nervously—"and you seem to have a way of bringing out the worst in me." Before she could argue, he pressed the length of his body against hers and kissed her with a fever that spread from his lips to hers and slid through her bloodstream to melt her very bones.

Breathing was difficult, pulling away impossible and she gave in to the hot impulses that fired her blood. She sagged against him, and as desperately as a starving person, she kissed him back, her pulse thundering in her ears, her breathing ragged and short. Her arms wound around his neck of their own accord and when he fit his legs between hers, his fly rubbing against hers, she felt a warmth begin to flow.

Somewhere in the distance bells began to ring and Ronni was vaguely aware of the noise. Travis lifted his head and cocked it to the side.

Another sharp ring and the scramble of anxious feet on the hardwood floor as she heard Amy race for the phone.

"Expecting a call?"

"No—" *Shelly!* "Oh, yes. It could be news about my sister."

It was. Victor, still at the hospital, was on the other end of the line and he gave her the sketchy news—that Shelly was all right, though still spotting. The doctor had ordered her to bed, no work, no frantic Christmas shopping and complete rest until the crisis resolved itself. There was still a chance she could lose the baby, early as it was in her pregnancy, but if she took care of herself, the risk was lessened.

"The boys will stay here." Ronni decided when Vic finished telling her as many details as he could remember. What she was going to do with two rowdy six-year-olds she wasn't certain, but somehow she'd figure it out.

"Oh, no, I can handle 'em," Vic told her. "They'll be with me at the lot and when I need a break, Mandy, our neighbor—she's divorced, you know—offered to help out. I figure we can trade off. I'll stack some cordwood for her and fix her kids' bikes in trade."

"But the boys are more than welcome here," Ronni insisted.

"I know, I know, and believe me I'll probably be askin' for your help, but now that Shelly's . . . well, laid up, you won't have a secretary or worker in the warehouse and you've already got your end of the business, the ski patrol and Amy and . . . Lord, girl, I think you're plate's about full, as it is."

"But Shelly—"

"She's right here. Hang on."

A few seconds later, Shelly's voice, filled with a falsely cheery ring, sang over the wires. "How are the boys? Have they worn you out yet?"

"Don't worry about them. How are you?" Ronni wound the cord in her fingers and glanced at Travis who had walked into the living room and was having a discussion with his son.

"I'll be fine. It's just the baby—they're not sure if, well . . . if I can go to term or even to the next trimester." Her voice cracked and she cleared her throat. "It's scary, Ronni," she admitted. "I know this baby wasn't planned and it's poor timing and everything but—"

"Shh. It's all right. The baby's going to be fine."

"I hope so," she whispered. "Anyway, I'm just about on my way home. Vic will come by and get the boys—"

"No way. Tonight they're staying here. We'll talk

more tomorrow morning. Go home and take it easy, Shell. You can call me when you're awake."

Shelly started to cry and Ronni wished she could console her sister. Obviously Shelly was worried sick and Ronni, too, felt a dull ache in the middle of her belly, a pain that she could only describe as dread.

"Problems?" Travis said once she'd hung up. She felt cold to the bone and rubbed her arms to shake the chill that had started in the middle of her heart.

"A few." She gave him a sketchy rundown of what was happening in her sister's life including Shelly's pregnancy and worries about having to move in order for Vic to find a steady job. All the while Ronni tried to keep her voice low enough so as not to be overheard by the boys.

While she spoke, Travis found a mug in the cupboard near the refrigerator and poured her a cup of coffee. "I could help," he offered, handing her the steaming brew.

"You? How?"

"Well, not with the baby, obviously. That's up to the doctors and nature. But Vic could work for me."

Ronni leveled him a look that was meant to convey, *Don't tease me on this one, Keegan.*

"I'm serious." He poured the remains of the coffee-pot into a cup and snagged a finished cookie from the drying rack.

Sighing across the top of her mug, she said, "I've seen the equipment you've got set up. Vic wouldn't know a fax machine from a word processor, and as for linking up to the Internet, forget it. He's a sawmill man. Born and bred for generations. He's not a three-piece suit kind of guy."

"I was talking about helping me get the house renovated and updated. I've had to hire contractors and subs for the tough jobs that require a lot of expertise and licenses and such, but there's a lot of work that I'd hoped I could share with Bryan which isn't going to happen for a while—at least not until he's off crutches—and some of the jobs won't wait."

She wavered as she sipped her coffee. It slid in a warm path to her stomach and chased away some of the cold fear that had settled there. Travis was offering a much-needed helping hand to a man he barely knew. "Vic's proud, almost to a fault. He won't want your pity or accept anything he construes as a handout."

"I think that can be managed," Travis replied, a mischievous light gleaming in his eyes. "Would you feel better if I promised to work off his behind?"

"Not me, but Victor would. A proud, stubborn, hardheaded man, that one," she said as if to herself, but inside, the wheels of her mind were turning ever faster. Travis's plan might just work. Business at the tree lot had slowed. With only a week before Christmas, sales had fallen off drastically and it was only a matter of days before her brother-in-law would be unemployed again. Tilting her face up, she eyed this complex man who could be hard-hearted and seemingly ruthless one minute, compassionate the next, and sexy as all get out, to boot.

"You don't know Vic."

"I met him the other night. Seemed conscientious enough to me—personable to the customers at the tree lot and someone who wasn't afraid of hard work. Unless he was just putting on a show for me by delivering the tree and sticking around to see that it fit into the stand."

"Don't be ridiculous."

"Then he's got a job if he wants one."

She was stunned. "That's how you hire people? From meeting them once?"

A small smile twisted his lips. "It's one way. When you can't get a resumé or don't have time to do background checks, then you have to rely on gut instinct." He lifted one shoulder. "Usually, it's right on."

"Oh?"

"It was right about you."

She squinted up at him. "How's that?"

"Pretty. Intelligent. Serious, with a wild side that needs to be explored."

"Oh, right," she mocked just as Kurt, struggling on tiptoe, crutches stretched out in front of him to accommodate his small size, fell into the room. He let out a yelp, then held his tongue as his brother, who was forever getting the short end of the stick, in Ronni's estimation, started to laugh.

"Kurt! Oh, be careful," she admonished, then picked

up her nephew and hugged him. For all his bravado, he was just a little boy and he sniffed loudly, though she suspected his pride was injured more than any part of his body.

Bryan sent his father a baleful look and Travis took the hint. "I promised Bryan he could rent some movies this afternoon."

"What? And give up entertaining the troops?" she said with a teasing grin. "I can't imagine why he'd want to do that."

Travis was suddenly sober, his eyes dark with emotion, his voice low enough so as not to be heard over the television. "It's all part of our new deal—peace treaty really. Bryan's agreed to spend the rest of the school year here, with me, then if things don't work out, he's moving to Europe to be with his mother."

"Oh, Travis." She read the pain in his eyes and knew that only a child could wound so deeply.

"I just hope he gives Cascadia a chance," he said, finishing his coffee. "Come on, Bryan, we've got money to spend at the video store." In an aside to Ronni, he added, "I could take the rest of the kids, too, if you want to go visit your sister for a while."

The truth of the matter was that she was itching to see Shelly, but she wasn't about to dump the load of kids on Travis. "I'll see her in the morning," she answered. "She needs to rest now and we've—that's a collective we, meaning the children as well as me—have a kitchen to clean."

"I'll call Vic," Travis promised. "Now, about those lessons?"

At that point, Bryan hobbled over to the front door.

"When do you get off the sticks?" Ronni asked.

"Probably next Monday," Bryan answered curtly.

"Two days before Christmas? Good."

"Yeah and I'm gonna try snowboarding that day!"

"I don't think so," Travis said.

"I'm not waiting a year!" Bryan insisted, glowering. "No way."

"We'll see what the doctor says. Hopefully snowboarding will be better on your knees. There's less chance of reinjuring yourself when you get good enough not to fall all the time. The problem with learning something new is that you're bound to fall over and over again. When you fall and lose control, that's when there's the danger of reinjury."

"Not me. You don't know, I could have a natural ability," Bryan said.

"It's possible, I suppose, but my guess is that you might land on your backside more often than not on the first day," Travis told him, setting his empty cup in the sink.

Bryan rolled his eyes.

"Don't forget what I promised about the horses," Ronni said, hoping to cheer the boy. "Anytime you're ready."

"I'll see you later," Travis said, touching her arm in a familiar gesture that caused her pulse to race.

"I'd like that," she admitted, surprised at her reaction. How could this man she barely knew make her heart thunder, her mind wander to long-forgotten fantasies, her lips curve into a smile? She wondered fleetingly if she was falling in love, then gave herself a quick mental shake. Love was an emotion that had to be nurtured over the years, that came with respect and trust. No, what she was feeling was lust—basic primal chemistry between a man and a woman. Travis was a sexy man with an easy smile, quick wit and quiet charm. She'd just been too long without a man—that was all there was to it. Nothing more. She stood on the porch, letting the cold winter air swirl around her as she watched him drive away. Silly though it was, he seemed to take a piece of her heart with him.

"I'm going to be fine and the baby's going to be fine, too. Just quit worrying," Shelly scolded from her worn plaid couch. From her position, she had a clear view of the side yard and the swing set where all three kids, despite the snow, were playing. Dressed in snowsuits, boots and stocking hats, they ran in crazy circles around the slide and teeter-totter.

"Worrying is what I do best," Ronni admitted as she set a red poinsettia on the coffee table near the platter of cookies the kids had baked.

"This is too much, you shouldn't have," Shelly protested, but she smiled as she fingered a silky scarlet petal.

"No way."

"It's not as if I can't do anything for myself, you know."

"I know, I know, but let me pamper you, okay?" Ronni hesitated at the front door. "Besides, I owe you. There was a time when I was a basket case. If it wasn't for you and Vic, I don't know what Amy and I would have done," she said, her heart squeezing when she remembered how Shelly, mother of two rambunctious two-year-olds, had put her own life on hold to help Ronni find herself in those brutal, dark days after Hank was killed. Vic, too, had stepped in awkwardly to provide whatever emotional support he could. "You just stay there on the couch for a second while I put a few things together," Ronni said.

She made a trip to the car and carried in a casserole dish filled with meat loaf and potatoes. After setting the timer and temperature, she shoved the dish into Shelly's small oven on timed bake. "That should do it. There's a green salad in the fridge, rolls in this basket and a chocolate cake on the counter."

"You're too much," Shelly said, her voice clogged with emotion.

"I just want you to get better and, with that in mind, I brought you my own special brand of medicine."

"Uh-oh."

"Oh, believe me, you'll love it." She ran out to the car and returned with the latest edition of Shelly's favorite movie magazine.

"You know my weakness," Shelly said, her eyes crinkling at the corners in delight. She'd given up her subscription when Victor had first been laid off.

Ronni handed her the slick magazine and sat on the corner of the coffee table. "Now, the truth, how are you feeling?"

Absently, Shelly thumbed the magazine, then looked across the room to a spot only she could see. "The truth?"

"That's right."

"Okay, I'm scared. I hate to admit it, but I am. I want this baby desperately but I can't afford to be off my feet, and Vic—he needs me healthy. He's coming around, though. The thought of losing the baby frightens him." She glanced down at the magazine cover with a picture of one of her favorite stars. "He's made a couple of calls to guys he knows who moved to California, because once the tree lot closes, he's out of work and his unemployment benefits ran out a long time ago." She let out a long sigh. "It's just a rough time right now, but I tell myself that we're all healthy—well, everyone else is, and this"—she motioned toward her belly—"it's in God's hands now, I guess."

"I might know of a job," Ronni ventured, unable to hold her tongue.

"For Vic? Around here?"

She hated the hopeful sound in her sister's voice. "I talked to Travis Keegan last night. He came over in the middle of our cookie-baking adventure." She went on to describe most of her conversation with Travis and Shelly's eyebrows drew together in concentration.

"It sounds good—too good," she finally said. "And if Keegan's doing this because he's seeing you, there's no chance it will work. You know Vic, he's prideful to a fault."

"Just have him talk to Travis."

Shelly rubbed her chin. "I still can't figure out why his name sounds so familiar, but it does, every time I hear it, I feel like I should know something more about him, that I *do* know something, but I just can't put my finger on it."

"If it's important, it'll come," Ronni said. She spent the next hour chatting with her sister.

By the time she was ready to pack Amy back in the car, Victor had returned from the tree lot with his check and word that he wasn't needed any longer, at least not until next year. "Decent of Delmer and Ed," he said, though his eyes gave him away and frustration clenched his jaw. "At least I'll have a job next December."

"Maybe you won't have to wait that long," Ronni said.

"Not if we move. Let's see, what's it gonna be? San Francisco or Seattle?" He found a coin in the pocket of his bib overalls and flipped it into the air.

"Talk to Keegan," Ronni advised.

"Why?" Victor was immediately suspicious and Ronni felt as if she'd been caught meddling. He scowled as she told him the work Travis needed help with. He felt in his chest pocket for a pack of cigarettes that didn't exist and scowled angrily. "I've always taken care of my family," he said when she'd finished her spiel. "Haven't taken a handout in my life."

"I know, I know. But just talk to him. If you think the job's bogus, then forget it, but see what he has to say," Shelly said, and the stubborn set of Victor's jaw softened as he stared down at his wife.

"All right," he reluctantly agreed.

"What have you got to lose?" Ronni asked.

"My pride. And when a man's pride and dignity are gone, he's left with nothing." He took off his old hunting hat and scratched his head.

"Victor," she reprimanded quietly.

"Okay, okay," he growled, snapping his hat against his leg. "You win. I'll see what the man has to say."

"So I'll need someone to help me with some of the refurbishing and cleanup," Travis told Victor as they walked through the third floor of the old house. It was filthy, some of the windows were cracked and rain and snow had blown in, destroying the hardwood floor. There were three dormer-style rooms tucked under the eaves and on the second floor, five bedrooms and three bathrooms. The interior in all cases was knotty pine, yellowed with age and battered by the elements where the wind and rain had permeated the old timbers. "The roof needs to be fixed, the moss killed, the gutters replaced. I could have a contractor do some of the work but I'd like to take a hand in it myself."

"I thought you were a businessman," Victor said, running the tips of his callused fingers on the old railing that wound down the stairs.

"I am . . . was, but I needed a break. Wanted to start a new life for Bryan and myself."

"This house is pretty big for just a man and a kid," Victor observed, and Travis was vaguely uneasy. His wealth had come through hard work, but it was there just the same, where a man like Victor worked day in and day out to scrape together a living for his family. The house, if it hadn't been in such disrepair, would have been ostentatious.

"Yeah, I know, but I fell in love with it. I wanted something different with enough acreage that we wouldn't feel cooped up."

"I don't think you'll have much worry about that."

The walk ended up in the front hall and the telephone rang. Travis excused himself and took the call in his makeshift den. Wendall was reporting in, offering suggestions on a new employee-benefit and healthcare package and explaining about one of the smaller skateboarding companies that TRK, Inc. was planning to buy. He listened, offered his advice and glanced at his watch. He was too young to retire and yet the business had started to bore him. He needed something new and fresh in his life, something he expected to find here.

Something or someone? his mind taunted. *Someone like Ronni Walsh?*

He hung up, feeling restless and frustrated. Trapped in a skin he was anxious to shed. Whenever he was reminded of his life in Seattle, he was disturbed and he longed to just cut the whole damned thing loose. His life here with Bryan seemed so far removed from the rat race he'd left.

He found Victor in the living room, staring through the windowpanes at the lake. "Just one thing I want to know about this job, Keegan," he said, frowning in concentration as he worried the brim of his hat in his work-roughened hands. "I'll work for you, do whatever it is you want done, but I have to know that I got the job because of me, not because you're interested in Ronni."

"This has nothing to do with her," Travis said. "This is business. I just happened to have met you through her."

Victor tugged on his lower lip. "All right then."

They discussed the terms of his employment and a smile of relief crossed Vic's features.

"Thanks, Keegan," he said, extending his hand.

Travis clasped his fingers over Vic's callused palm and gave it a shake. "I'll see you tomorrow at nine."

"I'll be here." Victor Pederson whistled as he left the old lodge and Travis ignored that irritating voice in his head that called him a fool for hiring Ronni's brother-in-law. His relationship with her was rocky already. What would happen if he was forced to fire Vic? He'd hedged when he'd confided to Ronni that he was hiring

Victor on gut instinct. It was more than that. He'd hired the man because of her, because he wanted to get closer to her, because he wanted to look good in her eyes.

Damn it all, what was happening to him? In years past, he'd hired and fired men and women because of their qualifications and performance, nothing more. Sure, people had given him names, but he'd always been careful, aware that hiring the friend of an employee could inadvertently cause problems between the two employees or with him. Oftentimes, professional jealousy developed or worse, and one of the two had to be let go. He'd rarely ever hired one person on the recommendation of an acquaintance unless that person was in the business.

But in one fell swoop of wanting to erase the silent worry in Ronni's eyes, he'd given up his objectivity and hired her brother-in-law.

He only hoped he didn't live to regret it.

CHAPTER 9

"A PUPPY FOR me and a new daddy for my mommy!" Amy announced. Clutching a candy cane in one fist, she balanced on the mall Santa's lap and cast her mother a superior, knowing look. Ronni wanted to fall through the tiled floor and die of embarrassment. Her face flaming, she grabbed Amy's little hand and led her away from the crowd that had gathered at the bench labeled North Pole at the south end of the shopping center in east Portland. She felt the eyes of other mothers watching her as she joined the clog of last-minute shoppers that bustled anxiously through the wide hallway outside one of the major department stores.

Shifting her parcels into her other hand, she said, "I think we should get something straight, Amy." She glanced down at her innocent daughter who didn't seem to understand what she'd done wrong. "I don't want or need another husband."

"Why not?"

"Because . . . because Daddy was special." Jostled by a group of teenage boys, she automatically said, "Sorry," even though the bump wasn't her fault. The kid that actually bumped her was six feet tall with shaved hair up the sides of his head, multiple earrings and a fluff of blond frizz on top. As he marched away in his army-style boots, he didn't bother turning around or acknowledging her.

Ronni ignored him.

Amy wasn't to be put off. "Just because he was special doesn't mean we can't have another daddy. Katie Pendergrass has two daddies, one that lives with her and one that lives . . . somewhere else."

"I know, but I just haven't met anyone who could replace your father," she said, cutting across the wide mall and through the undergarment department of one of the anchor stores. What was she doing having this conversation in the middle of a frantic throng of shoppers? "Come on, sweetie," she said, tightening her hold on Amy's hand as she shouldered open an outside door to the gray day. She searched the lot, trying to remember in which row her van was parked. Fortunately, the vehicle was big enough to stand out even in a filled parking lot and she dashed through the rain, keys in hand, packages rattling, Amy's little legs flying as the little girl kept up with her. By the time she'd gotten her daughter into the front seat, she was soaked and a woman in a small import was holding up traffic, waiting for Ronni's parking space.

Somehow, today, in the gray drizzle of Portland, the Christmas spirit eluded her. Slate-colored skies, pushy shoppers, picked-over merchandise and the continual clink of coins and cash registers reminded her how commercial the most sacred holiday of the year had become.

Easing out of the parking lot, she headed east, toward the mountains and home. Her shopping was done and, of course, the puppy, now weaned, was waiting to be brought home. Shelly had agreed to let Ronni put on Christmas dinner and she'd arranged her schedule at the mountain so that she had both Christmas Eve and Christmas Day off. Things wouldn't get hectic with her mail-order business until after the first of the year when people already started ordering items for Valentine's Day, but if Shelly wasn't able to help her, she'd have to hire extra staff.

Shelly. Ronni sent up a silent prayer for her sister and unborn baby. So far, Shelly was still pregnant and Vic had started working for Keegan. Things were working out, or so it seemed.

Suddenly, Taillights flashed in front of her. Tires squealed. A black dog came out of nowhere, galloping across several lanes of traffic up ahead. Automatically she stood on the brakes. The van fishtailed in the rain, its tires screaming in protest. The van stopped just before she collided with the car in front of her. She braced herself as she checked the rear view mirror and caught a glimpse of a silver sports car skidding sideways on the pavement behind her. "Watch out," she cried and the car missed her by inches.

"Thank you," she whispered in prayer. Adrenaline pumped through her and her heartbeat, normal only minutes before, began to throb wildly. "Oh, Lord."

"What happened?" Amy, round-eyed, her candy cane a sticky mess on her lap, asked.

"I think a dog ran out in front of one of the cars up ahead. The first car stopped and the next one nearly ran into it starting a chain reaction."

"Is the dog okay?" Amy's lower lip trembled and her worried eyes searched frantically through the foggy glass.

"I think so. He took off through those houses." Ronni pointed to the development just off the shoulder of the four-lane highway. Amy wiped away the condensation and her eyes searched the brush and path between the houses. "It's not his fault," Ronni said. "His owners should keep him leashed or fenced."

"But is he hurt?"

"I don't think he got hit."

"How do you know?"

"I don't, honey, but I saw him run past that fence. I think he'll be all right."

Traffic started moving again and the silver sports car roared into the lane beside Ronni. The driver laid on his horn, and when she looked at him, he glowered at her and used an obscene gesture before speeding away.

"Merry Christmas to you, too," Ronni muttered.

"You know him?" Amy peered through the drizzle and approaching darkness to stare at the car's bright taillights as they blended into the long stream of red beams ahead of them.

"No, and I don't want to know him. He's rude."

Amy picked up her candy cane and started working on it again. Ronni was about to protest as the sticky peppermint was already on the child's jacket and pants, but she kept her mouth closed and concentrated on the road that wound through the steep foothills. The suburbs gave way to rolling farmland dotted with smaller towns, then eventually the highway grew steeper and cleaved to the thick forest of the mountains. Rain turned to snow in a matter of miles and soon white powder piled high on the shoulders gave the dark night a small cast of illumination.

Amy glanced at her mother. "I still want a puppy for Christmas."

"I know you do, sweetie."

"And a daddy."

"Oh, honey, I don't think—"

"What about Bryan's dad? He gots no wife."

Travis. Funny, when she thought of marriage, his image always came to mind. "I don't think he's ready to tie the knot again—I mean, get married—either."

"Why not?"

"Oh, honey, I'm not sure." How did they get on this crazy subject? Amy seemed almost obsessed with thoughts of a father these days. The one thing Ronni couldn't give her.

With a theatrical sigh, Amy drew on the passenger window again, her small finger sliding through the condensation. "Everybody else has a daddy."

"Everybody? Like who?"

"All the kids in school and I told you about Katie."

"Yes, I know. She's got two." The lights of Cascadia loomed in the horizon just as the snow began to stick to the road. "I guess she's lucky."

"She likes one better than the other one."

"See, she's got problems, too."

"But Travis is nice."

Back to him again. "Yes, he is."

"He likes you."

"And I like him but that's not enough reason for people to get married, okay?"

"But—"

"Subject closed." She drove past the welcome sign and an old, empty sawmill near the railroad tracks. She could understand why Amy would try to pair her with Travis. They'd had dinner together the past three nights and had visited Shelly while Bryan watched Amy. They'd finished decorating the old lodge and celebrated by kissing under the mistletoe that Travis had hung in the foyer. Ronni had struggled with the idea of buying him a Christmas present, then decided to give Bryan and him a housewarming gift instead. It seemed safer and less personal. As each day passed, she and Travis were becoming closer. Just thinking of him caused a warm feeling deep inside, and whenever they were alone, the sparks flew.

She now knew the name of the company—TRK Inc., the holding company for smaller corporations—that he'd started and built into the empire that it was today. She'd also gained a little more insight into his marriage and why it had failed. Though he still blamed himself, it sounded as if his wife was as much, if not more, at fault for their union's slow and painful demise. Yes, Ronni and Travis had grown closer, emotionally as well as physically.

Never, since Hank, had she been tempted to make love to a man. She'd been a virgin when she and Hank had started dating and hadn't slept with anyone since her husband's death. She'd always just assumed she would never make love again, never wake up to the smell and feel of a man's arms around her, never experience a man's touch on her breasts or spine or—

She brought herself up short. Lately, her thoughts had a way of turning wanton, and she knew where to lay the blame for that. If Travis weren't so damned sexy . . . but it was more than his looks. There was the strong man with the soft center that appealed to her and touched her deep inside.

With a sigh, she wheeled the van into the parking lot of a local mom-and-pop grocery store and steadfastly pushed Travis Keegan out of her mind. She just didn't have time for a man in her life—no matter how fascinating he was.

"That's it then," Travis said, handing his son the thick sheaf of papers that had come from the school. Aside from health, registration and fee forms, there was information for all of the classes in which Bryan was enrolled. "Looks like a lot of work."

"Looks like a disaster!" Bryan corrected, eyeing the pages as if they were his death sentence. He hobbled over to the fireplace and sat on the raised hearth.

"They would have been here sooner, but they were sent to our address in Seattle and forwarded here."

"Great. Just goes to show you how on top of it the school is."

"Give the school a chance, Bryan."

"Why? So I can look like a freak to all the other kids."

"You won't look like a—"

"What about these, huh?" Lifting a crutch and swinging it in the air, he added, "What if the doctor doesn't let me get rid of them? I'll look like a geek. A weirdo—"

"A kid who had an accident," Travis said, trying to understand his son and yet remain firm. "I know it'll be difficult going to a new school, trying to make new friends, hoping to fit in, but you'll do just fine." He offered Bryan a smile. "You're worrying this to death."

"Because it's my life!"

"Your new life."

"I liked my old one."

"Did you?" Travis asked softly.

"Yeah, I did. And I liked living with Mom."

That was a lie, but Travis wasn't about to call him on it. Not while the boy was so upset.

"You know how weird it is living with your dad?" Bryan asked.

"No." Travis sat on the edge of a couch and let his clasped hands drop between his knees. "Why don't you tell me."

"It's way beyond weird. Guys live with their parents or their mother but no one lives with their dad."

"So that's it. You want a mom?"

"I've got a mom." He made a dismissive motion with his hand and bit his lower lip. "She's just not here."

"There you go, guys." Ronni shook forkfuls of hay into the manger and two velvet-soft noses began plucking at the dry blades. Contented snorts and the swishing of coarse tails contended with the rustle of straw as the horses shifted in their stalls.

Lucy, the white mare, was round with the foal she would deliver in the next couple of months, and Sam, the sire, a gray stallion with a black mane and tail, nuzzled her out of the way.

"Greedy," Ronni admonished. Liquid brown eyes blinked, dark ears flicked, but he kept on chewing and snorting, determined to get his share and then some. "Just like a man."

Ronni hung the pitchfork on two nails driven into the interior walls, dusted her hands and was ready to snap off the light when she saw the shadow. Her breath caught in the back of her throat and she reached for the pitchfork again as Travis stepped out of the doorway and into the lamplight.

She gasped, then shook her head. "You scared the devil out of me!"

"Sorry, just got here. I knocked at the house, but no one answered."

"Oh, well . . ." She had trouble catching her breath and her heart beat a little faster than it should.

"Amy's had a big day—shopping, Santa and all that—she's already asleep and I'm late with feeding the horses, so that's why I'm not in the house. . . ." Why did she feel the need to explain herself? Why couldn't she tear her gaze away from his mesmerizing stare? Why did her blood still race stupidly?

"How's your sister? Her husband's kind of tight-lipped about what's going on." In the shadowy light he looked more handsome than ever as he shoved his hands into the pockets of his jacket.

Ronni cleared her throat as it didn't want to work. "Vic's worried about her, of course, and the baby, but she's hanging in. Between her neighbor and me, she gets a little relief with the twins, but I think she's still on her feet more than she should be." She tightened the lid on the oat barrel, trying to regain some of her fast-fleeting composure. "But at least Victor's working and that's helped relieve some of the stress." She glanced past him to the darkness and prayed he couldn't hear the ridiculous hammering of her heart. "Are you here alone?"

Nodding, he said, "I finally got a packet from the school with information on Bryan's classes and they're different from the ones he was taking in Seattle, so he's doing some catch-up reading—Charles Dickens." His gray eyes touched hers again and lingered for a second. "Well, that's what he's supposed to be doing."

"So . . . you decided to take a walk," she guessed. Dear Lord, were her palms sweating? It was cold as ice out here, yet she felt a warm flush.

His smile was positively wicked as he snapped off the lights and the only illumination was the reflection of moonlight that bounced off the snow to shaft through the small windows and open door. "Actually, I decided to see you," he admitted with an edge of reluctance to his voice.

"Should I be flattered?" she asked, unable to stop flirting a little even though her heart was beginning to knock crazily in her chest.

"Definitely." He pulled the door shut behind him and they were suddenly alone. More alone than they had been.

"Why's that?" she asked, her pulse leaping wildly.

"Because it's been a long time since I wanted to be with

a woman," he said, walking slowly up to her. "Maybe too long." Stopping just inches from her, he wound his finger in the long braid that had flipped over her shoulder to curl around her breast. "You know, Ronni, I just don't know what to do with you."

"No?" she asked, the barn suddenly seeming to close, the air hard to breathe. "Why not?"

"You're not like any woman I've ever met."

"Is that bad?"

"Maybe . . . maybe not." She licked her lips nervously and a muscle worked his jaw. "I don't want this," he said.

"Want what?" But she knew. They both knew. Desire, new and frightening, yet as old as time, hung in the air.

Resting his forehead against hers, he whispered, "I don't know what it is about you, woman. Can't put my finger on it, but there's something damned irresistible." His arms circled her waist. "I just can't fight it," he said, "though God knows I've tried."

His lips brushed over hers and though she knew she was wading in dangerous waters, she couldn't stop. Wouldn't. It had been too long and Travis touched her like no other man. Ronni's breathing was already shallow, her heartbeat fluttering like the wings of a frightened bird. She gave herself without hesitation, kissing him, holding him, feeling his weight drag them both to the straw-strewn floor.

His lips were warm, the air cool and the quiet nicker of the horses in counterpoint to the soft hoot of an owl. Ronni closed her eyes and reveled in the feel of him, the way his lips touched the shell of her ear, the pressure of his hands as his fingers found the zipper of her jacket. She sensed the cold whisper of air caress her skin as he lifted her sweater over her head, and then, with weak moonlight filtering through the windows, unhooked her bra, letting her breasts spill into the night.

He kissed the deep cleft, breathed fire across the goose bumps that raised on her skin and touched a nipple that puckered and strained until his tongue encircled the taut point.

Writhing in sweet agony, she arched upward, her blood on fire, a dark need unfolding deep within. His hands reached behind her, pressing intimately on the naked small of her back, tracing the long depression of her spine as his lips surrounded one nipple and he began to suckle, creating a whirlpool of desire deep in the most feminine part of her.

"Travis," she cried when he delved beneath her jeans, his fingers grazing her buttocks, his hands hot and ready. The buttons of her fly opened in a sharp series of pops and soon, still making love to her breasts with his mouth, he skimmed the jeans down her legs, discarded her shoes and socks and she was suddenly naked in the dark barn. Burning and anxious and naked.

When he lifted his head, she cried out, but then he

moved lower, his tongue tracing a path along the center of her abdomen. She bucked, her hips rising off the floor with the want of him and he whispered, "Slow down, honey. Just slow down and enjoy."

She knew she should stop, that she was crossing an invisible and dangerous line, but she couldn't find the words and her voice was dry and hoarse as he continued kissing her and stroking her, spreading her legs gently, slowly finding that sensitive part of her that she'd sworn no man would ever discover again.

But she didn't stop him and as he touched her, slowly at first and then more rapidly, she found his rhythm and moved furiously with each magic stroke, inviting more, wanting more, gritting her teeth with the need of him, all of him. His hands and mouth were exquisite and she felt herself soaring ever higher like a shooting star careering across the sky until the release, when it came, rocked her so hard she would have sworn the heavens split and the world shattered.

Only when it was over, when he was holding her in his arms and kissing away the tears of relief, was she able to slow the beating of her heart and hear the soft sigh of the wind over her own ragged, desperate breaths. How could one man affect her so? How could she ever let him touch her again—how could she not? In a few short weeks, she'd come to rely on and trust him as she had trusted no one since Hank.

"Travis, I—"

"Shh, honey. No need for words." But his eyes had darkened as if there were unspoken gestures hanging between them.

She nestled in his arms for a minute before becoming aware of the sharp tensile strength of his muscles, the hard planes of his face and the very noticeable bulge in the front of his jeans.

Turning to him, she held his face in her hands and began kissing him, slowly at first and then more feverishly until he moaned with pleasure. With fumbling fingers she stripped him of his jacket and sweatshirt, her fingers playing softly in the swirling hair of his chest.

Strong and sinewy, his flesh was hot and firm. She kissed him on his bare skin, rimming one of his nipples with her tongue and letting her fingers explore him, the ridges and planes of his muscles, the slope of his back, the rounded firmness of his buttocks.

When she opened his fly, he didn't stop her and as she pushed off his jeans, he groaned in some kind of male ecstasy. Her fingers glided over the hard muscles of his thighs and she moved lower, but before she could pleasure him as he had her, he kissed her and his knees parted her legs. Eyes, seeking and dark, stared at her breasts as he poised over her. "You're sure about this?" he asked, sweat beading his upper lip.

"Yes," she lied. How could she be sure of anything? But she wanted him . . . maybe even loved him. . . .

"No regrets?"

"None," she promised.

Biting his lower lip, he fumbled in the dark, found his jeans and shook out his wallet. Deep within the leather he found the foil packet and opened it quickly.

Ronni was still breathing hard, her abdomen rising and falling, her breasts full and wanting as he kissed first one nipple, then the other. He lifted her hips with his hands. Eyes locked with hers, he entered her, so slowly she thought she would die in ecstasy, and then he withdrew just as lazily, as if he had all the willpower in the world. She would never have thought she could be ready so soon after being satiated, but her need was great and she moved with him, accepting his thrusts, yearning for more, wanting all of him.

His tempo increased. She moaned and cried out as he fell to his elbows and joined her in a fierce, ancient dance that caused the earth to shatter and the seas to part.

"Travis," she whispered, his name familiar and right. "Travis, oh, please—" And then it came, that sweet spasm of delight that caused him to collapse against her, crushing her breasts and jarring her to her very soul. This was how it was supposed to be.

She held him close, her heart pounding wildly, and a new sensation akin to love surrounded her in its gentle blanket. The horses snorted as if in disapproval, but she didn't care. For the first time in nearly four years, she felt like a woman, a full, complete woman.

"You're beautiful, Veronica," he said, his voice rough with emotion. He brushed a strand of hair from her face and when he stared at her, she saw deeper emotions in his eyes, as if he too felt the change in their relationship, he too realized there was no turning back, he too knew their lives would never be the same.

Levering up on one elbow, he stared down at her and touched the hill of her cheek with one long finger. "I . . . I . . ." He stopped, took in a deep breath and shook his head. "Look what you've reduced me to, woman."

A tightness was forming in her throat as she realized how serious he'd become. How sober. How intense.

A heartbeat, then his gaze locked with hers. Her throat turned to sand. Oh, God, she knew what he was going to ask before the words, those beautiful, frightening words whispered through the barn.

He took her hand in his as if afraid she might pull away, "I want you to marry me."

Chapter 10

"I . . . I DON'T KNOW what to say," Ronni whispered as Travis plucked a piece of straw from her hair.

A smile split his jaw and some of the tension drained from his face. "How about, 'Oh, Travis, I never thought you'd ask, I'll marry you and bear your children, clean your house, wash your clothes, kiss the ground you walk on and be devoted to you for the rest of your life?'"

Ronni, close to tears a moment before, laughed. "Oh, sure, that's what was on the tip of my tongue." Kissing him, she saw the merriment in his eyes and she hugged him closer. Marriage. To Travis. "I—I want to be sure," she said as the reality hit her.

"You aren't now?"

"For the moment, yes, but for the rest of our lives . . . ? I barely know you."

He smiled, his teeth flashing white in the darkness as

he stared at her. "I feel like I've been looking for you all my life."

"Really?" she asked and he laughed. "Be serious for a minute."

"I am. Dead serious. I want you to be my wife."

"I though that after your divorce you were through with marriage."

"But I didn't count on meeting you."

Sighing, she said, "I don't know if it would be fair— to you."

"I know what I want."

"Do you?" Still reeling from his proposal, she sat up and felt the cold air chill her skin. Never once had he said that he loved her, nor she him. It was just too soon, too early in their relationship. She'd known Hank for years before she'd married him and even now, almost four years after his death, she felt as if she was betraying his memory.

"I'm willing to take a chance."

"But I don't know if I can," she admitted. "There's Amy—"

"Who's crazy about me and Bryan."

"That much is true." Wrapping her arms around her legs, she stared at this wonderful man. Her first impulse was to say yes and throw herself into his arms and make love to him over and over again, but she had to be practical. She was a mother; he, too, had a child. It wasn't just the two of them, they weren't impetuous teenagers.

"How do you feel about my son?"

"Oh, that's not it," she said, reading his thoughts. "Bryan's a little on the surly side sometimes, but that's just the nature of the beast. A teenager suddenly thrown into a new situation—new home, new school. Then he wracks up his knee and feels like a fool so he covers it with bravado."

"Thank you, Dr. Freud."

"You disagree?" She arched a dark eyebrow high.

"Not at all, and I think you're just what he needs—a no-nonsense woman who likes kids."

"So that's what this is all about."

"No," he said quietly. "I'm not just looking for a new mother for my son. If that were the case, there are several women in Seattle who would have gladly done the honors." He looked away from her and she experienced a jab of jealousy for these faceless women who wanted him. "But they were more interested in becoming Mrs. Travis Keegan than being a companion to me or my son. I had the feeling that each of them had the same agenda—their first act as my wife would be to banish Bryan to a boarding school as far away as possible."

Had they slept with him? Shared his bed? Said they loved him? Had he promised them marriage? Told them he cared? "Then they were fools. Bryan's a great kid."

"You really think so?"

"I know so. He just needs some of his rough edges filed down, but it will all come in time." Reaching in the straw for her jeans, she added, "Look, I'd better go inside. If Amy wakes up—"

"You're ducking the issue."

Flinging her sweater over her head, she said, "I just can't make a quick decision like that. I mean, I never thought I'd marry again. . . ."

"Because you were still married to Saint Hank."

The accusation stung, but it was true. Years before, she'd believed that she would marry Hank, have his children, experience the joys and worries of parenthood, look forward to their grandchildren and eventually grow old holding each other's hands. Emotion clogged her throat. "When I took those vows, I was serious."

"But they ended with the 'till death do us part' bit." There was a trace of anger in his voice and he glared at her with hard, unforgiving eyes.

"I know. I've finally accepted it." She stuffed her bra into the back pocket of her jeans. "But it's taken a while. A lot longer than it should have." Only recently had the stones in her heart lightened. Only recently could she think of Hank's death and not be angry. "Come on," she said, shaking her hair loose, "I'll buy you a cup of coffee and you can try and persuade me that becoming the next Mrs. Travis Keegan is the sane, sensible and only path to take."

She started for the door but he tackled her and drew her down to the floor with him once more. "All right, Ronni, we'll play this game your way," he said, his nose touching hers, his eyes, bright and intense as he stared at her. "But I'm warning you, I'm not a patient man."

"Funny you should bring up your lack of that particular virtue," she replied with a giggle, "because I've been accused of the same thing."

"See. We're perfect for each other."

"Convince me."

"Gladly," he whispered and kissed her until the breath was trapped in her lungs and the world began to spin again.

"You're kidding!" Bryan said as he walked from one side of the room to the other. He was without crutches now and his gait was even and strong, with no hint of any lingering damage. The doctor had told him to take it easy, no strenuous running or jumping or skiing for a few weeks, but he was healing well and it looked as if he wasn't going to need surgery. He threw his hat onto a sofa in the living room and glowered at his father. "I'm *not* going to any dumb little Christmas pageant, Dad."

"Amy's expecting you," Travis said and swallowed a smile. Recently Bryan had begun to call him Dad again, though when it had first occurred eluded him.

"Geez!" Bryan flung one hand into the air in disgust. "Why'd she have to invite me?" he wondered aloud.

"Because she likes you."

"She's a runty little kid."

"Doesn't matter. She thinks you're great."

Bryan rolled his eyes and sighed theatrically. "She thinks everyone's great and I'm tired of her hanging around bothering me. Why is it we spend so much time with them, anyway?"

"Because I like her mother. And I like Amy and Ronni's going to be over here any minute, so try and paste a smile on your face, okay?"

He'd no sooner said the words than Ronni's van pulled into the driveway. She'd worked all day at the mountain and her face was still flushed from the cold as she entered the room without her daughter. Travis spun Ronni under the mistletoe, then as she giggled, kissed her lightly on the lips.

Bryan, witnessing his father's affection, looked out the window and glowered. He was talking about moving to France again and Travis figured he'd have to put up with the boy's insecurities and worries for a while longer. No doubt Bryan would be upset until he started school and then, hopefully, once he realized that he would be accepted and find friends, all this angst would abate.

"Look at you," Ronni said a trifle breathlessly when Travis set her on her feet. She was staring at Bryan as she stepped into the living room and tossed her purse onto the hearth. "No more crutches."

"Nearly a clean bill of health," Travis said.

"Yeah, but no basketball, skateboarding or skiing," Bryan grumbled.

"All in good time."

He made a sound of disgust as if he believed he'd never get to do anything the least bit fun again.

"So how were things on the mountain today?" Travis asked.

"Relatively calm considering it's Christmas break," she replied. "A few injuries, but not many, thank heavens."

Another deprecating noise from Bryan's direction.

Ronni ignored the boy's foul mood. "I wanted to make sure you know how to get to the church. The pageant's at seven, but I have to be there earlier since I'm in charge of the angel choir and getting the twins into their costumes."

"And Shelly? Vic seems to think she wouldn't miss this if she were on her death bed."

"She's coming. But just for the performance. Supposedly she's forgoing the party afterward that the parson always throws. She's even going to avoid the bazaar." Ronni's eyes clouded. "I hope she'll be all right." Forcing a smile, she attempted to hide the fact that she was worried sick. Shelly was still spotting lightly and Dr. Sprick was considering hospitalizing her.

Declining a soda or cup of coffee, Ronni explained that she had to pick up Amy who was playing over at her friend Katie's house this afternoon. "I'll see you at the church," she said as the doorbell rang and she ducked around the edge of the fireplace to retrieve her bag.

Travis opened the door and found Taffy LeMar, dressed in a business suit and high heels, smiling brightly as she stood on the porch. "Hi," she said to Travis and handed him a basket filled with sprigs of holly, two fluted glasses and a bottle of expensive champagne decorated with a wide gold ribbon. "From the firm. Just a thank-you for doing business with Mountain West Realty." A dimple creased her cheek. "And from me, too, I guess. I'm sorry I didn't deliver this earlier, but I've been out of town on business and . . . well, now I'm back." She forced the basket into Travis's hand.

"Thanks. This wasn't necessary."

"Of course it was," she said, touching his arm familiarly while her gaze, all blue and shiny, stared up at him. She walked into the entry hall without an invitation, and whether she realized it or not, stopped beneath the chandelier decorated with ribboned pieces of mistletoe. "This is a small town, Travis, and we're glad for new neighbors—especially someone who might bring his business here and revive a town that was so timber dependent. Dear God, this house is so beautiful. I knew you could—" Her words clipped off when her gaze slid around the room to land squarely on Ronni still standing near the fireplace. "Veronica!"

Ronni experienced a hard pang of jealousy.

Color washed up Taffy's neck. "I didn't expect to find you . . . but then you're neighbors, aren't you?" Recovering quickly, she said, "I tried to reach you, you know, to tell you about the impending sale, but with my schedule and yours, we never seemed to connect."

"It's all right," Ronni replied, gritting her teeth. Looking over Taffy's shoulder, she noticed Travis, still standing in the raised entryway, his expression drawing into a thoughtful frown.

"But I know how much the place meant, er, means to you," Taffy said, obviously flustered. "And I figured it was impossible for you to come up with a down payment on a place this size . . . oh, God . . ." She was digging herself a deeper and deeper grave and seemed to realize it. "Well . . . oh! You must be Travis's son!" Apparently anxious to change the subject, she crossed the living room and clasped Bryan's hand between both of hers. "Don't you just love it here?"

"I hate it," he said simply.

"Oh, well, I don't see why. It's so gorgeous by the lake, and inside, well, the decorations are fabulous."

"Ronni helped," Travis explained. He crossed the room and stood next to Ronni.

"Did you?" Taffy seemed to notice Ronni with new, calculating eyes. "Been here often?"

"Not as often as I'd like," Travis said, draping a familiar and possessive arm over Ronni's shoulders.

"Oh, well, I see . . . good. Since you're neighbors and all. How perfect." She leveled a surprised look at Ronni. "It's good you're finally getting out and seeing people. I was concerned, well, we all were, that you'd never snap out of mourning."

"It just took time," Ronni said evenly. "It was hard."

Travis's arm tightened around her as if offering her silent strength and she resisted the urge to sag against him.

"Well, merry Christmas to you all," Taffy said, making a hasty exit, her heels clicking loudly on the hardwood floors. "And a happy New Year, as well."

"And good riddance," Travis muttered under his breath once she'd closed the door behind her. 'That woman's a barracuda."

"She seemed to think you liked her."

"I did business with her. Period."

"You wanted to buy this place?" Bryan asked, eyeing Ronni suspiciously. "Why?"

"Sentimental reasons."

"Such as?" Travis prompted, his hand dropping to his side.

"Growing up here in the caretaker's house, I guess." She hoisted the strap of her purse to her shoulder. "I always felt at home here and I loved this old house, not that I was in it much, but it seemed special. I . . . well, it was silly really, because I never could afford it, but I always thought the estate would make a great bed-and-breakfast inn for skiers in the winter and sailboarders or hikers in the summer. Just over the mountain in Hood River, a town on the Columbia River, the sailboarders come by in droves. I thought Shelly and I could run the place and her family could fix up and live in the caretaker's house. It's empty now, but wouldn't take much . . ." Suddenly embarrassed, she added, "Oh, well, just a pipe dream."

"That I spoiled."

"It could never have happened. Really. It's better that

I let it go and deal with reality, which is"—she checked her watch—"that I don't have much time before I have to pick up Amy. So, I'll see you at the church and don't forget there's a party and bazaar after the pageant."

"Whoop-de-do," Bryan muttered.

"We'll be there." Travis walked her out to the van and as she started to climb in, he caught hold of her arm. "It's been a few days, Ronni," he reminded her. "Have you given any thought to getting married again?"

She laughed. "If it makes you feel any better, it keeps me awake nights."

His sexy, crooked grin slid into place. "I'd like to think *I* keep you awake nights." His gaze slid to her lips. "You seem to have that affect on me."

She grinned and kissed him lightly on the mouth. "Dreamer."

"Am I?" Gathering her into his arms, he kissed her. Instantly her blood was on fire, and desire, that beast that had slumbered within her for nearly four long years, was restless and ready to be awakened with just a touch, a smile or a sidelong glance.

When he lifted his head, she waited to hear the words, the declaration of his love, the vow that he couldn't live without her, but he just stared at her and gave her a quick little kiss to her forehead. "I can't wait forever," he warned her as she climbed into her van.

She rolled down the window. "Three days is *not* forever."

"Seems that way to me." He touched her face with

his fingers and she started the engine. Could she really marry him? Trust him to learn to love her? Maybe a good marriage wasn't necessarily founded on love, but on mutual respect, on a shared sense of humor and compassion, on like ideas. Maybe the hot-as-a-branding-iron kind of passion was close enough to true love. No way, she told herself. Ever since she was a teenager, she'd known the difference between love and lust, and what she felt for Travis was a blending of the two. True she wanted him physically and emotionally, but did she love him? Would she throw down her life for his? Walk through fire to be with him? Accept his son as her own? Have children and grow old with him? Yes! Yes! Yes!

But did he love her or did he want to marry her to add some stability in his life? Did he think of her as a stepmother to Bryan, a woman who would become an instant wife and mother? He now knew she'd hoped to buy the old lodge, maybe he thought living there would be an enticement. Maybe she was silly to hope to hear those magic words of love.

As she drove across town, maneuvering through the streets by rote, the nagging questions racing through her mind, she knew she'd come to a crossroads in her life and she couldn't take both paths without being ripped in two. What she'd wanted all her life was now in question. The past was the trail she'd already taken and to her left was a path she'd started down, a road of loneliness and devotion to a dear, dead husband; the second path stretched to the right and it was a brighter future, one with Travis and his son.

Without realizing what she was doing, she headed east and through gates on the outskirts of the city that opened to the cemetery. She parked, letting the engine idle and cool, then walked up the hill to a grassy spot with a simple headstone. Beloved Husband and Father, she read and felt hot tears well in her eyes. A blast of icy wind whipped around her and blew her hair into her eyes. "I loved you," she said to the plot where her husband lay buried. "I loved you with all my heart. I never wanted to let go. Never. But it's time, Hank. Way past time, and I think . . . no, I *know* that I've got to get on with my life, with the living part."

She waited, almost as if expecting an answer, but the only noise was the rush of the wind that blew through the surrounding trees. A few snowflakes swirled in the air and she shivered. "I'll never forget and you'll always be Amy's father, but there's another man, one I think I might be able to love and . . . and he wants to marry me." She sighed and lifted her face to the cloud-covered sky, as if she could glimpse heaven through the thick curtains. "I'm going to do it." Her fingers, frozen and bare, curled into determined fists. "By God," she vowed, "I'm going to marry Travis Keegan."

The pageant was a delightful fiasco. The angel choir sang the wrong song and the boy who played Joseph kept forgetting his lines. Fortunately, the girl who played Mary prompted him and when it was all over, the audience was smiling, the kids were relieved and they all celebrated at the party and bazaar.

Shelly managed to sit through the performance, but Vic whisked her and the twins away before she could get bogged down in any of the festivities. Amy was in her element, laughing and talking, still wearing the costume that she adored. She drank cup after cup of cranberry punch that drizzled down the white folds of her angel outfit and still managed to put away two slices of rum cake. By the time the party was over, she was pooped and Bryan was trying hard to look bored out of his mind.

"Let's go home," Ronni suggested.

"But you said we'd buy a star for the top of the tree." Amy's face, so sweet only seconds before, clouded over and her chin jutted stubbornly. "Or an angel or—"

"We will—"

"Tomorrow's Christmas Eve," Amy said.

"You're right. Let's look through the bins and see what we can find." She glanced up at Travis who was smothering a smile. "You've heard of the angel Gabriel, well you just met the angel Groucho."

Travis laughed and they followed Amy past tables laden with everything from gooseberry pies to quilted Advent calendars. Some of the local crafts were so intricate that Ronni made a mental note of them and thought they would make wonderful additions to her next year's winter catalog. She knew most of the local artists and craftsmen and women already but there were a few new and interesting pieces, created by artisans she had yet to meet.

"Here it is!" Amy found a table laden with hand-crafted ornaments and chose an angel made of a cone, netting, a hand-painted doll's head and gossamer wings. Pearly white beads and a loop of gold ribbon caused the angel's dress to glimmer and sparkle.

"Isn't she beautiful?" Amy breathed, holding the decoration as if it were made of spun gold.

"Gorgeous."

"Can we get her, Mommy?"

Ronni winced as she read the price tag, but realizing that half the proceeds went to the church, she agreed to make the purchase. "I think we'd better get out of here before we go broke," she said to Travis. "Oh, wait. I think you should meet some people who have kids about Bryan's age."

"No way," Bryan insisted, but Ronni wouldn't take no for an answer and within minutes she'd introduced Travis to the Carters and their son, Jake, and the Hendersons with their daughters, Becca and Sherrie. Bryan stared at the floor as if he found the yellowed linoleum fascinating, especially when he had to say something to the Henderson girls, but Travis and Ronni lingered, forcing the kids to interact.

Jake was interested in horses, skiing and basketball players and talked without seeming to take a break. The girls told him what to expect from his teachers at school. Bryan was nearly mute, answering in monosyllables, eyes nailed to the floor, but, Ronni figured, it was a start, a little inroad in that swamp of teenage relationships. The preacher's daughter, Elizabeth, joined them and encouraged Bryan to join their youth group, which met every Wednesday night and combined Bible study with fun, usually in the form of pizza parties, dances and trips skiing in the winter and swimming in the summer.

By the time they got into the parking lot, Bryan didn't even bother saying good-night, just slunk into the passenger seat of his father's Jeep and showed too many signs of teenage rebellion. "I hope he's all right," Ronni said.

"He will be," Travis assured her. "It's just going to take a while for him to change his mind-set."

"Good luck."

He kissed her lightly on the lips, then she walked to her van. Amy was yawning as Ronni helped strap her into the seat. "Is Travis gonna be my new daddy?" she asked, trying to keep her eyes open.

Startled, Ronni asked, "Would you like it if he was?"

"Mmm. Would you?"

Before Ronni could answer, the little angel with the cranberry-stained gown fell asleep.

"A puppy!" Amy squealed in pure delight. All the presents had been opened, and while Amy was playing with a new doll, Ronni had hurried out to the barn where she'd hidden the pup since five o'clock in the morning. Before that, she'd been up with the frightened little dog half the night as the animal had whined and howled and threatened to wake Amy. "You got me a puppy!" Amy fairly danced a special little jig and wiggled as much as the dog to get her fingers on the wriggling ball of fluff. "Oh, Mommy, he's beautiful!" Amy cried, entranced.

"She. It's a girl."

"So she can have more puppies someday!"

Ronni laughed. "I don't think so. One dog's going to be more than enough, I think."

After nearly squeezing the life from him, Amy let the pup down and the dog ran in circles, sped around the Christmas tree, under the table, into the kitchen and back again. Amy, in four-year-old heaven, raced after her and slid on the hardwood floors.

Ronni tried to drink a cup of coffee throughout the chaos. This—early Christmas morning—was their time together alone before Travis and Bryan and Shelly's whole family descended for Christmas dinner later in the afternoon. She couldn't believe how her life had changed in the past few weeks and she eyed the little Christmas tree under which the presents were spread. She'd even broken down and bought something for Travis and Bryan as they seemed already a part of her family.

"Let's name her Snowball."

"But she isn't white."

"Does it matter?"

"No, honey, I don't suppose it does. You can name her anything you like."

While Ronni picked up the litter and discarded wrapping paper from the Santa gifts, Amy busied herself by making a bed for the dog.

Once the house was cleaned and the pup was relegated during nonplay hours to a newspaper-strewn laundry room, Ronni turned on her favorite Christmas CDs and started stuffing the turkey. After plopping it into the oven, she even danced a little as she put together a molded salad, peeled white potatoes from her own garden and washed the yams. Yes, it was a time of new traditions, a new beginning. A new dog and a new extended family.

It was nearly four before she had time to dress Amy and get changed. Sitting at the vanity, slipping silver hoops through her earlobes, she heard the doorbell ring. "Coming," she called, following Amy down the stairs.

Travis and his son stood on the porch, their arms laden with packages. Ronni's heart kicked into double time at the sight of Travis in black slacks and a cream-colored sweater, his hair rumpled by the wind. Bryan, for the first time in ages, was without his baseball hat and wore clean jeans and a gray shirt tucked in at the waist. He managed a tight smile and Ronni was taken with how much he looked like his father. Once the soft flesh of youth gave way to harder planes and angles, he'd be as handsome as Travis.

"Come in, come in," she invited. "We have someone we'd like you to meet." From the laundry room, the pup gave an excited yip and Amy ran to get her.

"Lookie!" she cried, running with the little dog. "Her name is Snowball! Mommy got her for me."

Snowball wriggled and tried desperately to wash everyone's face. Travis and Bryan exchanged glances. "Uh-oh," Bryan whispered.

"What?"

"Well—" Travis rolled his eyes. "What is it they say about great minds thinking alike?"

"Oh no," Ronni whispered, fingers to her lips as she caught his meaning.

"What?" Amy asked, befuddled.

"May as well bring our surprise in now," Travis said and handed the keys of his Jeep to Bryan.

Ronni's gaze locked with Travis's. "I don't believe it."

"Believe."

A few minutes later, Bryan returned to the house carrying a half-grown pup.

"Wow!" Amy's eyes rounded.

"We got him at the local animal shelter," Travis explained. "His name is Rex."

"Is he mine?"

"If it's okay with your mother."

Ronni skewered him with a knowing look. "Oh, great, make me the bad guy."

"Can we keep him, Mommy?" Amy was dancing again, her eyes sparkling in anticipation, her cheeks rosy.

"I suppose."

"Yippee!"

Rex, black and white and looking suspiciously as if he had a Border collie in his family tree somewhere, bounded through the door as if he knew he was home. The smaller pup let out a worried woof, then dashed away to cower under the table.

Travis grinned sheepishly. "He's housebroken."

"That's the good news. One down, one to go," Ronni said. Yesterday she owned no dogs, today she had two. Unbelievable.

Travis kissed her cheek. "You'll survive," he predicted.

When Shelly, Vic and the boys landed, Ronni pointed a wooden spoon in her sister's direction. "Tell me you didn't buy a dog."

"I didn't," her sister swore, looking drawn.

"And you didn't pick up one at the animal shelter, humane society or a stray walking down the street."

"Scout's honor," Shelly said, hiding a smile as she held up two fingers.

"Good, then you can stay, but only if you promise to take it easy and put your feet up in Hank's recliner." Ronni wagged the spoon in front of her sister's nose.

"Yes, ma'am," Shelly replied with a mock salute. "But I thought you couldn't bear the thought of his chair empty in the living room. Wasn't it stored away?"

"I decided that was silly. Along with a lot of things,"

Ronni explained. "Besides, I wasn't really acting rationally, was I?"

Shelly didn't answer and plucked a cracker from a small bowl, then dipped it into the cheese spread.

"I mean, some of his things I kept around to remind me of him and others I hid away because I didn't want to think about what I'd lost." She shook her head. "I didn't realize how much of a basket case I was."

Shelly cocked her head to one side and munched on the cracker. "And now?"

"Now is tough, but I'm better. My New Year's resolution is to become whole again. To start over."

Folding her arms over her chest, Shelly motioned with her chin toward Travis. "I don't suppose this has anything to do with him."

"A little, probably," Ronni admitted, "but I'd decided it was time to rebuild just before I met him."

"And your war with the mountain?"

"Oh, it goes on forever," Ronni said. "As long as there are skiers trapped up there, I'm going to bring them down. Mount Echo will still win sometimes, but I'll fight her all the way."

"Her?"

"Her, it . . . does it matter?"

At that moment, both puppies galloped into the room, yipping and giving chase to each other. "My Lord." Shelly laughed. "What happened?"

"I think we're experiencing Amy's vision of heaven."

"And mine of hell," Shelly whispered with a chuckle.

Ronni laughed, too. This Christmas—the one she'd dreaded—was turning out to be the best ever.

They all ate around the table, though it had to be extended with a folding card table at one end and the tablecloth looked a little lumpy where the two tables butted up to each other. Candles graced the centerpiece and Christmas music filled the room. Ronni poured wine for the adults, though Shelly declined, then filled the children's glasses with sparkling cider. Travis was given the honor of carving the turkey and after everyone had eaten until they couldn't take another bite, they left the dishes and turned their attention to the Christmas tree and gift exchange between the families.

Kurt and Kent were thrilled with the new videogame system Ronni had bought for them. Even before the wrapping was totally off the package, they were fighting for the opportunity to play the first game. Shelly ended the argument by stating that if anyone was going to have the honor of using the new equipment first, it would be she.

Amy was so distracted by the puppies, she could barely concentrate on the intricate rag doll her aunt had sewn for her. "Just don't let any of those mongrels near it," Shelly teased. Bryan seemed, or at least pretended, to be interested in the instructional movies on skiing and snowboarding that Ronni had given him and Travis grinned over the books about the history and favorite recreational sports in Oregon. By the time everyone headed home, Ronni was exhausted and the house looked as if it had been hit by a hurricane.

After the first load of dishes was running in the dishwasher, she took the horses a Christmas treat of apples and carrots, then returned to clean up the rest of the house. Amy was so tired she could barely move, but she insisted on camping out on the sofa to be close to the puppies, who, now that they had each other, were curled in a ball of fur and fluff on a blanket in the laundry room.

Ronni had just hung up her apron when she noticed Travis on the front porch. His breath fogged in the air and his face was awash with color from the exterior lights. Catching her attention, he waved her outside and Ronni slipped through the door. After the warmth of the fire, the outside air ripped through her in a fierce gust of raw December wind. Nonetheless, her pulse raced at the sight of him. "Brrr," she whispered, rubbing her arms against the cold. "What are you doing here? Where's Bryan?"

"Back at our place watching the movies you bought him. I told him I'd be home in about an hour and he barely even said goodbye he was so engrossed."

"That's good, I guess, but it still doesn't answer my first question."

"I forgot to give you your present."

"No," she said, shaking her head. "I distinctly remember you handing me a leash, flea powder and twenty-pound bag of dog food."

His laugh was deep as it rumbled through the trees. "I know. That was your personal, intimate gift. Just for you."

"Thanks so much," she mocked.

"But I thought you needed something a little more practical."

"Like a shovel for scooping the you-know-what?"

His teeth flashed white. "No, something a little less personal than that."

"Oh, great."

He fished into the inner lining of his jacket and withdrew a long white envelope. "Careful," he said as she took it from his hands, her eyebrows knitting in concentration.

"What's this?" she asked. "Airline tickets?" She looked at him before fanning out the tickets and squinting to make out the destination.

"Lake Tahoe," he said. "For the four of us. You, me, Bryan and Amy. We take off tomorrow night."

"But why?"

He reached into the front pocket of his jeans and withdrew a small black box.

A lump the size of a golf ball filled her throat and she found it almost impossible to breathe. "It's not—"

"See for yourself."

Heart thudding almost painfully, she opened the

velvet-lined case and stared at a diamond ring that winked softly in the glow of the Christmas lights. "I—I don't know what to say," she whispered and Travis withdrew the ring from its softly lined container.

Taking her left hand in his, he said, "Tell me yes."

Her eyes searched his face, and she bit her lip for a second. "I—I—yes!"

"You'll marry me?" he repeated, seeming astounded.

She flung her arms around his neck. "Of course I'll marry you."

Laughing, he twirled her off her feet and kissed her head. "I was worried you'd say 'no.'"

She grinned and shook her head. "Oh ye of little faith," she teased. Again he kissed her, his lips filled with a sweet, gentle pressure. When he finally lifted his head, he sighed. "We'll elope tomorrow. Fly down to Tahoe and tie the knot, spend a few days there and come home just before New Year's."

"But—I can't leave. Shelly, my business, the dogs—"

"I've already talked to Victor. Shelly's doing as well as can be expected. It's just a matter of time and rest now and you can call her every day if you want to. Vic will look after the dogs and the horses. You already told me that your business is slow this time of year. As for the ski patrol, I talked to Tim Sether who said he could find someone to fill in for you."

"You were pretty sure I'd say yes," she said, still spinning in a rush of emotion.

"No, but I knew what I wanted." His voice deepened

and his eyes were suddenly serious. "And what I want is you, Veronica Walsh. Now and forever."

She almost cried tears of happiness. "You've got me, Travis Keegan, and if you ever try to get rid of me, you'll regret it for the rest of your life."

"Never," he vowed, and with his arms wrapped around her protecting her from the cold, she believed him. He slipped the ring onto her finger, kissed her until she no longer felt the cold night air. Then, once her bones had begun to melt, he lifted her off her feet, carried her over the threshold of her little house, locked the door, and while Amy slept soundly on the couch, mounted the stairs to Ronni's bedroom where, for the next hour, they celebrated Christmas alone.

CHAPTER 11

"YOU MAY KISS the bride!"

The preacher, Reverend Randy, as he insisted upon being called, lifted his hands as if he were addressing an entire congregation instead of the two witnesses Ronni had never met before, his wife on the piano and Bryan and Amy. The tiny chapel was wedged between two casinos and decorated more like an arcade than a church, but it didn't matter. Travis pulled her into the possessive circle of his arms and kissed her in that same breath-taking way that always caused her heart to skip a beat.

Amy, on cue, tossed confetti and rose petals into the air, and Bryan, trying hard not to glower, managed a grim, hard smile. Being his new stepmother wasn't going to be easy, Ronni told herself as she stared into the eyes of her new husband. Marge, Reverend Randy's wife, began to play and music filled the chapel. Ronni was ready for the challenge. Even if Travis didn't love her, she was certain he cared about her and Amy. Love would come later. It had to. They walked down the tiny aisle together and stopped at the back of the chapel when Marge stopped playing. A top-heavy lady in a polkadot dress, she scurried to the camera that was already poised upon a tripod and took some pictures of Ronni and Travis, the kids, even one with Reverend Randy.

Outside, the sun was just setting, and they walked the few blocks to their hotel. Sprawled along the shores of the lake, the hotel reminded Ronni of the old Johnson lodge—the place that would finally be her home with Travis. Living in and restoring the old lodge had been her dream for the past several years, except that in her dreams she'd never once thought she would share the premises or her heart with a husband and a stepson.

"Can I call you Daddy?" Amy, holding Travis's hand as they walked into the hotel lobby, wanted to know.

Travis grinned down at his new stepdaughter. "Sure. Why not?"

"Because you're not her daddy," Bryan said, the edges of his lips white.

"We're a family now—"

"No, Travis, we're not a family and this isn't the Brady Bunch. I've already got a mother." He glared at Ronni as if she were the devil incarnate.

"I wouldn't presume to try and take her place—"

"You couldn't, okay? No one can." With a furious

glance at his father, he stormed across the lobby and through French doors to the deck.

"I'd better handle this," Travis said. "I'll meet you upstairs." Ronni, still holding her bridal bouquet and feeling like a wretched fool, watched as Travis followed his son. "Come on," she said to Amy. "Let's get changed."

Once she and her daughter were in the suite, she peeled off her ivory-colored suit. Catching a glimpse of herself in the mirror, she remembered her first wedding, complete with a white silk and satin dress, long train, veil and Shelly as her matron of honor. The church in Cascadia had been filled with friends and good cheer, a long reception had followed wherein the timeless rituals of toasting each other, cutting the cake and taking the first dance together had been honored. This time, the wedding had been without all the trimmings—just the four of them, a pieced-together family who still weren't sure how they each fit with each other.

"Bryan hates us," Amy stated as Ronni hung up her clothes.

"No, honey, he's just not sure what to think of all this. It's happening too fast, I think. We should have waited until after the new year."

"I don't see why. I didn't have a daddy for Christmas and now I have one for New Year's and we're going to have a big party." Amy struggled to yank a barrette from her hair.

"Here, let me get that," Ronni said, helping her

daughter and laughing a little. "A party? Now, where'd you get that idea?"

"Travis—er, Daddy said we could."

"Oh. Then we will." Sitting on the edge of the king-size bed, Ronni kicked off her heels and massaged the aches from her feet. She thought about her friend, Linda, who was on her honeymoon at Timberline. Wouldn't she be surprised that she wasn't the only new bride working on Mount Echo? "You know what we should do," she said to her daughter.

"What?"

"Call Aunt Shelly."

"And find out how Rex and Snowball are?"

"Well, that's one reason." Rolling to the side of the bed, she reached for the phone on the nightstand. She punched out her sister's number and waited. The phone rang six times before an answering machine with Shelly's voice responded. After waiting for the tone, she said, "Hi, Shell, it's Ronni . . . I mean, Mrs. Travis Keegan. Can you believe it, I'm actually married again? It's so . . . strange . . . but so right." Stretching the phone cord to the window, she gazed past the snow-dusted branches of towering pine trees to the deep blue waters of the lake. "I just thought I'd share some of my happiness with you and I'll call you later—" She was about to hang up when Amy ran up to her.

"Ask about the puppies!" she demanded.

"Oh, and Amy would like an update on her new pets," Ronni said with a smile though she felt a vague sense of unease. Why wasn't Shelly answering? "She's going to want a full report."

She hung up telling herself that she was borrowing trouble again. Shelly had probably needed to get out of the house and had gone with Vic to take care of the horses and dogs, or the entire family had gone out for pizza or hamburgers. Being the vivacious person she was, Shelly couldn't very well lie on the couch day after day.

"Where was Aunt Shelly?" Amy asked as Ronni slipped into a pair of tan jeans.

"I wish I knew." She donned a cream-colored blouse with billowy sleeves and a leather vest. "Come on, let's get you into something a little less dressy."

Within minutes, Amy had transformed from an angel in pink velvet to a tomboy in a red jumpsuit who was not about to let Ronni comb out her hair. "It's okay this way," she said and Ronni decided it wasn't worth the trouble of chasing her daughter around with a brush.

"Fine, who cares?" Ronni said, tossing the brush onto the bed. "Let me know if you change your mind."

A key clicked in the lock and Travis, still in his black suit, walked into the room. Ronni's heart jolted. This man—this handsome man—was her husband. From now until forever. A flood of happiness swept over her until she spied Bryan, hands in his pockets, head slouched between his shoulders. "I—I'm sorry," he said, glancing at his father as if for approval.

"You don't have to apologize for stating your opinion," Ronni said.

"No, but he can't be rude. That's the rule we're going to have in this family. No one can be rude or cruel to anyone else."

Bryan winced at the word *family* and Ronni's heart went out to him. Obviously, his father's new marriage was tough on him, tougher than any of them could imagine.

"All right," she said. "But we all have to agree to listen to each others' opinions because I think it would be impossible for us all to think the same way. And"—she looked pointedly at her new husband—"everyone's opinion counts."

"Equal?" Bryan wanted to know.

"As equal as it can be," she replied. "For example, you might think you should be able to drive the car, and we don't—you'd have to give in. There are laws to consider and sometimes wisdom does come with age."

"I knew it."

"On the other hand," she said, wagging a finger at the two new men in her life, "your father and I promise to remember what it was like to be a teenager and will try to put ourselves in your place."

"As if you could."

"It won't always work," she admitted with a shrug. "But I'm willing to give it a shot. It's the best I can offer."

Bryan looked at her as if he wished she'd evaporate

on the spot and Ronni gritted her teeth. Being a step-mother was going to take a lot of determination, but she decided right then and there she'd be the best secondary mother any kid could ever want.

Scratching the back of his neck, Bryan asked, "Is the deal still on with the horses? Will you let me ride them if I take care of them?"

Finally, common ground. "You bet. And if your father says it's okay, you can have Sam—he's the stallion. Lucy is Amy's mare, but Sam, he was my husband's. Now he's yours."

"Are you serious?" Bryan asked, all pretenses dropped, his expression one of stunned disbelief.

" 'Course."

"Wait a minute—" Travis tried to intervene, but Ronni wouldn't hear of it.

"Consider him yours, Bryan, but remember to take care of him."

"Wow." He studied her for a moment, as if he was trying to determine if she was out of her mind, then shrugged and walked over to the window ledge where he'd left his CD player. Within seconds, he'd clipped on his earphones again.

From the corner of his mouth, Travis said, "You can't reward that kind of behavior."

"He just needs to know that he still belongs," she said, winking at her new husband. "Besides, Sam needs more exercise than I give him. It'll be all right."

"Will it?" he asked.

"Promise."

"You know what they say about promises," he teased, one hand touching her shoulder.

"What's that?"

"That they're made to be broken."

"Not this one."

Travis took them to dinner and a show and by the time they returned to the suite it was after midnight. Amy fell into bed and was asleep before her head hit the pillow. Bryan, rather than sleep in the same room with her, took refuge on the couch in the living area and plugged into the headphones of his CD player. Glowering darkly at the ceiling, he didn't bother to say goodnight.

"Maybe this wasn't such a good idea," Ronni said as Travis closed the door to their bedroom and bolted the lock. A fireplace gave off the only light in the room and flickering shadows seemed to climb up the walls and reflect in the windows.

"What? Getting married?"

"So soon, I mean. Bryan wasn't ready."

"Do you think he ever would have been?" Travis asked, stripping off his sweater and shirt. Firelight gleamed gold against his bare skin.

"I don't know."

"Give him time, he'll get used to it."

She worried her lip as his arms surrounded her. Travis pressed a kiss to her temple. "Bryan will be fine," he said. "He has a lot to work out, but we'll help him

along the way. Come on, wife," he whispered sugges-
tively against her ear. "Let me take you to bed."

"But—"

"Shh." He pressed a finger to her lips, then lifted her
from her feet. Kicking off his shoes, he carried her to the
bed and together they tumbled into the downy softness
of the comforter as man and wife.

"I just don't understand it," Ronni said the next
morning as she hung up the telephone in frustration and
chewed distractedly on her fingernail before catching
herself. "Why isn't Shelly home?"

"Haven't got a clue." Travis, barefoot in low-slung
jeans and no shirt, was leaning over the sink in the bathroom as he shaved. Fascinated, Ronni watched him
scrape the foam and whiskers from his chin and wondered why it seemed so sexy. As if reading her thoughts,
his gaze met hers in the foggy mirror. "Are you worried
about her?"

"A little," she admitted, thinking of the baby. *Please
see that she and the baby are all right,* she prayed. "I've
called three times and she's supposed to be resting so it
seems a little too coincidental that every time I phoned,
she was out."

"Or in the bathtub, or picking up the mail, or running the twins somewhere or buying groceries—"

"I know, I know, but the doctor told her to take it
easy." An ugly nagging thought crept through her mind,
but she steadfastly tamped it down.

"We're going home this afternoon. You can see her and catch up then." He shook the razor under the faucet. "Have you ever heard that you worry too much?"

"Only about a million times, but don't you start in on me, too."

"Are you ordering me around, woman?" The razor dropped to the counter.

"Me?" She spread a hand over her chest and angled him her most innocent look. "Wouldn't dream of it," she teased.

Toweling his face dry, he stared at her and her pulse jumped at the raw energy in his eyes. Tossing the towel to the floor, he grinned wickedly. Slowly he advanced on her. "I hope not," he whispered as his fingers twined in her hair.

"Why not?"

"Because I want a woman who knows her place." He kissed the shell of her ear.

She shivered as delicious little bursts of desire spread through her. "Do you? And . . . and where's that?"

His arms encircled her and his mouth was hot as it hovered over her lips. "Maybe I should show you." He brushed his lips across hers and her bones turned to jelly.

"Maybe you should," she murmured into his open mouth, and with the smile of a devil, he lifted her from her feet only to drop her back onto the bed again.

"You're wicked, Mr. Keegan," she said, suppressing a laugh.

"And so are you, love," he said as he kissed her. "So are you."

Amy was in seventh heaven. Her wishes had come true and she'd found herself a new daddy. Not so, Bryan. He acted as if he'd found his own personal hell. While Amy chattered and laughed during the flight back to Oregon, Bryan slipped earphones onto his head and, scowling darkly, generally avoided talking to anyone. His responses to questions were polite, short, to the point and muttered with a don't-bother-me attitude.

"I don't think he's crazy about the situation," Ronni said as they gathered their few suitcases from the baggage carousel and walked through the bustle of holiday travelers at Portland International Airport. Bryan lagged behind, listening to his music, making a point of not being a part of the family.

"He'll get used to it," Travis said. "He's just got to make a statement, but he'll come around."

"You're sure?"

"Positive." He kissed her temple. "I'll get the car." They walked through automated doors and then he was off, dashing through the rain to the long-term lot where his Jeep was parked. Amy, tired and bored with always being shepherded, let go of Ronni's hand and wandered down the sidewalk to stand next to her new stepbrother. Tugging on his shirt to get his attention, she said something to him that Ronni couldn't make out and he lifted one earphone to hear her.

For a fraction of a second, he smiled as if he enjoyed her precocious question, then glanced at Ronni, caught her eye and snapped the earphone back in place. Anger twisted his mouth and he ignored Amy, whose smile melted from her tiny face. Lower lip trembling, she wound her way back through stacks of luggage to take her place by Ronni. "Why does he hate me?" she asked, clinging to Ronni's leg.

"He doesn't."

"Yes—"

"No, honey." Ronni dropped her carry-on piece of luggage to the sidewalk as a jet roared overhead. Picking up her daughter, she sighed and hugged Amy. "It's not you he has a problem with."

"He's mean sometimes. Just like Kurt."

"Because he's hurting inside. You just keep being nice to him and it'll all work out. Now, don't you worry about Bryan for a while. We've got some puppies who are going to be mighty glad to see you."

Amy's face brightened and she wiggled to the ground just as Travis's Jeep rounded the corner.

The ride back home was slow and tedious. Along with the usual crush of vacationers on the road, enthusiastic skiers were heading to the mountain as seven inches of new snow had fallen in the Cascades over the weekend. The roads were icy and treacherous, with snowplows and sanding crews unable to keep up with the dropping temperature and increased snowfall.

"Looks like a good night to build a fire and curl up on the couch with a glass of wine."

"Mmm," Ronni agreed, glancing at the backseat where both Bryan and Amy had fallen asleep. Bryan's head was propped against the window and Amy had slumped against him, her forehead touching his sleeve. "I'd feel a lot better if I could talk to Shelly."

"You could try using the cell."

"No, I'll wait. We're almost home."

"That we are, Mrs. Keegan," he said with a smile. "That we are."

They stopped at Ronni's house and a groggy Amy collected the pups while Ronni gathered a few more clothes and Travis and Bryan fed the horses.

Again Ronni tried to reach her sister and this time her brother-in-law answered. "Oh, Ronni," he said in a voice that was flat and lifeless. "How was the trip?"

"Fine, fine, I'm a married woman now," she said brightly, though the serious tone in Victor's voice was enough to scare her to death. "I tried to call a couple of times but no one answered."

"We were at the hospital," he admitted.

Ronni's heart plummeted. "The hospital?"

"That's right. Look, Shelly's not in the best of shape right now. She's home and physically she's gonna be fine, the doctor assured her that she could still have more kids but . . . "

"Oh, my God," Ronni whispered, clutching the receiver and bracing herself against the refrigerator.

"Yeah," he said, and his voice cracked a little. "She lost the baby."

"You go home," Shelly admonished, squeezing Ronni's hand. She. was lying in bed, her face drawn, the sparkle missing from her eyes as Vic and the boys watched television in the living room. "You're a new bride and you need to be with your husband—keep celebrating your honeymoon."

"Don't be silly."

"Not silly, just practical," Shelly said with a weak smile that didn't add any life to eyes that were puffy and red-rimmed from tears. "I'm going to be fine. The doctor said to take it easy for a few days, but I'm not bedridden and I should bounce back in no time."

"But . . . I feel so bad." Ronni sniffed to keep from crying.

"We all do, and even though I've got two healthy, wonderful boys, this was . . . well, a loss. I just have to think of it that way and get over it." Dragging her gaze away from Ronni's, she cleared her throat. A tear gathered in the corner of her eye, but she quickly dashed it away with a finger. "I'm going to be fine. It'll just take a little time to get used to . . ." A long, heavy sigh escaped her. "Oh, damn, maybe I'll never get over it."

"You will."

"I hope. The good news is that Victor wants to try again—can you believe it, after his reaction when he learned I was pregnant?" She gave a short, brittle little laugh. "He's come around and wants another baby."

"Of course he does."

"I wouldn't have believed it, but then he was out of work and now, thanks to Travis, he feels better. They've talked, you know, about him staying on after the work on the house is finished, and about fixing up the old caretaker's house for us. Travis said that Vic could either be a caretaker of the grounds like Dad was or he could work for Travis's company in some capacity—I don't know exactly what, the vice president in Seattle sent Vic some information . . . it's there, I think, on the bureau." She waved at a small stack of papers tucked behind her jewelry box. "I guess you married a millionaire."

"Maybe," Ronni said, embarrassed that she didn't have a clue as to Travis's holdings, that she didn't really care. She realized he had money, of course, and plenty of it, but she hadn't worried about how much and he hadn't bothered with a prenuptial agreement.

"No maybes about it—your husband is loaded." Shelly sighed dramatically. "It would be nice, but then again, money isn't everything." Tears filled her eyes once more as she absently touched her belly, but she pressed the silent drops back into her eyes. "Have you found that stuff yet?"

Ronni picked up the brochures and typed pages introducing Victor Pederson to TRK, Incorporated. Along with employee information, there were advertising sheets and lists of products with a letter of introduction signed by Wendall Holmes.

Ronni's heart nearly stopped.

Wendall Holmes!

She swallowed and stared at the signature. So bold. So precise. So damned familiar. "Oh, God," she whispered. She'd heard the name Wendall and once Travis had said something about Holmes, but she hadn't, until this very minute, put two and two together to get four.

"What?" Shelly sat straighter in the bed.

For a second, her vision blurred and she was sure that she'd made a mistake, she couldn't be reading the same name that had signed so many letters, but no matter how often she blinked, each time she looked at the letter, the name and the signature remained the same. Wendall Holmes.

"I've talked to this man before," she said, and her voice seemed disembodied, as if it belonged to another person in another time.

"Where? How?"

"Wendall Holmes was the vice president in charge of consumer relations for SkiWest," she said, her voice barely audible.

"Oh, Ronni, no." Shelly bit her lip.

"He was the guy I was writing to about Hank's equipment." The brochures balling in her fist, she sank onto the corner of Shelly's bed. "Those bindings . . .

they were SkiWest 450's. Travis's company manufac-
tured them."

"You don't know that," Shelly said, reaching forward and clasping Ronni's arm. "Holmes could have
changed companies—"

Ronni shook her head. "No, I asked about him once.
Travis told me they've worked together for years." Pain
cracked through her heart and she bit down on her lip
to keep from crying.

"Let it go," Shelly advised.

"I can't."

"You have to."

"Hank died, Shelly! He died!" Ronni said, shooting
to her feet and reaching for the doorknob, but Shelly's
silent, sad gaze held her in the room. "I can't just forget it."

"You have to put it aside."

"But he's dead."

Shelly's eyes lost all of their sparkle. "So is my baby,
Ronni."

Travis drove the last nail into the new railing of the
back porch. Bryan, against his better judgment, was
helping out, using a square and a level, making sure that
his father's work was precise. Ronni was visiting her sister and Amy was napping inside. "Better, don't you
think?" Travis asked as he stepped away from the porch
and looked at the bare fir two by twos.

A table saw screamed in the garage where Vic had set up shop and was cutting lengths for the next section of the rail. The old, sagging wood had already been hauled to the pile behind the garage and it was Bryan's job to take out all the old nails and stack the used lumber in the kindling pile. "It's okay."

"Just okay? Not terrific?"

Bryan stared sullenly at him. "Okay, it's terrific. Feel better?"

Travis's temper was already stretched thin. He hated walking on eggshells around his son and decided that it was now or never—time for another father-son show-down. "Are you going to tell me what's eating you or do I have to guess?"

"Whad'ya mean?" Bryan grabbed his hammer and tried to wiggle nails out of a piece of old railing.

"You've been in a bad mood since we moved here and every time things improve and I think you're set-tling in, we take a backspin."

The boy's jaw tightened. "So?"

This wasn't going to be easy. Travis straightened and rubbed the kinks from the small of his back. Frowning, he eyed the sky, a storm had been predicted, a big one with the promise of high winds and more snow. Already the tops of the taller trees were moving with the breeze. "You aren't very friendly to Ronni."

No answer. Another nail squeaked as Bryan yanked it out of the rotting wood.

"You know she's been nothing but nice to you. First

she gets you down the mountain when you hurt yourself, then she offers to teach you to ski and now she's
given you one of her horses. She's bent over backward
to be friendly to you and all you've done in response is
give her the cold shoulder."

"Big deal."

"That's right. It is. A very big deal. I assume you're
not happy that I married her."

"What does it matter what I think?"

"A lot, Bryan."

"You didn't even ask me," his son mumbled, reaching
for another rail. "You marry her and don't even ask me."

"I didn't know I had to."

"Don't I count?" Bryan wanted to know.

"Of course."

"And my opinion, too, right? That's what Ronni
said."

"Yes, but—"

"Then what was all this talk about you and me
being a family, huh? Just the two of us." In anger,
Bryan threw the rail into the woods. "Was that all a
bunch of baloney?"

"No, but—"

"What did we need her and her stupid little girl for?
All they're gonna do is mess things up . . ." His voice
trailed off and he looked away sharply. Travis heard a
gasp and turned to find Amy standing in the partially
open doorway. The puppy was in her arms and her face
was twisted in silent agony.

"Amy," Travis said, but she ran away, the puppy yipping wildly. Travis turned on his son. "What were you thinking?" he demanded.

"You wanted to know," his son said. "I just told you what I thought."

"You hurt her feelings!"

"Yeah, well, you hurt mine." Bryan tossed another rail into the rapidly growing pile, and Travis, muttering under his breath, hurried into the house.

"Amy! Amy!" he called, walking through the lower level and up the stairs. If it weren't for the barking on the upper floor and the sound of dog toenails digging into wood, he might not have found her huddled in some old blankets on the floor of a closet in the attic.

"He hates me!" she said when Travis located her and the two dogs.

"He's just confused. Come here."

"Bryan," she said, her little jaw quivering. "He hates me."

"He's just not used to things the way they are right now."

"He's mean!"

"He's not trying to be." Travis gathered her into his arms and held her close. The dogs scrambled out of the closet and ran in circles through the pine-walled room. "This is hard for Bryan, too, honey. Being a new family isn't easy."

"I thought we were supposed to love each other."

Crystal-like tears tracked down her face. She began to sob.

"We do all love each other, but sometimes . . . sometimes people inadvertently hurt the ones they love. They don't mean to, they're just shortsighted."

She sniffed loudly and the smallest dog bounded onto her lap to wash her face with her long tongue. Amy couldn't resist and giggled wildly. Travis's heart warmed at the sound and he wondered how he'd lived his life without hearing the happy ring of her childish laughter. One step at a time, he told himself, one step and one day at a time. "Come on, short stuff, let's take the mutts outside."

The lights flickered and Amy let out a whimper.

Travis hugged her. "Don't worry."

"Ghosts," she said, shivering.

"Just the wind, honey. Let's find some candles and kerosene lanterns in case the electricity decides to give out."

She carried the small puppy, he carried her and Rex bounded along behind as they made their way down to the main floor. Bryan, flopped on the couch and staring at the television, glanced their way and his eyes darkened in silent fury.

"I think we'd better scrounge up some flashlights," Travis suggested, but his son didn't budge. "Bryan?"

"Yeah?"

"You know where the flashlights are?"

"Yeah."

"Then find one before we lose power."

Bryan rolled his eyes, shot Amy a look that could kill and sauntered to his bedroom. Whistling to the dogs, Travis carried Amy outside and into the garage where Vic was just putting away his tools.

"Better get home," he said half-apologetically. "Shelly isn't happy when we don't have power."

"Don't blame her."

"But I'm leavin' early—"

"Doesn't matter. The weather service seems to think we're in for the storm of all storms, so you'd better get home before it breaks."

"Kind of ya," Victor said. "I'll be in early tomorrow." He unbuckled his tool belt and rumpled Amy's hair.

"Don't worry about it." Travis slid a glance to the slate-colored sky. Dark clouds skudded over the tops of the highest trees and snow had begun to fall in tiny, hard flakes. Victor turned his collar against the wind and strode to his truck. Still holding Amy, Travis watched him leave and hoped that Ronni would return home soon.

Thank God she wasn't on ski-patrol duty today. Against the horizon and through the thickening snowflakes, Mount Echo loomed like a specter, tall and dark and threatening. "Come on, let's get you inside," he said, bundling Amy into the kitchen and calling for the dogs. The puppy, scared of the rising wind, didn't need any encouragement. She dashed through the drifting snow and scurried up the slick steps.

Rex, still sniffing trees in the forest, was more difficult to corral, but eventually he followed.

Bryan had found a couple of flashlights and Travis gathered an old oil lantern, matches and a few candles. He couldn't help glancing at his watch and then peering through the windows, all the while hoping Ronni would return soon.

Obviously still miffed at her stepbrother's unkind remarks, Amy stayed close to Travis and he was just about to break down and call Shelly, interrupt his wife's sister-to-sister talk when he spied Ronni's van rolling slowly down the driveway.

Relief swept through him and he was at the front door, holding it open, drinking in the sight of her running up the broken path in the snow, her hat pulled low, snowflakes catching on the tips of her eyelashes, when he noticed something different about her. Gone was her easy smile and the twinkle in her warm eyes. Her mouth was pulled tight, her nostrils flared, her expression grim as death.

Because of Shelly and her loss of the baby.

"I take it things didn't go well," he said, trying to reach for her, but she stepped quickly out of his arms.

"Shelly's upset," she said, rubbing her arms. "I'm upset. It's . . . it's not right."

Knowing instinctively that she didn't want to be placated, he held his tongue and didn't say that things would turn out, that her sister would have more babies, that it just took time to get over these things. She and Shelly had to grieve.

"I'm sorry," he said softly and she stared up at him with eyes that seemed to glisten in the night. Somewhere far away a horn honked and a lonesome dog barked. Closer to the house, the wind picked up, starting to whistle through the trees.

Again the lights flickered, this time causing darkness for a few seconds as the string of Christmas bulbs and the porch lamp died before blinking back on.

"There's a big one brewing," he said, reaching for her again as the lights winked again. "I've got a fire started, candles and flashlights ready. Come on in, I'll buy you a drink." Smiling, he touched her lightly on the shoulders, but she drew away and reached for the door-knob. Before shoving against the panels, she paused, her shoulders bunched tight, and she hung her head for a second, as if gathering the strength to fight a new battle.

"Ronni?"

"Wendall Holmes."

"What about him?"

She closed her eyes for a second. "He's worked for you for a long time, hasn't he?"

"Nearly twelve years." Was it his imagination or did her face wash of its usual color?

"I thought so."

"He's buying me out—"

Holding up a gloved hand, she nodded. "I know."

Slowly she turned, and when she stared up at him, he felt something wither in his soul. "Then you were the owner and president of SkiWest Company?"

"Still am." Why did he feel as if he were signing his death warrant? Her eyes were full of silent condemnation and her lips were white as the snow that was blowing across the porch.

"I was afraid of this."

"What? What's wrong?"

"SkiWest bindings 450's were the kind that Hank was using—compliments of the company—when he was killed. The bindings didn't release." She reached for the door again but this time he caught her and grabbed her shoulders.

"You blame the bindings?" he demanded. "You think faulty equipment was the reason that your husband was killed?"

Sighing, she shook her head. "I don't know," she admitted and his heart felt as if it might crack. How much she'd loved Amy's father, how deeply she'd cared. He could never hope to fill the huge shoes left by Saint Hank and she'd never love him with the same fervor. "No . . . not really . . . but I just needed someone, *something* to blame."

"It was an accident. You said so yourself. The mountain reacted before they could make it avalanche-proof. He was unlucky, so were you. Even if his bindings had released, even if his skis had been stronger, even if he were the fastest skier in the world, he couldn't have outrun that wall of snow." Travis's throat twisted into a painful knot and his voice was strangled when he spoke. "Let it go, Ronni." He folded her into his arms and she shivered, burying her face in his neck, holding him, letting out the dry, wracking sobs that tore at her soul. "If I could change the past for you I would, but it's just not possible."

"I know," she said and it was as if the starch slipped away from her, as if an old dam she'd constructed had cracked and a tide of emotion swept through her. "I do know."

He kissed her hair. "I'm not the man he was, Ronni," he said and she let out a choked sound. "But I swear to you, I'll be the best husband and father I can be. I'll never leave you, never let you down." His arms tightened around her. "No one can bring Hank back."

"I know."

"He's gone and so is Shelly's baby. It's not fair, it's not right, but there it is. I can't promise you to be like Hank—I wouldn't even try."

"I wouldn't want you to."

"Are you sure?" He held her at arm's length and stared deep into her eyes.

"Yes."

The door opened. "Mommy?"

"Oh, sweetheart." Ronni dragged her gaze away and reached for her daughter who was still holding the pup.

Extracting herself from his embrace, she picked up Amy. In the semidarkness, she transformed from a grieving, unhappy woman to a concerned mother. "Let's go inside and light all the candles and have a party."

"A party?" Instantly Amy grinned, her fears forgotten as she squirmed to the floor and raced into the house.

Ronni stomped the snow from her boots and shook her hair out of her stocking cap. Travis was right, life marched on, and though she still grieved for Shelly's loss, there was nothing she could do but help her sister get well, both mentally and physically. As for Hank, she would always love him, there would always be a special spot in her heart for him and his family, but she was married to Travis now, her life was with him, and though she hated to admit it, she felt as if her love for him was deeper than it had been for Hank. Maybe because she was older and more mature, perhaps because her memories had faded over time. Whatever the reason, she loved Travis and, in his own way, he loved her.

She filled several kettles and the bathtubs with water as the pump for their well was electric and without power they'd have no water source for drinking, washing or flushing the toilets. Travis understood the problem, but Bryan, the city kid, lying on the couch and fiddling with an old Rubic's cube as he watched television, didn't pay much attention when she described what it was like in the mountains without any energy.

She heated soup and bread while Travis found down-filled sleeping bags that he brought into their bedroom, which had a lower ceiling than the living room and a huge fireplace for warmth. They'd just finished eating when it happened—the lights didn't even wink, just went dark. Amy whimpered, Ronni held her close and the wind howled around the house, rattling the window panes and screaming through the trees.

Travis snapped on a flashlight. "I think we'd better move into our room," he suggested.

"Why?" Bryan asked.

"To keep warm."

Bryan made a sound of disgust. "I'm not moving into your bedroom."

"Just until the lights go on."

"No way, Travis," he said, no longer calling him anything but his given name.

"Listen, we should stick together."

"Forget it. I'll hang out in my own room."

"There's no fireplace," Travis argued, but his son had already grabbed one of the flashlights, his blankets and headed off to his bedroom.

Ronni was about to protest, but Travis grabbed her arm. "He'll be all right. We'll check on him later." They gathered the candles, lantern and flashlights and, after locking the dogs in their pen in a room off the kitchen, they headed for the bedroom. Amy, wrapped in her thick sleeping bag, her ratty stuffed tiger tucked under her chin, was asleep within minutes and Travis and Ronni snuggled close together, watching the fire cast warm golden light around the walls and on their faces. She sighed against his chest, resting her head in the crook of his neck, and they couldn't resist kissing and whispering to each other as the flames crackled and hissed against the dry oak logs.

Outside, the wind moaned and snow fell in a blizzard. Inside, the old lodge was warm and dry and cozy.

They fell asleep as the fire died, and over the howl of the wind, they didn't hear the footsteps in the hall, didn't realize their door was pushed open, didn't know they were watched for a few long minutes.

They slept on, uninterrupted as the front door opened and closed. And Bryan escaped into the night.

CHAPTER 12

"BRYAN'S GONE."

Travis's voice, deep and urgent, permeated her brain and Ronni roused herself from a deep sleep. Blinking, she found her husband dressing rapidly, stepping into ski pants and sweater, jacket and boots.

"What do you mean, he's gone?" she asked, her mind still blurry with the soft cobwebs of sleep.

"Just that. He left sometime last night."

"Left? As in left the house?" Suddenly, she was instantly awake.

"I've looked everywhere from the attic to the cellar, even the out buildings and his backpack is missing along with his portable CD player. I think he took off."

"But how? Why?" she asked, throwing off the pile of covers that had been tossed over their king-size bed. But before he could speak, she knew the answer. "This is because of me, isn't it? He's run away because you and I got married and he feels like he doesn't have a place in the family anymore."

"I don't know why he left, I'm just sure he's gone."

Sick inside, Ronni threw on her ski jumpsuit and found her goggles. She glanced outside and saw that the storm was still in full force, snow blowing against the windowpanes, the wind screaming wildly. The power was still off and the temperature in the house had dropped, the fires mere embers. Fortunately, the phones still worked and Travis was able to get through to the sheriff's department. Every deputy was already on duty, trying to help people stranded in vehicles that couldn't get through the snow-covered roads and shut-ins without electricity.

"They'll start looking for him," he said as she lit the gas stove with a match and warmed water for instant coffee. He glared outside to the beauty and treachery of the storm. "What the hell was he thinking?"

"He wasn't."

The phone rang and Travis nearly jumped out of his skin. "Keegan," he answered curtly and Ronni watched as he steeled himself for bad news. The lines near the corners of his mouth and eyes deepened to crevices and his lips flattened into a worried scowl. "Just a minute." He handed her the phone. "It's your sister."

"Shelly! How are you?" Ronni asked, crossing her fingers and hoping beyond hope that there was word of

Bryan. Maybe he'd made a friend of Victor and had walked the two miles into town. But when she asked about Travis's son, Shelly knew nothing.

"I was just calling to see if your power was out," Shelly explained, "and to tell you that I'm feeling better, but, no, we haven't heard from Bryan."

"I was afraid of that," Ronni said, her eyes meeting the distress in Travis's. "Look, we're worried sick and don't want to tie up the phone lines so that if there's any news, the sheriff's department can get through."

"Okay, but if you want a place for Amy to stay, bring her over and I'll watch her. Believe me, I need some distraction. Of course, Vic will help with the search. Oh, Lord, I hope that boy wasn't so stupid as to take off in this weather."

"Me, too," Ronni replied as she hung up and tried to ignore the horrid feeling of desperation that burrowed deep in her heart.

While Travis searched the buildings outside again, Ronni started in the basement and looked in every nook and cranny in the old lodge, hoping Travis had missed a hiding spot during his first search. Closets, laundry chutes, cupboards, crawl spaces, stairwells, coal bins, every inch of floor space was inspected. But by the time she reached the attic, she was as certain as Travis that Bryan was gone.

She returned to the kitchen where Travis had poured himself a cup of coffee. His face was red from the cold, his hair wet with melting snow. "Nothing?" he asked and she shook her head.

"I found footsteps near the garage that look fresh, but they disappeared so quickly where the snow has fallen there's no way to know which way he went."

"I'll call the search-and-rescue team," she volunteered just as Amy, dragging her tattered blanket and stuffed tiger, bounced into the room.

"It's cold," she complained.

"That it is. How about a cup of hot cocoa?" Ronni offered and in silent agreement with Travis didn't mention that Bryan was missing. There wasn't any need to worry her. "I thought maybe you'd like to go visit your cousins this afternoon."

"Can I take the puppies?" Amy dashed to the pen where the dogs were playing with each other, growling and knocking over their water dish.

"Aunt Shelly can't have them at the duplex, honey, but another time the boys can come here and play with them."

Amy's face twisted into a knot of frustration and she appeared about to argue, but Ronni handed her a cup of dog food and more water and, for the moment, Amy was distracted.

Travis was fit to be tied, pacing and glaring at the phone as if by staring at it long and hard enough, the telephone would ring. Ronni could barely think straight, her mind racing with images of Bryan in the snow, hitchhiking back to Seattle, walking through knee-high drifts, alone, cold, miserable. *Please keep him safe,* she silently prayed while going through the motions of fixing Amy breakfast and locating her clothes. Even though she'd been trained to deal with emergencies on and off the mountain, her calm fled when it came to her own family.

She dialed Tim Sether and explained the situation, then took Amy over to her sister's.

"Any word?" Shelly asked as she answered the door. Wearing jeans and a heavy sweater, she offered her sister a cup of tea or coffee, but Ronni couldn't stand the thought of sitting around and waiting. Outside, the temperature was barely twenty degrees and the winds and snow weren't supposed to let up for another day. Power outages were still widespread and a few of the smaller roads were closed. When Shelly asked about Bryan, Ronni felt an ache deep in her soul.

"We haven't heard anything."

"Fool kid," Shelly said, eyeing the sky through the window and shivering though a fire was blazing in the grate and the little duplex was warm enough. "Well, don't worry about Amy. She'll be fine here. Besides, I owe you, big time."

"You don't owe me anything. Are you feeling okay?"

"Right as rain," Shelly said with a sad smile. "Things have a way of working out. I'm still upset about losing the baby, but I've got to remember I've got the twins and they're healthy as all get out. If we want more kids later, we'll have another baby. Vic and I have already talked. Now, you find that boy of Travis's."

"I will," Ronni promised as she reached for the door-knob. She only wished she knew where to start looking.

Before returning to the lodge, she stopped by her house, the cabin she'd shared with Hank, then with Amy. Her life with her first husband seemed so long ago now as she stared at the hardwood floors, old couch and Christmas tree that had yet to be taken down. She picked up some camping gear, her snowshoes, skis and first-aid kit. Then she packed three bags of warm garments including her ski clothes and long underwear, loaded everything into the van and walked through the snow to the barn to feed the horses.

It was dark inside, but an anxious nicker called to her as she fumbled for the pitchfork and shone her flashlight around the barn. Lucy, always the more nervous of the two, whinnied softly. "How're you guys, hmm?" she asked, feeling as if something wasn't right, yet unable to put her finger on the problem. "Cold enough for you?"

Another nicker and she directed the beam of the light into the stalls. Lucy tossed her white head, then blinked against the glare of the light as she stood in the thick straw. Her ears twitched nervously as Ronni draped a red horse blanket over the mare's back and snapped it into place. "You'll be okay," she said, moving to the next stall and stopping short. The enclosure was empty, the gate unlatched. "What the devil?" Sam had somehow escaped, and he hadn't done it alone. A bridle, saddle blanket and saddle were missing. Her heart lurched. It didn't take a genius to figure out that Bryan had walked over here last night, saddled the gray and ridden off on him.

But where?

And why in the middle of the worst storm in five years?

She was about to run to the house and call Travis when she noticed a piece of notebook paper, folded neatly and left in the manger. Heart racing, she smoothed the creases and began to read Bryan's sloppy scrawl.

> *Travis*
> *I'm leaving. I know you won't understand, but I just can't take it anymore down here in the middle of nowhere and you don't need me, anyway. You've got your new wife and your new kid. I don't know how many times I heard Amy say she wanted a daddy for Christmas, well, it looks like she got herself one for New Year's. Don't tell Mom.*
> > *Bryan*

"Dear God," Ronni whispered, her heart pounding, tears burning the back of her eyes as she dashed out of the barn, leaving a bewildered and hungry Lucy. In the house, she had to keep her fingers from shaking, then punched out the number for the lodge.

Travis was quick to answer. "Hello?"

"He's run away. On Sam. He left a note and took a saddle and bridle and—"

"Whoa, slow down." Travis's voice was grim. "Now, take a deep breath and start over. What's this about Bryan leaving a note and running away?"

Trying to stay calm, Ronni repeated everything, reading him the note and hearing the soft groan of denial from the other end of the line. "I'll be home in five minutes," she said.

"I'll call the sheriff again."

She hung up and felt the breath of doom on her neck. It was her fault Bryan had run away, her fault that at this moment he could be lying near death, freezing on the damned mountain. *Just like before. Just like with Hank.*

By the time she'd thrown Lucy two forkfuls of hay and driven to the lodge, a search party had formed. Tim Sether, Vic, Travis and a few other men and women who worked with her promised to gather volunteers and comb the surrounding woods. A deputy from the sheriff's department stopped by and helped organize the search.

Meanwhile, Travis read his son's note, once, twice, even a third time before crumpling the sheet of notebook paper in his fist. A muscle tightened in his jaw and his eyes narrowed in determination. "I'll find him," he assured Ronni. "Or die trying."

"Don't even say it."

"Let's just hope he sticks to the main roads," Tim said, his round face creased with concern. "What's he wearing?"

"I'm not sure, I didn't see him leave, but his navy ski jacket and pants are missing, along with the red stocking hat and face mask he wears up on the slopes." Travis's face was drawn, his eyes cloudy with worry.

"Hang in there," Ronni encouraged, though she couldn't force a smile. "He's going to be fine."

"Okay, everyone gather 'round." Tim laid out maps of the area on the kitchen table and Ronni heated hot water for tea and instant coffee. They discussed their plan of attack, called the weather service for conditions and coordinated the search with the sheriff.

Most of the searchers would start on foot, helicopters would be called in when the storm let up and snowmobiles and four-wheel drive rigs would be used where possible. They'd form a grid and work their way south, covering as much ground as possible with the men and women they had.

Ronni was elected to stay at the lodge near the phone and she protested violently. "No way, I know this mountain better than anyone."

Travis would hear none of it. "Someone's got to remain here."

"But he's my son now."

"And you've got a daughter who needs you. We can't risk losing you . . ." His eyes touched hers. "I can't risk that."

"I can help. Here I'm trapped," she whispered as one of the searchers raised an eyebrow and shot a look in her direction.

"I know, but I couldn't stand it if I lost you, too."

"Damn it, Travis, you can't force me to stay here."

"It's important that someone oversees the phones. What if Bryan calls? What if one of the searchers finds him? What if they need an ambulance? Someone's got to be here to receive and relay messages."

"It's best this way," Tim agreed and Ronni wanted to throttle him. She couldn't sit idle and twiddle her thumbs, staring at her watch and worrying herself to death.

"Please, Ronni, just this once, do as I ask." Travis's eyes searched hers and despite the clamoring in her heart that she was making a mistake, that she could help more by combing the lower slopes of the mountain, she nodded.

"If you think it's best," she said, hating the words.

He kissed her on the temple so gently, she thought her heart would crack.

"Okay, let's do it," Tim said. Everyone on the team carried flares and tracking devices, most had walkie-talkies. By nine o'clock, they left, fanning out from Ronni's place and the lodge, braving the storm and hoping to find a scared teenage boy in a whiteout.

Ronni wrapped her arms around her middle and stared outside. She couldn't shake a horrid premonition as she watched Travis leave. He was headed around the lake to search the forest around the base of Mount Echo and Ronni experienced a sickening sense of déjà vu, that this was the last time she'd ever see her new husband or his son, that the mountain would win again.

"Bryan!" Travis's voice boomed through the forest and echoed back at him. He stopped in his tracks, listened, but only heard his own words over the force of the wind. He moved forward and with each step, his heart shredded. How could anyone survive in this? He could barely see four feet in front of him and the cold air froze against his nose. "Bryan! Bryan, can you hear me?" he yelled, trying to keep the edge of panic from his voice. In his mind's eye, he saw his son's broken body, heard him whimper in fear, knew he could be dead. *"No!"* he yelled, and again his voice came back to him without an answer. He stumbled forward and for the first time in twenty years, he prayed.

"I couldn't stand it, just sitting in the house waiting to hear so I bundled up the kids and drove over. The car is stuck at the end of the lane. It couldn't make it up the last hill," Shelly explained as she walked through the front door, her eyes sweeping the dark interior of the lodge. Amy ran inside followed by her cousins and they made three beelines to the puppy pen.

"I'm glad you're here," Ronni admitted. "Now you can take care of the phones. I've called most of the teen shelters between here and Portland on Travis's business line, but none have taken in a boy of Bryan's description."

"He could have stopped by a house or a barn or anywhere," Shelly said. "Try not to worry."

"Impossible, but now that you're here and can handle the calls—"

"Me? What about you?"

"I'm going to join the search."

Shelly hazarded a glance to the window, where snow had drifted against the panes. "Wait a minute. Shouldn't you leave this to the men?"

As she began gathering her jacket, flares, flashlight and survival gear, Ronni shot her a look that could cut through the base of an old-growth fir tree. With a sound of disgust, she said, "The *men* need all the help they can get. And I think Beverly Adams, Maude Lindsay and JoAnne Rodgers would be offended if they thought you didn't think they, as women, were doing a good enough job."

"But—"

"All you have to do is be the information center. When a call comes in, you spread the word. Almost everyone in the groups has walkie-talkies and here's yours." She gave her sister quick instructions on how to run the equipment and before Shelly could put up any further protest, Ronni kissed Amy goodbye and was out the door.

Snapping on a belt, she tested her walkie-talkie and discovered she could hear the other groups of searchers. Much as she didn't want Travis to know that she'd gone against his wishes, she advised the other searchers of her plans. The only area that hadn't been covered when Tim's teams had marked their territory on his maps had been an old logging road, long overgrown, that wound up the lower slopes of the eastern face of the mountain. It was treacherous going, portions of the road had washed or eroded over the past twenty years, but it was the only unsearched spot. No one in his right mind would ride up that old trail, but then, she was dealing with a teenager unaccustomed to the mountains in winter.

She didn't think twice about saddling poor Lucy and starting to ride the old trail. Although she was wearing her ski jumpsuit, goggles and a huge poncho, the wind pierced through her clothes, and her face above her ski mask was raw, but she rode by instinct, urging Lucy through the deep snow, her eyes straining as she looked for any trace of her stepson.

"Come on, girl, you can make it," she whispered and the horse kept plodding forward, ever upward, her breath steaming from her nostrils. Ronni brushed the snow from her goggles and tried to call other members of the rescue team on her walkie-talkie again but heard only static. Giving up on the device, she concentrated on her search. "Bryan," she called, crossing her gloved fingers as she held lightly to the reins. "Bryan?" And then more softly. "Where are you?"

The road narrowed and dipped but the old bridge that had once spanned the gully had long ago rotted through. Lucy picked her way down one steep slope and over a trickle of water that had iced over, only to slip while trying to climb the opposite side. "You can do it, girl," Ronni encouraged, squinting hard and searching the snow-covered undergrowth. Berry vines and ferns, brush and saplings were bent with the weight of their wintry blanket.

They kept plugging on, passing old, abandoned equipment, searching the trees. Once she stopped by an old logging camp that was deserted, the remains of the buildings only wooden skeletons. Bryan wasn't there.

By one o'clock, Lucy was breathing hard and Ronni stopped just a few minutes to rest the horse, then mounted her again and started through virgin forests of old growth that had escaped being eaten by the huge saws of the timber industry.

The afternoon wore on and Ronni's spirits sank with each of Lucy's plodding steps. It had been hours. How could he survive? She checked the walkie-talkie again but she couldn't hear much and what she did pick up suggested that the boy hadn't yet been found.

She thought about Travis and Amy and Bryan. If only she could turn back the clock forty-eight hours. Things would be different.

Lucy struggled to the top of the ridge where the wind

was more fierce, the roar deafening. "Bryan?" she yelled and heard no response, but Lucy's ears pricked forward and she neighed anxiously. "Bryan?" Ronni screamed again, her voice hoarse. "Can you hear me?"

Lucy snorted and through the curtain of snow, Ronni saw a shape, a dark looming shape. Her heart leaped for a moment when she recognized Sam, her gray stallion. "Bryan, thank God—" Her prayer froze on her lips as the horse trudged through the snow and Ronni realized that his saddle was empty, the reins of his bridle dangling unattended to the ground.

Her heart plummeted. She'd held out a ray of hope that Bryan would be all right with his surefooted mount. Sam was familiar with these old mountain trails even if his rider wasn't. But the horse ambled forward riderless and now Bryan, lost somewhere in this frigid wilderness, was completely and utterly alone.

Dismounting, she snagged Sam's reins. She'd ride the stallion for a while, giving Lucy a break. "Let's go," she said, holding on to two sets of reins and turning Sam around. For as long as she could, she'd follow the trail Sam had broken in the snow. After that, she'd have to rely on luck.

"We're going to have to call off the search until the storm blows over," the deputy said over the crackle of static on his walkie-talkie.

Travis gritted his teeth. "No way. I'm in this until we find Bryan."

"I can't risk these people's lives. It's nearly dark and we're turning back. The storm's supposed to move north by tomorrow. We'll resume then."

Fear clutched Travis's heart in a stranglehold and wouldn't let go. In eight hours he could lose his son. "I'm not coming in. Tell Ronni I'll be back when I find him."

There was a pause on the other end, just the sound of crackling static. "Weren't you listening? Ronni's out here," the deputy finally said. "She called but something's wrong with her walkie-talkie. It looks like she took off after Bryan, too. Near as we can tell, she's on horseback. We're trying to reach her to call her in, but so far she hasn't responded."

His heart nearly clutched. "What?"

"You heard me. Took off and left her sister here to oversee the phones."

"Damn," Travis growled, his eyes searching the woods, his feet and hands nearly frozen despite his insulated boots and gloves. That hardheaded woman! Her image came to mind, her dark hair, warm brown eyes, smiling full lips. Oh, God, he couldn't lose her. Frantic, he plowed forward. Somewhere out here, somewhere in this damned wilderness, was his wife and kid. He only hoped they were still alive.

"Bryan!" Shivering from the cold, Ronni rode as darkness began to creep over the mountains. She had two choices—to keep searching or ride back. She couldn't stop for any length of time and build an ice cave because the horses wouldn't survive. She'd followed Sam's broken trail for over two miles, up a canyon and down a draw to the trickle of a creek flowing sluggishly between icy shores. When the trail had given out, she'd let Sam pick his way, hoping that the horse would understand and locate the boy. So far, it hadn't worked.

Be with him, please, keep him safe, she prayed, then squinted. For a second she thought she was seeing things, creating a happy mirage in her mind—a mirage of her stepson propped up against the spreading bows of a fir tree—but as Sam trudged through the drifts, she made out a navy jacket and a body. Swallowing hard, she yelled out. "Bryan? Are you okay?"

The body moved. She let out her breath. Bryan turned, waved frantically, and her heart soared.

"Oh, honey," she cried, jumping from Sam's broad back and taking the last steps through the snow on her own. "Are you all right?"

He managed to look sheepish though his teeth were chattering and his face was red from the cold. "Twisted my ankle when Sam spooked and I fell off," he admitted. "Can't walk and I was in so much pain, it hurt to ride, so, um, I, uh, stopped to rest and . . . Sam took off on me." His lip trembled, either from the cold or some strong emotion. "Guess I'm not much of a cowboy."

"That's not such a crime, is it?"

He stared down at his hands, his young pride bowed.

"Don't worry about it. You're all right now. We're going to get you home and warm and safe and . . ." She saw the doubt in his eyes and took his gloved hand in hers. "I know it's been rough and that your dad and I have been so wrapped up in each other that we inadvertently left you out, but you have to know that both of us love you so much. Your dad . . . he's frantic with worry and . . ." Rocking back on her heels, she looked him squarely in the eye. "I believe we can work this out—all of us. But if you're unhappy, if you think that Amy and I don't belong in your family, well, then maybe something will change."

"Meaning?" he asked suspiciously.

"Meaning that I'd be willing to move out, at least for a while, until you and your dad figure out what's best for you two."

"You're serious?" he asked, disbelief threading into his hoarse voice.

Her heart nearly broke at the sound of hope in his words. "Yep," she admitted, then slapped him gently on the leg. "But first things first. We have to find a way to get you out of here. Can you ride?"

"I—I think so."

"Good, 'cause there's not much light left. We'll ride back close to the stream, follow it downhill and we should either end up in town or at some shelter, an old logging camp or mine or something." She paused to try to call on her walkie-talkie, but the battery had worn down and she couldn't reach anyone. She set off flares in the small hope that someone who was still searching the mountain might come across their trail.

"Okay, let's go." Helping him hobble to Sam, she acted as a brace. He winced as he climbed into the saddle, but eventually they were both mounted, the wind was at their backs and with the gray leading, they headed downward. Ronni crossed her fingers as they rode and hoped that they would find civilization before the horses or Bryan gave out.

Travis couldn't believe his eyes. The sizzling red light of a flare guided him and he shouted, his voice ringing through the woods. He followed the light from the small beacon, but when he reached the sputtering embers, he found himself alone. Gritting his teeth, he stared at the ground. There was a fresh trail broken by two horses. One that came down the ridge to the stream base, the other following along the dark, nearfrozen water. With a flashlight he checked the depth of snow in the trails and decided to follow the stream. He plunged forward, yelling and hoping beyond hope that his family was safe. "Bryan! Veronica!"

"Travis?" Ronni's voice was faint but sure and he raced forward, plunging through the stream, running and mindful of nothing other than seeing his son and wife again. Tears burned in his eyes, the dark forest rushed past in a blur, and as he rounded a bend, he saw them, two dark shapes on horseback. Ronni was off her mount in a second, running to him, flinging herself into his arms, sobbing in relief.

"He's all right. He's gonna be all right," she said over and over again, and Travis, still holding on to her, approached his son.

With tears in his eyes, he looked up at his boy. "Don't you ever scare me like that again," he said, blinking and sniffing. "I was worried sick about you."

Bryan fought a losing battle with tears.

"Don't you know I love you?" Travis said. "That I'd do anything to make you happy? God, Bryan . . ." His words faltered and he felt Ronni slip out of his embrace.

"Dad—" Bryan's voice cracked as he slid off the horse. Travis held him close, afraid that his son would disappear again. The sheer terror of losing him washed over him in an icy wave.

"We're a family, son. All of us. Just because I love Ronni and Amy doesn't mean I love you less. If you only knew how scared I was, if you only knew how much I care about you and your happiness."

"I'm sorry—"

"Shh. We're gonna work this out." Travis looked at Ronni over his son's shoulder. "All of us."

Bryan nodded against his chest, then glanced over his shoulder to his new stepmother. Through his tears, he offered her a small smile. "Thanks," he said gruffly, his chin angling upward again. "I—I was stupid."

"I love you," she said simply and he squeezed his eyes shut. "I will love you as my own son, if you'll have me. And I won't stand in the way of your relationship with your dad or your real mom. Never."

He stared at her a second and then to Travis's surprise, he reached forward and hugged her. "I'm sorry for everything I said, everything I thought . . . I . . ."

"Shh, it's all right. Let's get out of here and get you home."

He blinked hard and nodded. " 'Kay, Mom," he whispered, wiping the back of his glove under his nose, and Travis felt the scars in his heart begin to heal.

The surprise party was over, the guests, rounded up by invitation from Shelly and Vic, had long since left. Balloons and streamers still rose to the ceiling of the lodge and the Christmas tree was lit, but the surprise wedding reception/New Year's Eve party had ended and Ronni kicked off her shoes. Two bottles of champagne still rested in a bucket of ice. "Here's to us," Travis said, clicking his glass to hers. "All four of us."

"To us," she agreed and took a swallow. The past couple of days had been a whirlwind. The blizzard had ended and finally, they were a family again. Bryan had only sprained his ankle and didn't even have to use crutches. He'd finally accepted Ronni and Amy to the point that Amy tagged after him wherever he went. He'd quit talking about moving away and had even deigned to meet some kids from the local church group. There was hope, Ronni sensed, and there was happiness.

Travis slipped his arm around her waist. "So what's your New Year's resolution?" he asked and she smiled.

"Well, Amy's is that she's going to be good so she can keep you as her daddy." She reached into her pocket and dragged out a scrap of red paper with childish handwriting. "I think Bryan helped her with it."

"A smart girl," Travis said, his eyes misting as he read the note.

"And Bryan said he wanted to learn how to ride a horse, snowboard and play an electric guitar."

Travis winced. *"Electric?* Why not acoustic?"

"And he's agreed to visit his mother at least once a year. Maybe twice."

"That's progress."

"I think so. Vic and Shelly plan to have another baby," Ronni said.

"And you?"

"I thought I might go along with my sister. It sounds good, you know."

"What? To have another baby?"

"Our baby, half sibling to each of our kids. Kind of a knot to hold us together."

"Do we need one?"

She laughed and sipped the champagne. "Suppose not, but it would be nice."

"I guess so." He nuzzled her neck and caught a glimpse of Bryan and Amy staring down at them through the rails of the landing.

"I'm not talking about right away," she said. "We need time to grow as a family, just the four of us."

A muffled bark from the area of the kitchen made her laugh. "Okay, just the six of us," she amended. "But, by the end of the year . . . "

"It could be a possibility." Travis's eyes sparkled.

"So right now I resolve that I'll be the best mother in the world to our two kids and the best wife on this earth to you."

"Hear, hear." He started to take a sip, but she caught his wrist.

"Not so fast, mister. What's your resolution?"

"Mine?" His grin stretched wide. "That's easy." He set his glass on the mantel and circled her waist with his strong arms. Intense eyes stared down at her. "I'm going to love you forever, Ronni," he vowed, saying the words that she'd longed to hear ever since first meeting him. "My resolution isn't for a year, it's for the rest of our lives."

EPILOGUE

THE CLOCK STRUCK twelve.

"Happy New Year!" Amy sang out, proudly displaying a front tooth that wobbled precariously on her bottom gums.

"Same to you," Ronni said with a yawn. She hugged her daughter as Bryan clomped down the stairs. The first signs of stubble covered his upper lip and his voice cracked whenever he talked. "Where's your father?" she asked. "I didn't think he wanted to miss this."

"In the bedroom," Bryan and Amy said in unison, then exchanged knowing glances.

"I should have guessed." Ronni pushed herself from the couch and walked past the embers of the fire in the grate to the master bedroom where Travis was reaching into the bassinet.

"You wake her and I'll strangle you," Ronni warned, but it was too late. Travis, fascinated with his two-month-old daughter, picked up the infant and held her close.

"Happy New Year," he whispered to Andrea and she made little sucking motions with her lips. With a proud smile, he looked up at his wife and winked. "You know she's the most beautiful baby in the world, don't you?"

Ronni grinned. "Don't tell Shelly. She thinks Kevin's got that award all sewed up."

"Well, she's wrong. Besides, he's bald."

"He's only two weeks old," Ronni said, but laughed when she thought of her sister and small family all tucked into the caretaker's house on the lake. Victor was working for Travis full-time and had added two bedrooms and a bath to the house where Ronni and Shelly had grown up. Now, all their lives had settled into a comfortable, contented routine. Ronni had moved from her little cabin and rented it to a young couple. She'd transferred her business to an old storage building near the lodge and the horses had moved, as well, to new stables Travis had insisted upon building. Bryan had learned to snowboard this season and had reconciled himself to having a stepmother and a few new siblings. He even called his mother in France every once in a while and planned to visit her again this summer, as he did last.

Amy, growing by leaps and bounds, was in seventh heaven with her new sister, two dogs and Lucy's half-grown colt, and Ronni was happier than she'd ever been in her life.

"I guess you're right," she admitted, gazing down at her infant daughter's precious face. "She's probably the prettiest baby ever born."

A thunder of footsteps announced Amy's arrival.

Andrea blinked and stretched a little fist, as her father, reached forward, grabbed the belt surrounding Ronni's waist and pulled her close.

"Aren't we gonna have champagne?" Amy demanded.

"Your mother and I are. You'll have to settle for sparkling cider. You, too," he added when Bryan poked his head into the room.

"I know, Dad," he said and Ronni smiled inwardly at the familiarity and love that had grown between father and son. Bryan was starting to talk about cars and getting his driving permit and some girl name Julie and Travis, bless him, was handling being a father of a teenager.

"We'll be there in a minute," Travis promised. "You guys find the corkscrew."

Amy was off on her new mission with Bryan in tow. "Now," Travis said, shifting the baby so that she wouldn't get squeezed, "I just wanted to make our private New Year's resolution."

"Oh? And what is that?"

"That we have a baby every year."

She laughed. "Only if *you* go through pregnancy, gain thirty pounds and then suffer with labor."

"Spoilsport."

"How about we have one this year and then decide?"

"As long as we can have at least one more."

"Mmm, I might be able to be convinced."

"I was hoping . . ." He loosened the belt of her robe and touched her breasts.

"Watch out," she warned, kissing him. "You might be getting yourself into big trouble."

"That's what I'm aiming for," he whispered, brushing his lips across her ear.

At that moment Andrea decided to wake up and let out a squawk loud enough to rouse the dead in three counties. Amy and her dogs thundered back toward the room. Ronni quickly adjusted her clothing.

"Later," she said, taking the baby from her husband's arms.

"I'm counting on it."

She grinned and winked. "Good. I think we'll both have to learn a little patience."

"No problem," he drawled. "The way I figure it, we've got the rest of our lives."